Murder
in
Fourth
Position

Murder
in
Fourth
Position

An On Pointe
Mystery

Lori Robbins

LeVel
BEST BOOKS

First published by Level Best Books 2023

Author Photo Credit: Alice Kivlon

First edition

ISBN: 978-1-68512-448-9

Cover art by Level Best Designs

This book was professionally typeset on Reedsy.
Find out more at reedsy.com

To Glenn

Praise for the On Pointe Mystery Series

"Robbins, a former ballerina, steeps the novel in the glamorous grunge of the dance world...The result is a suspenseful romp with loads of atmosphere. A highly entertaining whodunit with a twisty plot and plenty of biting ballet intrigue."—*Kirkus Review* [starred review]

"Robbins does an outstanding job of juxtaposing the ballet world with the investigative process that challenges Leah's set roles, forcing her to new heights of realization about the world of dance, her colleagues, and her own ambitions. This makes for compelling reading... the tension is finely drawn and the movements between dance and death assume their own form of masterful entwining that keeps readers involved in a realistic character's moves. Exquisitely complex, nicely steeped in both drama and the competitive atmosphere of the dance world."—D. Donovan, Sr. Reviewer, *Midwest Book Review*

"Robbins delivers another brilliantly crafted On Pointe Mystery with *Murder in Fourth Position*. Leah Siderova is back in this latest book of the series, still squaring her shoulders and pirouetting across the stage, but this time as the lead dancer in Mad Music, Broadway's most anticipated new musical. Her true role is a clandestine one. She agreed to take the part only to conceal her undercover investigation of the online threats against the show's star, Amber Castle. Stunned to discover that the threats they all feared had become a reality on the first day of rehearsal, Leah is determined to uncover the truth as intrigue and danger grow. Masterfully written, Robbins takes you on a journey through every stunning leap and down every dark path to the end. I couldn't put it down!"—Cynthia Tolbert, writing as C.L. Tolbert, author of the Thornton Mystery Series

"With a narrative as deft and agile as a prima ballerina, ambition and jealousy embrace in a lethal pas de deux in this no-holds-barred clash between ballet and Broadway."—Gerald Elias, author of the Daniel Jacobus mystery series and Silver Falchion finalist.

"Prima ballerina Leah Siderova makes the leap from ballet to Broadway in Lori Robbins's twisty *Murder In Fourth Position*. Going undercover as the alter-ego dancer of the star of *Mad Music*, Amber Castle, accidents plague the production right from the start. After Amber winds up in the hospital, things go from bad to worse. Will the show be a no-go? Or, will Leah discover who's behind the threats? You'll be turning pages as fast as you can to find out!"— Cathi Stoler, award-winning author of The Murder On The Rocks Mysteries

"Peek backstage at rehearsals for a Broadway musical, as jealous dancers and actors vie for attention and praise. In *Murder in the Fourth Position*, the newest addition to her On Pointe series, Lori Robbins again entertains and surprises us. Ballerina Leah Siderova, selected for a central role in the show, learns the star actress has received threats. Who wishes her harm? Her ex, her understudy, her boyfriend? Who will find the culprit first, Siderova or the police? Readers will love this mystery on its own, while reaching for the other On Pointe books."—Marlie Parker Wasserman, author of *Inferno on Fifth*

"Award-winning author and former professional dancer Lori Robbins doesn't miss a step in her latest delightful On Pointe Mystery, *Murder in Fourth Position*. From the opening sentence of the novel, 'I'm a ballerina on the wrong side of thirty, with a future as uncertain as the A train during rush hour,' you'll find yourself captivated by the self-deprecating humor and colorful observations of ballerina Leah Siderova, who manages to solve crimes while on the job as a professional dancer. There are so many reasons to love this novel, including its page-turning suspense, fascinating look at what goes on behind the scenes of a Broadway musical, and a wonderful cast of characters. Most of all, though, is the unforgettable voice and heart of Leah, whose talents as an amateur sleuth easily rival her artistry as a ballerina."—Lynn Slaughter, award-winning author of *Missed Cue*

"Raise the lights! When Lori Robbins' favorite Lincoln Center ballerina picks up her toe shoes and goes undercover for the NYPD as a Broadway star's dreamy alter ego, she quickly discovers that enduring torn ligaments and resentment by jealous cast members are the least of her worries. *Murder in Fourth Position* puts Leah Siderova center stage in the midst of a desperate hunt for a sadistic killer. Bring on her secret weapons and readers' favorites, a mystery writing mother, acerbic aunt, and three elderly, loveable 'Weird Sisters', and Lori's fourth On Pointe Mystery proves she knows how to bring down the house with another Tony-winning performance. First rate!"—Judy L Murray, award-winning author of the Chesapeake Bay Mystery Series.

"Crimes in the glamorous world of ballet take center stage in this very compelling mystery. Leah Siderova, a talented sleuth in toe shoes, returns with another intriguing case, a cast of memorable characters, and a perfectly paced plot. The author's insider knowledge shines through the sharply drawn settings and scenes, creating an impressively authentic and entertaining tale."—Cynthia Kuhn, author of the Agatha Award-winning Lila Maclean Academic Mysteries

Chapter One

Beauty, of course, is the most important requirement and the paramount asset.
—Florenz Ziegfeld

I'm a ballerina on the wrong side of thirty, with a future as uncertain as the A train during rush hour. Onstage, I can still reel off thirty-two fouettés without fracturing any of the really important bones. Offstage, my qualifications were less impressive. These assets included a high school diploma, two surgically reconstructed knees, and the survival instincts of a woman whose career outlived multiple attempts to write its obituary. Perhaps this was why no one questioned my decision to leap from ballet to Broadway while I still had the legs and the guts to make a go of it.

Even before opening night, *Mad Music* was the buzziest new show of the upcoming season. The choreographer tempted me with a hot score, a cool director, and a starring dance role. When I signed the three-month contract, not one of my rivals at American Ballet Company suspected me of an ulterior motive.

Most of what I told them and the press was true. Unless I blew my cover, only the NYPD and a few trusted friends would ever know the whole story of how and why I swapped Lincoln Center for the Great White Way. As a dancer closing in on the end of her career, every performance felt like a matter of life and death. This time around, it really was.

The first rehearsal left me bruised from my hips to my ankles, thanks to a series of acrobatic moves that should have been assigned to a stunt double.

The second day was similar, except I was already exhausted and in pain when we began.

Although complaining about injuries and muscle fatigue constituted at least half of every dancer's conversation (romantic and professional gossip accounted for most of the rest), no one at *Mad Music* was sympathetic. Choreographer Bryan Leister, seeking to capitalize on my fame among ballet fans, had demoted the dance captain to the chorus, in order to give her starring role to me. That he'd done so less than two weeks before opening night earned me a frost-bite cold reception from her loyal friends.

The social temperature was in single digits, but Bryan kept us in a state of sweaty, perpetual motion. My knees were on fire, and when the wardrobe mistress interrupted the thirtieth repetition of my solo, I silently cheered the opportunity to take an unscheduled break.

Lynne Heller ignored the music and Bryan's feeble attempt to continue practicing. She whipped out a tape measure and said, "I'll start with Leah." Everyone, except for the anxious choreographer, greeted her decision with unaffected enthusiasm.

I stood on aching legs as Lynne took precise measurements before trying out a selection of wigs. Most of the cast idled by the refreshment table or stretched out on the floor. In retrospect, that would have been a good time to observe more closely the people around me.

If I had been paying attention, I would have realized sooner that an atypical silence blanketed the room. Instead of talking to each other, everyone was staring at me, as if witnessing a ghostly apparition and not a routine costume fitting.

Natalie Stevens, my lone friend and ally, said, "This is creepy. If I didn't know you were Leah Siderova, I'd think you were Amber Castle." With a smile that wasn't entirely pleasant, she added, "Or maybe her younger sister."

I didn't think I looked anything like the starring actress of *Mad Music*, but when Natalie handed me a mirror, I had to agree. A crown of red-gold curls transformed me so thoroughly, I didn't recognize myself in the glamorous image. The wig effaced tiny differences between my face and Amber's, and the result was slightly unnerving. It was as if the real me had been erased.

2

Natalie shook her head, which sent her long braids flying. "I've heard everyone has a twin. I think you've met yours."

Amber put down her coffee cup and pushed past Natalie to examine for herself the success of my disguise. The actress placed her face next to mine and smiled into the mirror's double image. "I've always wanted a sister. I didn't think I'd have to wait so long to get one." She put her arm around my shoulders. "I knew you'd be perfect as the Dreamcatcher. The audience won't be able to tell us apart!"

She was right. My role as her alter ego required me to reflect in movement what she expressed in words, and from the audience's perspective, it would indeed look as if we were two sides of one person. A closer examination, however, revealed many differences between us. My forehead was higher, and my cheekbones sharper. But the curve of her fair eyebrows and my black ones was uncannily alike. We were the same height, and our costumes had been cleverly designed to minimize the dissimilarity in body type.

Lynne stepped between us and snapped her fingers. "Marty! Where are you?" She looked around and said to no one in particular, "He better not be taking another cigarette break, or he's going to be New York City's newest unemployed wardrobe assistant."

A skinny guy, whose matchstick arms were inked in elaborate tattoos, emerged from the group that had congregated around the coffee pot. He waved away Lynne's threat and said, "Gimme two minutes." Marty poured four packets of sugar into his drink, tasted it, and scowled. "This tastes like yesterday's garbage."

Natalie stirred her coffee and took a sip. "It tastes fine to me, and you can't argue with the price. If you want better coffee, you're going to have to pay for it."

While Lynne and Marty poked and combed and tugged, the rest of the cast continued to help themselves to the free drinks and pastries. I wondered whose idea it was to provide the refreshments. If I were with my friends at American Ballet Company, the sweets would have gone uneaten. The dreaded "fat clause" in our contracts kept vulnerable dancers on perpetual diets, including many ballerinas who were vanishingly thin.

I sat in the folding chair Lynne offered me, happy to have the chance to rest my sore knees and resume my observation of the *Mad Music* cast. Most stayed in a tight circle around the donuts, but Carly Messina, the disappointed dancer whose starring role was now mine, stood apart and whispered to Natalie in a corner of the room.

Their conversation appeared amiable, even confidential. On my first day of rehearsal, Natalie gave me the impression their relationship was, at best, frosty. What clues had I missed? The intimate way the two women stood, with their heads inclined toward each other, indicated they were good friends.

I wondered if they were talking about me. In my position, this was a prudent, not paranoid, reaction. Backbiting and backstabbing were as common as joint problems and more popular than over-the-counter pain relievers.

Lynne took back the wig and turned her attention to another dancer as Bryan's voice cut through the growing noise. "Back to work, people. We'll start with the opening of the Dream ballet."

The score for most of the show was a compilation of jazzy, familiar, big-band tunes, but Bryan had commissioned new music for my solo. The melancholy waltz began slowly and gained intensity as the melody fractured and became increasingly discordant.

The eerie sound of an instrument I couldn't identify moaned and wailed as the chorus closed in on me. They flicked their arms in my direction, as if throwing imaginary projectiles. I responded to each pantomimed attack with a dramatic fall to the floor that annexed more territory to the map of bruises across my legs. The drafty windows of the rehearsal studio revealed dark clouds that dimmed the room, and a flash of lightning and crack of thunder added to the ominous atmosphere of an approaching storm.

Absorbed in the music and the movement, I wasn't aware of much, other than my reflection. Not until high-pitched screams pierced my concentration did I break out of character. Startled, I lost my balance when

CHAPTER ONE

Amber crashed through the circle of dancers. She fell to her knees, clutching her stomach. Her breathing was labored, and she seemed not to hear our frantic questions.

Amber's collapse marked my first failure.

Chapter Two

Words...can get in the way of dancing.
—Jennifer Homans

Red blotches stained Amber's pale skin, and her eyes watered. Bryan propped her up and tried to help her to a chair, but she slithered away from him and ran out of the room. I ignored the growing frenzy and raced after her. With surprising energy, she sprinted past the elevator, turned the corner, and kept going.

Amber's legs failed her a few feet from the bathroom door. I caught up with the actress in time to break her fall and cushioned her head in my lap. Surely, one of the distraught people we left behind would have the presence of mind to call nine-one-one.

If we'd been rehearsing in the theater, my shouted pleas for an ambulance would have gotten a swift response. Unfortunately, we were in the D'Anconia, a building that housed numerous practice studios, which were mostly soundproof. The bathrooms were in a separate alcove, off the main corridor. She couldn't have chosen a worse place to lose consciousness. Although I could hear the muffled music of other rehearsals, the performers inside wouldn't be able to hear me.

I didn't want to leave Amber's side, but her shallow breathing scared me into action. Slipping out from underneath her, I rose to my feet.

Bryan must have followed the sound of my voice, and we collided as he turned the corner. I couldn't keep up with his long stride and shouted, "Stop! Get an ambulance. I-It's bad, Bryan. I think she's been poisoned."

He froze. "Made the call right after you left. They should be here soon."

"Bring me a coat. Anything to keep her warm."

"I'll be right back." He did an about-face and ran toward the studio.

With growing dread, I tried to keep Amber comfortable as she shivered in my arms. Without a phone or a watch, I had no sense of time, other than a terrified consciousness that the beautiful, talented woman lying on the floor was fading fast. Her trembling increased, and I waited in an agony of impatience for Bryan to return with something warm to protect her from the cold, hard floor.

The faint sound of a siren penetrated the interior corridor. Amber's eyes fluttered open, and I said, "Did you hear that? An ambulance is on the way." With more confidence than the situation warranted, I added, "Hold on, my friend. You're going to be fine."

Her eyes were glazed, and her breath had a sickly sweet smell. "Need Lynne. I'm too high."

Those last three words negated every assumption I'd made about Amber's condition. Maybe what made her ill had been self-administered. Maybe she hadn't been poisoned. And maybe I wasn't guilty of failing to protect her. My undercover role was to investigate threats against her. It didn't include protecting her from herself.

She licked her lips and groaned, over and over, "*Need Lynne. Get Lynne.* In the bathroom. Have to…"

I was frantic with worry. Could Lynne actually help? Or was this panicked request for the costume mistress a sick person's delirium?

My knowledge of illegal and off-label drugs was limited, and without my phone, I couldn't google her symptoms. Some of my ballerina friends resorted to weight loss drugs, but Amber's distress didn't square with an overdose of black beauties or Ozempic, satirically known among hardcore dieters as Slimfast Premium.

After an eternity of waiting, I was relieved to hear a chime that heralded the arrival of the elevator, but when the medics charged into the hallway, the sound of receding footsteps told me they were headed in the wrong direction. Again, I cried for help. Again, no one answered.

Bryan must have told the medics where we were, because a few seconds later, a burly guy turned the corner and came to the rescue.

He crouched next to us and put his fingers on Amber's neck and his ear to her mouth. After sniffing her breath, he spoke in a reassuring, matter-of-fact tone. "Yep. Take it easy. We got this."

He opened her eyelids to shine a light in them, then rubbed his knuckles over her chest. She moaned in pain. He reached for his bag and pulled out a plastic device with a small screen. He pierced her fingertip with a needle and drew a small amount of blood.

I was on fire with nervous energy. "She said she's high and wants me to get Lynne. I can be back in two minutes."

The medic ignored me and spoke into a walkie-talkie. "Booker here. Got a female, about forty-five years old. Probable DKA. Bring a stretcher and bag of NS. Stat." He lifted Amber's shirt, withdrew a second needle from his bag, and stabbed her in the belly.

Most of what he said was incomprehensible to me, but his competence and calm were reassuring. I hovered over his shoulder. "What's happening? Is she going to be okay?"

He kept his eyes on her while answering me. "She needed insulin. Not Lynne."

I was weak with relief. Amber hadn't overdosed. And she hadn't been poisoned. But after the medic jabbed her, relief gave way to dizziness at the sight of the needle. While our hero waited for his colleagues, I bolted and took refuge in the bathroom.

On the shelf above the sink sat a red leather makeup bag that looked familiar. A mini pack of tissues was stuck halfway out of the bag, and I used a few to wipe my eyes.

For the second time that day, my image shocked me with a reflection I didn't recognize. This time, however, it wasn't because I was a more glamorous version of myself. Oddly, my bloodless skin, sweaty forehead, and teary eyes again resembled Amber's. Only the long, tangled mane of dark brown hair was identifiably me.

I pressed my lips together, and when I was reasonably certain I wouldn't throw up, exited the bathroom. A second medic arrived, and the two hoisted Amber onto a stretcher.

I kept pace with them. "Can I ride with her?"

They answered in unison. "No."

I called to her, "I'll meet you at the hospital."

She opened her eyes a fraction of an inch. "Bring my bag. My phone. Get me…" Her voice was so low I couldn't hear the name of the person she wanted me to contact. I reached over the safety bar and squeezed her hand.

A third emergency worker was waiting by the elevator. He kept the door open while Booker wedged Amber inside. It was a tight fit. He had to maneuver her around a second stretcher, which held an unconscious guy with spindly, tattooed arms.

I felt my stomach drop. There were two victims. Not one.

Chapter Three

To dance, put your hand on your heart and listen to the sound of your soul.
—Luigi

The cloud of guilt that lifted, when the medic diagnosed Amber's collapse as insulin-related, descended again when I saw Marty's unconscious face and limp body strapped to the stretcher. Unless the wardrobe assistant succumbed to a diabetic reaction at the same time Amber did, a substance more deadly than sugar had to have made them ill. Anxious to check on the condition of both victims, I returned to the studio and searched for the actress's elegant, red leather tote.

Bryan pushed past the people clamoring to speak to me and ordered them to step away. He grabbed my shoulders. "What happened? Is Amber going to be okay?"

I twisted out of his grasp. "I think so. Help me find her bag. I told her I'd bring it to her. I'll call you as soon as there's news."

He joined me in the hunt, and while I picked through a pile of shoes and discarded warm-up gear under the grand piano, he found Amber's red bag behind the coffee pot. In my haste to grab it, I overturned a cup that was left on the windowsill. The few drops that were left dripped onto the floor.

I tossed jeans and a sweater over my leotard and tights. "What happened to Marty?"

"After Amber left the room, he fainted and hit his head against the radiator. I have no idea what knocked him out." Bryan took a deep, loud breath. "Can you imagine how horrible it would have been if another performer got sick?

Lynne can hire a wardrobe assistant by tomorrow and not miss a beat, but I'm at my wit's end."

I bit back my instinctive reaction to Bryan's heartless dismissal of another human being. Instead of chiding him, I went with the second thought uppermost in my mind. "Where were you? I asked you to bring Amber's coat. And I didn't want to be alone with her. I thought she was dying."

He held his hands out, palms upturned. Perhaps sensing his mute plea for sympathy was getting him nowhere with me, he said, "Marty fainted, people were screaming, and I was on the phone with the nine-one-one operator. It was total chaos."

I didn't have time to query him further and headed for the door.

Bryan held onto my sleeve. "You can't leave yet. We haven't finished blocking your solo."

"You can't be serious. Look around you. Rehearsal is over, Bryan."

He peered over his shoulder, where he found the assembled cast of *Mad Music* staring at him with the same loathing a group of trick-or-treaters gave my mother that awful year she handed out toothbrushes on Halloween. Carly stepped away from them and stood so close to Bryan she could have kissed him, although romance was not on her agenda. I thought the dance captain was going to poke his eyes out, but I was wrong.

Carly spoke softly to Bryan. "I got you, Boss. Leave this to me."

She addressed the angry crowd in strident tones. "I don't know about the rest of you, but I'm gonna do whatever it takes to get this baby some Tonys. You want to help Amber? Give her a show that'll run forever. And if you don't want to do it for her, do it for yourself. If this show folds, you could be looking at months of cattle calls before you land another paying gig."

Her appeal to their self-interest was more effective than Bryan's desire to fine-tune the choreography for my solo.

Carly turned her marble-hard eyes toward me and said, "Leah, you can go. I'll take over your role." The dance captain went back to Bryan, and the two exchanged a long look.

He didn't hesitate. "Carly, you're on. If I win for best choreography, you'll be my first shout-out." Beckoning to Natalie, he said, "You're on too. Take over for Amber." He clapped his hands. "Places, people. From the top."

The dancers scrambled to take their positions. And just like that, Amber and I were out, and Carly and Natalie were in. There was no guarantee they would make it to opening night. There was no guarantee they'd make it to the next rehearsal.

But it's like the song says: There's a broken heart for every light on Broadway.

I closed the door to the studio, but a chilly breeze and the haunting notes of a melancholic fragment of music—my music—trailed after me. The soundtrack changed as I moved toward the elevator. Our *Mad Music* rehearsal was one of many taking place on each floor of the D'Anconia. The aging building was long past its glory days, but an eclectic group of performing artists continued to rent space there, from tiny practice rooms for individual musicians to large, cavernous studios for Broadway shows and visiting dance companies. When I turned the corner, I was serenaded first with the notes of a Mozart aria, next, by the twang of a guitar, and lastly by the *rat-a-tat* of tap shoes. It was a Petri dish of art.

Unlike the itinerant performers at the D'Anconia, American Ballet Company dancers had a permanent workspace that occupied several floors of an Upper West Side building. Despite the presence of other tenants, the ABC studio felt like a private island in the middle of the bustling city. It was my home, and with a sudden rush of emotion, I missed it. Although the company was on tour and my fellow ballet dancers were living out of suitcases, I was seized with a desire to return to the place where I belonged.

If *Mad Music* was successful, my contract stipulated a minimum three-month performance commitment. No time off for good behavior unless I lost my role to Carly, who made no secret of her fierce desire to unseat me, as I'd unwittingly done to her. Under other circumstances, the prospect of being replaced by the dance captain would have upset me, but not anymore. Flaming out on a Broadway stage paled in comparison to blowing my covert mission.

A breakout role in *Mad Music* had the potential to open up opportunities beyond ballet, with significant financial rewards. But who was I kidding? If I wanted to be rich, I wouldn't have become a ballerina.

With growing impatience, I waited for the elevator, which rivaled the one at ABC in pokiness. Taking the stairs would have been faster, but I wasn't tempted. Aside from a general and not entirely irrational fear of being attacked and dismembered in a deserted stairwell, my knees ached more going down than they did going up.

Amber's bag buzzed and vibrated every few seconds. I didn't want to infringe upon her privacy by checking out her phone, but I also didn't want to miss a call from her. If she was trying to reach me, calling her number was a logical decision.

There was a second and equally compelling argument in favor of sneaking a peek. Perhaps if I'd been more aggressive earlier, Amber and Marty wouldn't now be on their way to the emergency room.

Having quelled my unproductive distaste for prying into other people's personal lives, I fished Amber's phone from her bag and scrolled through a line of messages. Most were from people I didn't know, but many were from cast members, including Bryan and the wardrobe mistress. I didn't look enough like Amber for the photo ID security system to unlock, but with my phone, I took a picture of the names on hers.

Jagged bolts of lightning illuminated a window at the end of the hall, and I steeled myself for a sprint to the nearest subway station. In the middle of a storm, and with rush hour well underway, a train would be the fastest, if not the most comfortable, method of transportation.

Unfortunately, when the elevator doors finally opened, Fate provided yet another roadblock in the form of two police detectives. The last time I saw Jonah Sobol, he had one of my pink towels knotted around his waist and wore a much less grim expression. The last time I saw Detective Farrow, he was fully dressed and equally stern.

I pushed against the closing doors, but it was too antiquated a mechanism to respond to the presence of a human obstruction. Since neither detective made a move to assist me in my effort to keep the doors open, I gave up the unequal contest and saved myself from being crushed.

Farrow spoke first. "We meet again, Ms. Siderova. I don't know where you think you're headed, but you're going to have to talk to us first. Perhaps you could begin by explaining how two people ended up leaving the rehearsal in an ambulance. I want to know every detail of what happened before, during, and after."

When Amber first reported the online threats against her, the older detective argued against Jonah's suggestion that they appease her by using me in an undercover role. My job was to determine if someone in the cast was guilty of sending the intimidating posts and to protect her from further harassment. Since I had no official capacity, Farrow had limited his opposition to a few grumpy complaints about amateurs. I swallowed his implicit criticism, because amateur or not, I deserved it.

I kept my face composed but couldn't control the wobble in my voice. "I don't know what happened. I should have paid closer attention. That was my job."

"Yes, it was. Do you have anything to show for it?"

His gruff response stiffened my spine. "You were the one who thought this assignment was a waste of time. I believe you called me a babysitter and Amber, a spoiled starlet. I'm not alone in misjudging the situation. Those threats against her were real."

While he searched for a suitably cutting comeback, I sent Jonah an oblique glance, hoping he'd hear my wordless message.

Jonah's face didn't give any indication he'd received my telegraphed plea, but I was well acquainted with his ability to hide his emotions. "Farrow, why don't you get started with the others? I'll talk to Leah and catch up with you when we're done."

His partner wasn't ready to give up so easily. "Are we going to have the added benefit of Mrs. Siderova's reports and advice in addition to Leah's?" He turned back to me. "Or has your mother decided to stick with writing and turn today's events into a book?"

My mother wrote crime fiction. Although Barbara's knowledge of detection was limited to online searches regarding knife wounds, obscure poisons, and untraceable handguns, she considered herself an expert. One of my fondest memories was listening to her explain to Farrow how her amateur detective, a professor of literature, went about solving crimes. In the end, Barbara failed to convince him that the literary analysis she used to unmask a killer in *A Midsummer Night's Death* applied to his pursuit of real villains.

I overlooked his sarcasm, which I suspected hid more complicated feelings about my mother. "Thanks for asking, but I'm flying solo this time. I'll let Barbara know you were asking about her."

"Please don't." With a sudden blush and an awkward bob of his head, he left.

I couldn't wait any longer, not even for Jonah. "Please. You have to let me go."

Although no one was in the hallway, Jonah spoke with professional detachment, as if dozens of officers from the New York Police Department of Investigation were taking notes on our conversation.

"I can't let you do that, Leah. You have to give us a statement. We didn't take those threats against Amber seriously. That was my fault, as much as Farrow's. Until we know more, we have to treat today's incident as an assault. Could be attempted murder."

I dropped the two heavy bags, which were digging twin trenches into my shoulders, on the floor. "That's all the more reason to let me go. I can call you from the hospital with an update. Amber doesn't have so much as a cell phone with her. She's all alone."

"Trust me, Leah. She's not alone. Officer Morelli is with her, and she's in charge."

This was good news for me, but bad news for the police officer in question. Francie Morelli and I spent time together during a previous investigation at American Ballet Company, which was when I learned of her ballet-phobia. That phenomenon wasn't uncommon among women forced to take lessons as kids. Guarding the temperamental cast of a Broadway show was unlikely to constitute an improvement for her.

"Poor Francie. Maybe next time, you could assign her a post at the WNBA."

Jonah's inflexible posture indicated he wouldn't release me or allow himself to be distracted until he got what he wanted. With as much brevity as I could manage and still deliver a coherent story, I gave him a summary and description of the events that transpired over the course of the day, from the first *plié* to my recent conversation with Bryan.

He was similarly terse. "Thanks, Leah. This will help when I talk with the others. I'll be in touch later."

I snaked my leg around his and pulled his face toward mine for a kiss, but Jonah remained in Cop Mode and resisted temptation, other than a single word: *Later.*

Chapter Four

I'm the original take-orders girl.
—Judy Garland

When I arrived at the hospital and asked for a visitor's pass, the nurse on duty kept her eyes on her computer and said, "You have to be a family member."

I didn't miss a beat. "Tell Ms. Castle her sister is here."

The nurse swiveled in her chair to examine my face. "I didn't know Ms. Castle had a sister. Except for the hair, you look just like her!" She handed me a paper mask and a visitor's badge and directed me to her room.

Unlike Amber, I wasn't famous enough for ordinary people to recognize me. Every once in a while, I'm met with the kind of look that says, in true New York City fashion: *Hmm. Looks like she could be someone, but I'm too cool to admit I've seen her, whoever she is.*

I edged down the hallway, keeping my arms close to my sides and barely breathing through the itchy mask. I hate hospitals. The needles, the tubes, the beeping sounds, and the smell of disinfectant made me feel ill. I fought against the lightheadedness, afraid that a medical professional would impound my visitor badge and replace it with a hospital wristband and a bed in the emergency room.

I forced myself to breathe more deeply and made it to room 507 without passing out or having a panic attack. Compared to the rest of the day, that achievement counted as a major victory.

Francie Morelli stood at attention outside Amber's private room. She inclined her head, which sat atop a six-foot-tall body, and said, without detectable humor, "We've got to stop meeting like this."

I put my hand to my heart as if wounded. "Don't freeze me out, Francie. I'm legit now. We're practically coworkers."

She scanned the empty corridor. "In that case, you won't mind me telling you that when you're working undercover, you don't make announcements about it. The entire ward now knows you are, as you say, legit."

"Unless the nurses at the front desk have bugged the hallway, I think I'm safe." I hesitated before entering the room. "How's she doing?"

The police officer was her usual taciturn self. "You want a medical report, talk to a doctor. Or to Ms. Castle. I think she's awake now."

I knocked softly and tiptoed to where Amber lay, her red curls vivid against the white pillow. Her eyes were closed, and the ghastly pallor that had so frightened me was gone. The windowsill held a vase filled with roses so fragrant they overpowered the scent of eau de hospital.

Hovering over her was the most beautiful man I'd ever seen in real life. Unlike most, the director of *Mad Music* looked better in person than in his publicity shots. I wished I did. Face to face, I didn't look nearly as good as in American Ballet Company's professionally produced photos.

Sam Flannery straightened up and greeted me with an easy smile. "Leah Siderova. I regret we had to meet for the first time like this, but Bryan needed a few more days with the dancers before we have a full-cast rehearsal."

"Thanks, Sam. I'm looking forward to working with you." I wrenched my eyes from his face to Amber's. "I've been worried sick about her. How's she doing?"

Amber opened her eyes and briefly smiled. Her voice wasn't as slurred as the last time I saw her, but it was still weak. "Did you bring my bag and my phone?"

I patted her carryall, but her phone had entered the black hole that resided at the bottom of all handbags. It was hiding under a lunch bag, an empty, orange plastic medicine bottle, and a jeweled dog collar that spelled out *Farley*. A half-eaten candy bar was stuck to the back, and I wiped off the sticky mess before giving it to her.

She was too weak to hold the phone and motioned to the nightstand, where I put it in easy reach.

"Why don't you two get acquainted while I take a short snooze?" She fell asleep almost before she finished talking.

Sam bent down to kiss her and beckoned me to follow him into the corridor, where Francie was still on duty. He smiled a greeting at her and guided me a discreet distance away.

The director clasped both my hands. "I can't thank you enough for taking care of my girl."

I wasn't impressed by people whose claim to fame was their good looks. Every day, I danced with men of extraordinary beauty. American Ballet Company was full of them, as was the cast of *Mad Music*. My work environment was not as enviable, however, as one might think. Physical perfection warps the brain, which was why I avoided entanglements with the drop-dead gorgeous. This ban applied equally to men and women. How can you be friends, or fall in love, with people whose deepest affection and loyalty is to their own image?

In other words, I shouldn't have been held spellbound by the charismatic director of *Mad Music*. But I was. Lost in the depths of his gray eyes, I almost forgot to answer him.

I slipped my hands out of his. "It, er, it was n-nothing. I wish I could have done more." I swallowed hard to dissolve the lump in my throat. "I was supposed to protect her."

He leaned with graceful ease against the wall. "It's not your fault. You're looking out for her, which is all we want."

I blinked back guilty tears. "I don't understand what happened, or why it happened. I'm so—I'm so sorry."

Sam's voice was husky with emotion. "Don't say that, Leah. Don't even think it. Amber's diabetic. It was an accident."

Of course he was going to say that. It didn't make his claim true, although it did make me feel a tiny bit better. "The police don't think it was an accident. Did she get sick from something she ate? Or a missed dose?"

He held his hands wide. "She thinks she drank someone else's coffee that

19

had real sugar instead of the fake stuff. What other explanation is there?"

I could think of at least two other scenarios. Someone could have deliberately switched Amber's cup. Or, someone could have spiked her coffee with real sugar.

I kept those fears to myself. "I should have remembered she was diabetic. Amber has done so much work raising money for her organization. She's almost as famous for that as she is for acting. But it all happened so quickly. When she said she was high, I didn't realize she was talking about her blood sugar. She kept asking for Lynne, and I was too clueless to understand she was telling me to get her insulin. I thought she wanted Lynne Heller, our wardrobe mistress."

I remembered, as if it had been years instead of hours ago, the red leather makeup bag in the bathroom that matched the larger one I'd brought to the hospital. No wonder Amber ran down the hallway. She must have left her supply of insulin in the bathroom.

Sam brushed back a lock of hair that hung across his perfect brow. "The diabetic community has its own language, including a million insider names. Amber might tell you she's roller-coastering or that she's zombied. 'Lin' is her personal nickname. There's no way you could have known that."

Little by little, I started to relax. "What happens next? Will she be able to return to the show?"

He laughed. "What do you think? They'll keep her here overnight, but I'd bet good money our girl will be back, if not tomorrow, then the next day for sure. Being onstage is Amber's life. It keeps her going as much as insulin."

"What about Marty? Was he admitted to the hospital?"

Sam worked his jaw, which did nothing to diminish its chiseled appeal. "The wardrobe assistant? I'm sorry to say that Marty isn't doing nearly as well as Amber. He's in intensive care. I don't know what knocked him out. We'll have to hope for the best."

Before leaving the hospital I stopped by the front desk, where a different nurse was on duty. Like the woman he replaced, the new guy was as eager to deliver information as a billionaire being questioned by a Congressional oversight committee. I'd have to wait for Jonah to learn anything further.

I went to the gift store and spent a small fortune on two bouquets, one for Marty and one for Amber. There wasn't much more I could accomplish until Amber was strong enough to talk, so I left the hospital and headed home. With Sam and the imposing Francie guarding her, Amber would be well-protected.

I picked up a microwave meal at my favorite bodega, and when I got home began an online investigation of Sam. Maybe a little more thorough than if I was interviewing him for a job as a schoolteacher, but far short of the stalking I would do if I'd made a date to meet him after swiping right.

Most of what popped up I knew. Sam's acting career, his achievements as a director on Broadway and in Hollywood, and his two divorces were common knowledge. Also well-documented was his brief romance with Rose Summerson, a young performer with the cast of *Mad Music,* who'd had a freak accident a few weeks earlier.

Sam Flannery had no reason to hurt Amber or Rose. From a professional standpoint, the loss of either one would hurt him, not help him. He might be an unfaithful lover, but he hadn't been anywhere near the room where Amber and Marty fell ill.

I crossed him off my list of suspects for a crime that might not have happened.

Chapter Five

If you don't challenge yourself and risk falling...it's not interesting.
—Julie Taymor

My last task was to file a report for Jonah and Detective Farrow, but the day's events evoked emotions too raw for me to write a dispassionate summary. I couldn't do it. Instead, I delayed recording what happened in the previous ten hours and reread the report I'd completed a day earlier, before everything I thought I knew unraveled. Unsure of what the proper procedure was, I hadn't yet sent it to Jonah and Detective Farrow.

Day One

Met the cast. Contradicted rumors about a romance between me and Bryan. Got pranked. Had drinks with Amber, who was a no-show at the rehearsal. She thinks her online troll is either Rose or Natalie. Definitely not Carly.

I read the report twice, with growing dissatisfaction. My grocery lists were more inspiring and informative. I deleted every word and rewrote the journal as if it were happening in real time. If yesterday's events held any clues to the horrific conclusion of today's rehearsal, they'd be in the details, not in a cold recitation of facts. I organized this new effort into three parts.

Without stopping to think or edit, I let my unfiltered memory guide me. What follows is what really happened on the day before Amber and Marty collapsed.

Day One/Part 1: Behind Enemy Lines

Dance captain Carly Messina welcomed me to my first rehearsal by hammering home the distance, and the difference, between life as a ballerina and life as a Broadway hoofer. She reminded me of a morbidly sadistic kid who'd made my sixth-grade life miserable, and the glare she sent my way made me wonder if I reminded her, in a similar fashion, of a childhood enemy.

With the same marble-hard eyes, mousy hair, and thin lips as my elementary school antagonist, Carly possessed a bully's mystifying ability to intimidate. Standing against the mirror of a drab rehearsal studio, she addressed the assembled dancers with the enthusiasm of a cult leader but without the charm that inspires people to hand over their life's savings.

She pointed to the large picture window, which offered a view of some of Broadway's most famous stages, and said, "I've been dance captain for six shows, and I promise you, this one's a sure hit. We've had a few bumps along the way, but that's in the past. Next week, we bring them to their feet on opening night."

Carly's defiance of theatrical superstitions alarmed me. I expected to see at least a few faces reflect my irrational fear that predictions of good fortune would end up delivering the opposite, but most were unmoved.

Bryan was one of the few to react with visible displeasure, although the young choreographer didn't voice his dismay. A series of unfortunate events, from random injuries to financial instability, had dogged this production for months, and Carly's blithe prediction clearly grated on him. I caught his eye and mouthed *merde*, which was how dancers wished each other good luck.

With clenched hands, he crossed his arms and made an X in front of his chest. I got the joke but was careful not to register amusement. Bryan was using ballet pantomime, and his pose was how dancers delivered a death threat while onstage. Offstage, the crossed-arm pose was shorthand for a much milder wish for another person to stop talking.

Unaware of the pained reaction she'd elicited in two of her listeners, Carly segued into a rambling story about a conversation she'd had with Bette Midler during a revival of *Hello Dolly!*

A dancer with large dark eyes and a cascade of braids that extended to her waist leaned into me and said, "If I have to hear one more time about how Carly and The Divine Miss M bonded, I'm going to lose my breakfast. And unless I'm missing something, Amber Castle's last two shows closed in less than a month. She and Carly are like the kiss of death."

Cheered by the presence of a like-minded cast member, I introduced myself. "I'm Leah Siderova, and I'll be dancing Dreamcatcher."

She stared at me with comical intensity. "Really? Totally didn't see that coming, Ms. Prima Ballerina. I'm Natalie Stevens. Most days, I'm holding up the scenery as the second-worst dancer in the crew, but I'm also Amber Castle's understudy. My acting and singing are a lot better than my hoofing."

I was pleased to find a friend so quickly. "In that case, we're even. My dancing is a whole lot better than my acting and singing, which is why I'll be talking with my feet. Any chance you'll get to move from the back row to the spotlight?"

"Amber would miss giving birth before skipping a performance. She's banking on this role to put her back on top. As you can see, though, she's not as dedicated to showing up at rehearsals as she is to self-promotion, which is driving Bryan crazy."

Natalie put a hand across her mouth to mute the rest of her complaint. "What made you, of all people, decide to get on board this sinking ship? Most of the rats have left. There was a huge casting call last week for another revival of *Fiddler on the Roof*. That's the show that's going to run forever."

I'd prepared an answer for anyone who questioned my motivation to join the cast, but I didn't have to use it. Carly paused in her long-winded recital about Bette Midler to glare at us, which spared me the need to explain. My new friend met the dance captain's gaze with a mock-serious salute, but I adopted a contrite expression and sat at attention. It would do me no good to make one friend if, in doing so, I made a more powerful enemy.

Bryan, oblivious of any tension, edged the touchy dance captain aside.

"Thanks, Carly. Great story. I'll take it from here. Okay, people, I'll begin by introducing Leah Siderova, who is joining us as the new Dreamcatcher. Most of you probably know her work with American Ballet Company. We're lucky to have her. Obviously, she's a pro. The put-in will be a piece of cake."

The same people whose faces had radiated sympathetic attentiveness when Carly was talking regarded me with less kindness. I'd danced in front of thousands at Lincoln Center, but braving those two dozen critical cast members was more daunting. Did anyone suspect I was there to spy on them? Or was my outsider status the problem? I waved at the hostile circle and said something eloquent along the lines of *um, hi, great to be here.*

If Bryan was conscious of the sub-zero reception my presence inspired, he didn't show it. His posture, the result of a lifetime spent in ballet class and onstage, was easy and graceful, and his blue eyes didn't blink. When Carly attempted to interrupt him and take charge again, he ignored the obvious sentiment in the room that favored her and said, "Save the rest of what you have to say until later. We have work to do, and the clock is ticking."

She flexed arm muscles that bore witness to a lifetime in the gym and winked at the dancers. "Whatever you say, Boss."

A ripple of muted titters followed Carly's words, and Bryan's face turned pink. He was accustomed to the iron discipline of ballerinas. They could be counted upon to follow every directive, even if it led them off a cliff. Carly's cheeky answer rattled him.

With no great show of haste, the dancers took their places for the opening number. As the first beats of music echoed through the studio, Bryan regained his dictatorial manner, and he made adjustments to the spacing and choreography with unsmiling efficiency. The dancers' mild rebellion ended without a single shot fired.

I'd had several private rehearsals with Bryan in advance of this first meeting when he taught me most of the steps and gave me a video to study the rest. It hadn't taken long for me to memorize the choreography, but the challenge of integrating myself in the larger group, which was the "put-in" he'd referenced in his introduction, proved tricky.

Most of the dancers were seasoned veterans, but one or two looked as if they'd wandered into the studio from Dolly Dinkle's School of Ballet. It was no easy feat to earn a spot in a Broadway show. They were supposed to be the best of the best. But they weren't.

At the end of my first solo, I exited from the center of the room, stepping backward and pausing to balance every four counts with my leg stretched high over my head. Bryan was focused on the entering chorus. That's when I turned and tripped over a large, heavy dance bag, which hadn't been there when I began.

Muscle memory, honed over many years of dance training, saved me. I managed to fall on my hands, which prevented my fragile knees from further injury.

Bryan furiously kicked the bag out of the way. "What the—"

Carly stepped between Bryan and the bag. "Hold your horses, cowboy. Accidents happen. That's why God made understudies."

I didn't yet understand the laughter that followed, but everyone else did.

Chapter Six

I wasn't naked. I was completely covered by a blue light.
—Gypsy Rose Lee

I closed my laptop, too tired to keep writing. Pulling the blankets over my head, I tried to stop thinking about *Mad Music*, but the remainder of that first day of rehearsal unspooled in my mind's eye, a movie that refused to turn off.

I gave up on sleep and restarted my journal, again writing down the events as they happened.

Day One/Part 2: Gossip Girls

When I tripped over the dance bag, the dancers' amused reaction bruised my feelings, although not as painfully as the crash-and-burn fall hurt my body. I, however, would doom myself to a lifetime of blisters on my big toe before revealing physical or emotional weakness. While Bryan fumed and everyone else smirked, I arched my back and curled my fingers into claws. "It's a good thing I have eight more lives."

The tide of public opinion appeared to shift a few millimeters in my favor, but I was too intent on hiding my sore hands and pounding heart to care what my catty coworkers thought of me. I brushed myself off and returned to the center of the room. When it came time to repeat the back-facing exit, I did so without a wobble or stumble.

Although *Mad Music* was my Broadway debut, Bryan and I had collaborated many times during his tenure at American Ballet Company. His choreography was filled with tricky balances and off-kilter turns, and the role of Dreamcatcher was an endurance test on par with Act II of *Swan Lake*. By the end of the day, my muscles ached with strain. Neither this nor the painful fall I took was the worst part of the rehearsal process, which was emotional and not physical. Carly continued to snipe at me, and any hope I might have harbored about blending in with the cast went down in her sarcastic flames.

I have a high, light jump, which two knee surgeries had not yet destroyed. Bryan, as he had in the past, took advantage of my natural affinity for the air. After making some minor adjustments to the choreography, he left for a meeting and let Carly take over the rehearsal.

The dance captain stopped me mid-leap. Speaking with exaggerated patience, Carly said, "Dig your heels in. You were chosen for this role because you look like Amber Castle, not because you dance like her."

A ripple of laughter greeted this comment. Was Carly mocking me? Or was she taking aim at Amber, who hadn't shown up for my first rehearsal? Despite her celebrity status, Amber didn't have a diva's reputation, but that persona, perhaps, didn't match her real-life actions. Not that this mattered much. Once you make it to the top, jealous competitors itch with the desire to push you off.

Carly yawned. "I'm sorry, Ms. Prima Ballerina. I must have dozed off waiting for you to get moving."

When Natalie called me a prima ballerina, it was a compliment. Coming from Carly, it was an insult, but I remained outwardly impervious. The dance captain's snide antics paled next to what I'd endured over the course of my career. Although her acid remarks made my undercover job more difficult, they didn't dent my confidence. If there's one thing I can do better than most people, it's dance, and I proved it when I went through the routine again, pushing and bending deeper into the ground.

Again, Carly stopped me. "Your arms are all wrong. You've got them in a weird fourth position instead of extending them straight in front of you."

I returned to my starting position for another attempt, but she shoved me out of the way and showed off her cat-like jump. Her muscular arms stabbed the air in front of her, fingers held straight, long legs scissoring the air. She was terrific.

Without comment, I mimicked her stretchy landings and powerful arm movements. My growing mastery of the choreography pleased her less than the earlier, more tentative efforts.

Several hours later, the problem of my too-airy jump ended when my knees and my will to live weakened to the point of no return. With the union clock ticking off expensive overtime minutes, Carly dismissed us. All the dancers except Natalie exited in a clubby group and made loud plans to meet for drinks. My new friend detached herself from the others and linked her arm in mine. She followed me to the dressing room.

I took out a jar of my favorite liniment and showed Natalie the label. "Consider yourself warned."

She waved her hand to indicate an immunity to the stink of camphor. "I'm not sensitive. And speaking of being sensitive, don't let Carly or any of the other dancers get you down. It's not personal. She's upset because she was supposed to dance Dreamcatcher. She was going to hate anyone who got the part over her. The rest of the cast will follow her lead at first, but they'll get over it."

"I wish I could tell you how sorry I am to hear that. Maybe I should talk to her. I know how it feels to get pushed aside for someone else, but this wasn't my call. I didn't ask for the role. It was offered to me."

"Not sure that'll make any difference, but you could try." In a casual tone that didn't match her words, she said, "No offense, but Carly told us you and Bryan are hooking up, which is why he bumped her and chose you."

Hah. Turned out ballet and Broadway had more in common than I anticipated. "I am not, nor have I ever been, romantically involved with Bryan Leister. We danced together at American Ballet Company and became friends. Nothing more."

I didn't mention the more complicated aspects of my relationship with the young choreographer. For anyone still interested in that ancient history, a two-minute online search would yield plenty of information about the last time we worked together, when he cut me from the cast of his new ballet. If

Natalie didn't know the whole story, I wasn't going to be the one to tell her how my rival ended up dead. Especially since the real reason I joined the cast of *Mad Music* in the first place was to make sure history didn't repeat itself.

Chapter Seven

I wanted to make people happy, if only for an hour.
—Busby Berkeley

I dozed off and didn't wake again until the rumble of sanitation trucks outside my window began their early morning song. I staggered into the kitchen, made some coffee, and plugged in my dying laptop. Almost done. Before starting my third day at *Mad Music*, I was determined to finish documenting the first one. Day Two could wait.

Day One/Part 3: Some Like It Hot

Amber didn't attend my first rehearsal but texted an invitation to meet at the end of the day. Natalie and I exited together, which was trickier than I anticipated, as the star of the show was standing outside the D'Anconia, signing photographs.

"Ms. Castle! We love you, Ms. Castle!" A crowd of fans thrust old programs, photographs, and pads of paper in her face. Others waved phones and tried to get selfies with her and with her dog Farley, who was almost as famous as she was.

Amber acknowledged Natalie with a curt nod, but when she turned her lovely face in my direction, she broke into a smile. In a voice that cut through the surrounding chatter, she said, "I'm so happy to see you! Meet me at Joe Allen's. I'll be in the back room in fifteen minutes." A few of her admirers aimed their cameras at me in case I, too, turned out to be famous.

Natalie saluted me with the same ironic gesture she'd given Carly earlier in the day. "I knew you had friends in high places. I didn't know The Castle was one of them."

I wished Amber had been more circumspect in her greeting. "Neither did I."

A handful of customers sat at the bar at Joe Allen's, and the back room was equally quiet. The restaurant catered to theater people, but it was too early for the post-performance crowd and too late for pre-theater drinks and dinner. When I told the guy at the front desk I was meeting Amber Castle, he welcomed me as if I were a long-lost rich uncle and brought me to a corner table in the rear.

Wearing dark glasses and a scarf pulled up to her nose, Amber joined me a few minutes later, along with an adoring employee, who brought two martinis. I hadn't eaten enough food to make martini drinking safe, but I didn't want to seem ungrateful.

She removed a shapeless black stocking cap from her head, and those much-photographed red-gold curls cascaded down her back. She was so beautiful, so vivacious, it pained me to think of her as she looked twenty-one hours later, lying in a hospital bed.

Stop. Regret wouldn't help her or me. I gulped down more coffee and continued the summary of my first meeting with the glamorous actress, which, in hindsight, was more revelatory than it first appeared.

Amber hugged me and said, "I wanted us to have a private space where we could speak freely. I spend so much time here. It's practically my living room." The actress flashed a smile. "Sorry to keep you waiting, but I had to hand off the mutt."

I was disappointed not to see her dog. "I was hoping they'd let you bring Farley inside. Where is he?"

"My assistant is taking him to a very expensive pet hotel. It's like the Ritz-Carlton for dogs. Thanks to my publicist, that mangy animal is getting more popular than I am."

She took out a compact to inspect her face. "I had a meeting today with Detective Sobol, which is why I couldn't make it to rehearsal. In my humble opinion, he belongs in the centerfold of a sexy cop calendar. It was worth getting trolled to spend time with him."

When Jonah briefed me, I hadn't yet met the magnetically beautiful Amber. Now that I had, a sting of jealousy bit. I hid this reaction with a veneer of polite interest. "What did he tell you?"

She leaned back and drank deeply from the frosted glass. "He assured me you'd be discreet and that you knew what you were doing."

Her next words had an ironic weight that wasn't apparent until I wrote them down.

"To be honest, Leah, I'm not sure anyone understands how dangerous my situation is. Detective Farrow blew me off, saying online threats were the price of fame. I couldn't get a read on Jonah, though, and I'm a pretty good judge of character. I'm hoping you can persuade both of them to take me seriously."

Amber's inability to analyze what Jonah was thinking was typical of most people. When he got his inscrutable gaze on, it was tough to know what was going on behind those dark eyes.

I didn't have to imagine Detective Farrow's response. I'd already heard it. "Since the police department refused to open an official investigation, why not hire a private detective? And while you're at it, a security guard as well."

She bit her lip. "Believe me, I've tried, but it's not as easy as you think. The last guy I hired was secretly feeding the trolls. That's why I needed someone I knew I could trust."

She tilted her head and gave me a knowing look. "I've heard Mr. Hot Cop and you have quite the history together, and it's common knowledge Bryan wanted you to dance Dreamcatcher from the start. He said he choreographed the role with you in mind."

Unlike Amber, who wove together her personal and professional life in one seamless public relations package, I preferred to keep mine separate. "It's true, Detective Sobol and I are friends, but we're not romantically involved. As for Bryan, his offer of a contract was a lucky coincidence because without it, we wouldn't have been able to get me into the show at this late date. He offered me the role months ago, but I was in the middle of *Nutcracker* season, and I wasn't sure if I wanted to leave the company for so long."

I ignored further queries regarding Jonah and said, "None of that is important. The threats against you are. If you'll allow me a few days' access to your social media, I've got a good friend who works outside traditional channels who may be able to help. I've had to battle my own virtual demons, which is why I'm happy to be working under the radar this time around."

She raised her glass in a toast to our shared misery. "Yeah, I know all about what you went through, and you have my sympathies. I can't remember the name of the hater who trashed you, but I haven't forgotten what a bad rap you got."

Savannah Collier. She was the ex-dancer and would-be social media influencer who'd built up her reputation by attempting to destroy mine. I drew some consolation from the fact that my nemesis hadn't yet achieved the heights of name recognition she so desired, but it wasn't for lack of effort.

I again pressed Amber for details. "Do you have any idea who's behind the threats? If it isn't some random lowlife, like a guy who didn't get your autograph and is now nursing a grudge over an imaginary insult, who could it be?"

"I wish I knew. It started with anonymous posts. Some of it was stupid stuff, claiming I wasn't doing my own vocals and that I should quit the show. Then, the threats started. As soon as I reported them and the accounts were taken down, new ones took their place. Very quickly, the whole thing got out of control. I realized the guy sending me direct messages knows me, knows where I am, and knows what I'm doing. Here's the latest DM."

She held up her phone. It read: **I'm getting closer**.

Amber's eyes were glassy with unshed tears. "It had a photo of me with blood spattered on my face, but the picture disappeared after I opened it."

The message sickened me, but I kept my voice and manner under control. "Let's not get ahead of ourselves. The person who sent this could be miles away and afraid to leave his house."

She buried her face in her hands. "What if he isn't miles away? What if he's outside right now?"

That was a chilling thought. Fifteen minutes earlier, she'd been surrounded by fans who posted pictures of her and her location to untold numbers of people. Her stalker could be loitering beside the entrance to the restaurant, waiting for her. Waiting for us.

If what she suggested was true, perhaps her tormentor was someone she knew in real life. "Could the sender be a cast member? Or maybe your stalker has a close connection to someone in the show. It's also possible a jealous coworker is playing into the hands of someone dangerous. That's what happened to me."

Her face hardened. "If we discount my cheating ex-husband, Natalie is at the top of the list. Don't let her fool you with that nice-girl, innocent way she has. I've been in this business a long time, and I can spot her type from a mile away. She'd stop at nothing to star in this show, and I'm standing between her and her ambitions. We've both seen that story play out a thousand times."

It figured. My only friend was Amber's prime suspect. But surely there were others. "What about Carly? She seems more the type. I'm pretty sure she'd take me out in a heartbeat and possibly you as well."

Amber tipped her glass to drain the last few drops and delicately patted her mouth. "Carly is a little rough around the edges, but underneath her tough exterior, she's a cupcake. And even if she wasn't, she's not going to go after you. It wouldn't be worth it to her since even if you left, they'd have to find someone else."

Given Carly's talent, I wasn't ready to credit Amber's analysis. "Why would she get passed over? She may not have a big name, but mine isn't exactly a household word. Carly knows the role inside and out, and although she's a miserable person, she's a terrific dancer."

Amber dismissed this argument with a wave of her well-manicured hand. "Carly is way too tall. Bryan wanted someone who looked like me for the Dream sequences."

She cut me off when I tried to point out the logical flaw in her argument. "Carly and I go way back. Trust me, Leah. She's no backstabber."

From what I saw of her in rehearsal, Carly had enough fiery ambition to fuel a Space X mission to the outer reaches of the galaxy, but I didn't debate the issue. Amber trusted her, and I put aside my hasty judgment of the dance captain. You can't evaluate a woman fairly when she's smarting from rejection. I'd been in that position several times. Getting left at the altar might be worse than getting cut from a ballet you love, but not by much. My experience with the latter left me with wounds as deep as any jilted bride.

Perhaps others, besides Carly and Natalie, had been slighted or passed over. When I asked Amber, her tone became cool. "There's a chorus kid I have my eye on. Like Natalie, Rose Summerson is a nobody who thinks she's going to be a star. Her strategy is to have sex with guys she thinks will advance her career."

I was inclined to side with Rose. "At her age? She's probably more a victim than a predator."

She set her mouth in a stubborn line. "Rose Summerson—who's no Anna Pavlova, by the way—is smarter, tougher, and more devious than she looks."

I studied Amber's face, with its mobile, delicate features, while she signaled to the server to bring another round. Her porcelain skin was mostly unmarked, aside from a slight droop beneath her chin and a network of fine lines that circled her eyes. From a distance, she might be in her thirties. Up close, I could see she was at least ten years older than that.

When I pushed her again for more information, Amber admitted, "If you must know, Rose and Sam Flannery were hooking up for a while. The whole stupid affair is now well and truly over."

Relationships between powerful men and vulnerable young women were too commonplace to make headlines unless there was some unique angle. I didn't meet Sam until the day after this conversation with Amber, so I wasn't yet convinced of his good intentions. I also didn't yet know that Amber and Sam were an item. If I did, I would have phrased my next question more diplomatically.

"There are a few girls in the show who are weak dancers. Did Sam have sex with all of them?"

She put her martini down so forcefully a few drops sloshed over the wide brim of her glass. "No! You've got the totally wrong idea about him. Rose seduced him, not the other way around."

I fished three olives from my drink to appease my empty stomach. "I'll take that under advisement. In the meantime, I'll use Natalie to find out more about the others, and I'll use Bryan to find out more about Natalie. Did you have something particular you want me to do?"

In light of what happened to her the following day, the memory of what she said next pained me and shamed me. "I want you to watch my back. And I'll watch yours. I don't know what life is like in a ballet company, but in the theater, you have to remember that everyone's acting a part."

Amber's observation ended my Day One journal. Unlike the rest of my gifted family, I wasn't a writer, and I had serious misgivings about submitting the document. There was almost as much conjecture as information, and it was thick with details that might not be important.

I deleted everything except the cold, hard, impersonal facts. The parts about Jonah were the first to go, and quite a lot of the rest also failed to make the cut. I emailed a much shorter and less emotional version and got back to dancing, the one thing that came naturally to me.

Chapter Eight

No dance has ever turned out the way I thought it would.
—Mark Morris

Subtle differences in behavior emerged on the day after Amber and Marty went to the hospital. These minute changes manifested themselves in a more watchful attitude, an absence of gossipy laughter, and, for me, a heightened sense of isolation.

One alteration was easy to spot: there were no complimentary pastries or donuts on the table below the windowsill. Carly put her cup under the spout of the coffee urn and lifted the tab, but it was empty. She clinked a spoon to get everyone's attention. "This empty coffee pot tells us more than that stupid email we got. You'd think someone would have the courtesy, or the guts, to let us know what happened to Marty and Amber. I couldn't get a word out of that detective...what was his name? Sobol?"

Bryan cut her short. "It was Amber who provided the free coffee and donuts, and since she's in the hospital, you'll have to do without. No one's keeping any secrets from you."

Carly walked away from the table and stopped a few feet in front of me. "Maybe Leah can fill us in." She cocked her head and pursed her lips in a showy display of innocent inquiry. "I've heard you and Sobol are friends. *Very* good friends. So don't hold back on us. We're like a family, including the fights over who's the favorite kid."

I resisted the itch to speak my mind. "I met Detective Sobol and Detective Farrow when they worked a case at American Ballet Company. They're both good cops, and I trust them to get to the bottom of what happened yesterday."

With false friendliness, Carly poked me with her index finger. "I think you're holding out on us." She spun around to point the same finger at Bryan. "You're also good friends with Sobol. The guy definitely gets around."

Encouraged by a round of laughter, she continued, "Anyone besides me notice how these bunheads have taken over? I mean, if I wanted to hang with that crowd, I would be doing this—" She broke off to do a perfectly turned-out double pirouette. "Instead of this." She bent one knee and spun around twice, her legs in a parallel position.

There were many feats of skill Carly could have selected to prove her superiority over me. Skiing, ice skating, sky diving, and softball would have been good choices, since I loathe cold weather, am afraid of heights, and lack the hand-eye coordination necessary for most sports. Electing to compete in the realm of dance technique wasn't a good move on her part. I placed my feet in fourth position and did a classically perfect triple pirouette. Without pause, I stepped toward her and echoed her parallel turn, spinning four times before coming to a slow stop and sliding into a split.

I looked up at her red face and echoed her prehistoric insult. "Don't underestimate a bunhead. You never know when you might need one."

I had no desire to further antagonize her and held out my hand. She grabbed it to pull me to my feet. "Not bad. For a ballerina."

I nudged her with my elbow. "Not bad. For a hoofer."

Her peace offering didn't fool me. The woman was as adept a shapeshifter as the most craven politician. She'd turn against me as soon as it benefited her. For the moment, however, the dance captain had given me an opening. If I could breach the close-knit clique of dancers and actors, I had a better chance of finding out if one of them was hiding a deadly grudge against Amber.

I quieted the butterflies waltzing inside my stomach and spoke in a mild, affable tone. "I was in the middle of my solo when Amber and Marty got sick. Did any of you see what happened? I have no idea why Marty collapsed, but we all know Amber has diabetes. Did she drink from the wrong cup? Did anyone, er, accidentally, of course, put sugar in her drink?"

Rose Summerson stepped forward. The harsh words, coming from her angelically young face, startled me. "Are you accusing one of us of tampering with her drink?" A growl of support thrummed from the group.

Unwilling to let the fragile warmth between me and my colleagues recede back into the Ice Age without a fight, I spoke without rancor. "That wasn't an accusation. It was a question. What happened to Amber was probably an accident."

I raised my voice a notch. "Just like the accident that sent me crashing to my knees in the middle of my solo. Or the accident that put you, Rose, out of commission for over a week."

No one answered. People looked at the floor and their phones but not at each other.

Carly, unwilling to yield her position as the center of attention, pounced on Bryan, although with the opening Rose gave her, she couldn't resist another dig in my direction. "Since Leah can't tell us anything, maybe our leader can shed some light. Bryan, the least you can do is tell us how our friends ended up in the hospital and how they're doing."

Bryan tried to deflect her by changing the subject. He took out a clipboard and began reading us notes on the previous day's progress.

It didn't work. He was drowned out by a flood of protests. Bryan ignored them and strode back and forth across the room, his long legs eating up the space with ravenous energy. "That's enough. I'm not going to comment until I have more information."

He clapped his hands. "Let's go, people. We have work to do." The choreographer resorted to the one person he knew wouldn't fight him. "Leah, we'll start with the Act I ballet."

I took my place in the center of the rehearsal studio, and the others followed suit. The cliché that time is money was especially apt in the performing arts, and social media was roiling with gossip that claimed *Mad Music* was running low on both. For once, the rumors were true. If we didn't pull together, the show would open and close before my fellow dancers accrued enough weeks of work to qualify for unemployment.

I regretted not having the opportunity to eavesdrop on the intense, whispered conversations taking place along the sidelines but hoped Natalie could clue me in later.

Carly, having once again been relegated to obscurity, waited until our first break to continue her argument. "Bryan, I'm not giving up. You owe it to us to let us know what went down yesterday."

He fought back. "How many times do I have to tell you the same thing? Health records are privileged information. I can't tell you what I don't know. Even if I knew, I don't owe you anything."

Cool sarcasm was Bryan's usual mode of intimidation, but Carly wasn't cowed by his heated response. She railed against him with ill-concealed bitterness. "I'll stop asking when you start respecting how we feel. We've got as much riding on this show as you do. Maybe more."

Other than a telltale flush around his ears, Bryan suppressed further proof of his emotion. "Believe what you will. But this is my rehearsal, and I'm going to run it my way."

The dramatic reversal from the previous day's détente between the choreographer and the dance captain was breathtaking in its vitriol. I spent most of my career working with unpredictable and tempestuous artists but was hard-pressed to find its equal.

This time, Carly didn't look to the other dancers for support. She knew they wouldn't risk the loss of a well-paying job for an unwinnable argument. Bryan's next gig might be as the choreographer of another production they hoped to join. No one burns those kinds of rickety bridges.

Carly executed a sharp about-face. "Listen, Boss, please understand how we feel. We're terrified." Her hard eyes turned liquid, and her strong shoulders shook. "This is no joke. Who's going to watch over us? Who's going to protect us?"

Interesting question. It was supposed to be me.

Chapter Nine

Creation is a drug I can't do without.
—Cecil B. DeMille

Despite the drama that rocked the morning rehearsal, we resumed working as if our lives depended on it. Which, from a financial standpoint, they did. *Mad Music* was paying the bills.

Self-interest, however, couldn't dispel the lingering resentments that cast an uneasy pall over the rest of the day. I fought to keep my concentration from fracturing into a thousand tense fragments, and the strain was evident in others as well. Bryan barely noticed me fumble a series of turns, and he watched the men form a ragged line without a single derogatory comment.

Running like a dark current below the surface was our worry about Amber and Marty and the more selfish concern that we, too, might be in danger. At the end of the work session we received a single update, which was delivered via email. The brief missive cited privacy issues and stated that Amber would return soon and Marty at an indeterminate future date. I knew, thanks to a late-night call from Jonah and an early morning text from Amber, that she planned a dramatic entrance. Her message began with a line of hearts and said: **My peeps need to know the show will go on!**

As we danced the final steps of the Dream ballet, with Natalie again subbing for Amber, the actress swept into the room on the arm of our director. They were both so beautiful, they glowed. She stepped away from Sam, twirled around, and stretched out her arms as if to embrace us all. "I'm so happy to be back! Thank you, everyone, for the lovely flowers and notes."

Her cheerful greeting broke the jittery silence. We dropped our poses and rushed to her. Sam, after complimenting us on our work, let Amber take center stage while he spoke to Bryan, who listened but didn't say much. The choreographer, whose balletic grace and camera-loving good looks earned him modeling gigs in the off-season, faded in comparison to the director. Sam's brilliant gray eyes, fringed with black lashes, blazed across the screen in his film roles. In person, his charisma made everyone around him look pale.

Everyone, that is, except for Amber.

While the star of our show chattered gaily about how well she felt, Rose eyed Sam. Like the rest of us, though, she didn't approach him. I wondered again about their relationship.

Natalie also stood apart. She circled the room to stand next to me and pointed to Rose. "If looks could kill, Sam would be the next one carted off to the hospital. Or the morgue."

Despite Rose's harsh words, I felt sorry for her. "Amber said Sam's relationship with Rose is over, and I think she's right. Poor kid."

Natalie dabbed an imaginary handkerchief to her dry eyes. "Before you start crying a river over poor, heartbroken Rose, remember that she took advantage of him. So don't let it keep you up at night."

"Amber said the same thing, but I don't believe it. He's a powerful guy, and she's a struggling kid. Not what I would call a level playing field. I especially hate the fact that Sam has taken up with Amber. It's bad enough having your heart stomped on. It's worse when it takes place in public."

Transactional relationships in the performing arts were common and drearily predictable. Someone got used. Often, someone got abused. Sometimes, both parties got what they wanted, but it was rarely without cost.

Amber was reticent about her health scare, but unlike Bryan, she didn't hold back from telling us how Marty was faring. She dropped her breezy manner and with a sober look, said, "I met Marty's parents this morning. They're devastated. The poor guy suffered a brain bleed. When he fainted, he hit his head pretty hard. It's truly awful. The doctors say it may be a while before he recovers. He could end up with permanent damage."

Carly elbowed Rose out of her way and said, "Do the doctors know why he fainted? Did it have anything to do with why you got sick?"

Natalie cut in before Amber could answer. "We shouldn't jump to conclusions. It could have been something totally random. Maybe he was hungry. Marty was so skinny, he probably couldn't skip a meal without feeling faint. It's lucky the ambulance arrived as soon as it did."

Amber looked fragile, but her voice, which was famous for reaching the back row of every theater, was strong and sure. "I drank coffee that had sugar in it instead of Splenda. If it wasn't for my diabetes, nothing bad would have happened to me. But Marty's parents told me his coffee was roofied. I can't remember the name of the drug that knocked him out, but it was strong enough that he lost consciousness."

Carly asked the question that hung over us. "Does Marty have any idea who did it?"

Amber shivered. "His parents said his memory is starting to come back, but it's still spotty. He can't recall anything that happened yesterday, but it's possible that over time, it'll come back to him."

She lifted her chin and tossed back her flaming curls. "Most of you know me well. For those who don't, I can tell you this: I'm not going anywhere. And I'm not giving in to the haters." Her eyes grew liquid with unshed tears. "You guys are my family. You're like the brothers and sisters I never had, and I won't let you down."

Amber knew the person who spiked the coffee was among the group of people that she, like Carly, called her family. With respect to recent events, the only way the familial comparison worked was if the two women had relationships similar to the fraternal bond between Cain and Abel.

Amber was neither gullible nor naïve. Her blind spot was her belief that her coworkers, like her fans, loved her. As I watched her laugh and joke, however, a different rationale for her proclamation occurred to me. If Amber suspected Natalie, perhaps she was sending her an implicit warning not to attempt another attack.

While everyone except Natalie and Rose offered protestations of loyalty and love, and the men vied to embrace her, I stood apart from the rest and watched the two women who remained outside Amber's charmed circle. Natalie's reticence was probably a function of Amber's cold attitude toward her. Rose presented a different problem. I couldn't decide if she was jealous of Amber, afraid of her, or simply heartbroken over Sam's defection.

Amber and Natalie, who rarely agreed on anything, both thought Rose had schemed to entrap Sam. I wanted to hear from the young actress herself what transpired. This move proved difficult, as every time I got close enough to speak privately, Rose slipped away.

Bryan broke off his conversation with Sam to dismiss us. The actors, whose role during the dance scenes was mostly decorative, executed a swift exit. The dancers lingered, rubbing down their muscles and packing away shoes and warm-up gear. I retreated to a corner to mull over the paltry facts in my possession.

Amber's indiscreet discussion of Marty's health troubled me. Despite intense pressure, Bryan had been far more prudent. Now, however, whoever drugged the coffee cups knew Marty might recover his memory and help identify the culprit. I picked up my phone to text Jonah, but with magical prescience, he texted me first. **My place at 8?**

I jumped when I realized Amber was peering over my shoulder.

"Don't panic, girlfriend. It's just me." Her heart-shaped face showed amusement but no self-consciousness about reading my messages. "I was going to suggest we meet for dinner, but it looks as if you're booked for the evening. How about tomorrow? Or the next day? Let's have breakfast at Beaulieu. Their coffee and croissants are the best I've had this side of Paris."

A breakfast meeting would prevent me from taking a ballet class, which was a non-negotiable part of my life. Rehearsals were no substitute for that necessary ritual.

"Make it brunch. Or lunch. My teachers are all on tour with ABC, so I keep in shape with an early morning ballet class at Studio Dance. Why don't you come with me?"

She lifted one leg a few inches off the floor and pointed her foot, stretching it as far it would go in its narrow, spike-heeled boot. "Studio Dance is too hardcore for me. Unless you're taking a beginner-level class, I wouldn't last five minutes. And anyway, I need to take advantage of tomorrow's day off to recover from this traumatic experience. The doc wants me to take it easy for a few days. But brunch is fine. I don't eat breakfast until noon, at the earliest."

A slight vibration alerted me to another text and, immediately after, two more. I slipped the phone into my bag until I could read them in private.

When Amber bent closer to the mirror to touch up her lipstick, I checked the screen to see if I'd missed anything important. The first message was from Bryan. The choreographer was standing ten feet away and must have texted because he didn't want anyone to know about his invitation, which read: **Meet me for dinner? Made reservations at Paradox. My treat.**

I'd made plans to meet Jonah but knew he'd understand why I had to cancel. I answered Bryan with a like and glanced at him. He gave me a wink and a thumbs-up. The messages that followed were from my mother and from Gabi, my best friend. Those could wait until later.

Sam fist-bumped Bryan, and the two men joined Amber and me. If the director was apprehensive about the continued problems and delays surrounding his show, he covered it well. With a brilliant smile, Sam said, "How's our local hero doing? I managed to catch the end of your solo." He kissed my hand, which I hoped was not as sweaty as the rest of my body. "You're a star. Even better than Bryan promised."

His praise pleased me, and the knotted muscles in my neck relaxed their grip. "I'm looking forward to seeing the whole show."

Sam ran his hands through shoulder-length dark hair. "It's still a work in progress. We had it on the road for a good long while, and although we've still got some work ahead, opening night is looming." He put his arm around Amber. "My girl's gonna be great."

A slight movement from behind Sam caught my eye. Rose Summerson was in the doorway, fists clenched, listening to every word.

Chapter Ten

Ballet technique never becomes easy, it becomes possible.
—Agnes de Mille

Rose was nearly at the elevator by the time I gathered my belongings and said a quick goodbye to those who had lingered after the rehearsal ended. She didn't respond when I called her name and instead bolted through the exit door to the stairway. Her long legs took the stairs three at a time.

My knees stung with repeated shocks of pain as I raced after her. "Rose! Wait!"

She yelled over her shoulder, "Leave me alone!"

I almost caught up with her at the bottom of the stairwell, but she shoved open a grimy, creaking door, headed toward Eighth Avenue, and kept going.

Running wasn't as hard on my knees as tearing down the stairs had been, but at the end of a long rehearsal, a prolonged sprint was not on my list of preferred pastimes. I slowed to a walk when it occurred to me that I would see Rose the following day. She couldn't avoid me forever. If she didn't want to tell me about her relationship with Sam, inevitably, someone else would be happy to deliver the latest gossip.

At the crosswalk, she turned to see if I was still following her. Interestingly, she didn't keep walking and instead waited at the corner. People don't like being pursued, but they also don't want to miss out.

I stayed put and waved, trying to convey the type of smug goodwill a passenger on a swanky ocean liner might feel upon seeing a less fortunate friend stuck on the pier. It wasn't a difficult posture. I was in a position of power, both short and long-term, with dinner reservations at a trendy restaurant and a starring role on Broadway. She'd been publicly dumped by the fickle director of *Mad Music* and was toiling in the back of the chorus.

Rose walked back. Her face was streaked with tears. "Why are you following me? Can't you see I want to be alone?"

I wasn't winded, but I wasn't popping with energy, either. "I don't want anything from you other than a few minutes to talk. Maybe I can help. You look like you could use a friend."

Rose's lower lip trembled. "Any friend of Amber's is no friend of mine. And I don't know why you think you can help me. I have nothing to say to you." She emphasized the word "you" each time, a clear indication that of all the people who could have offered help, I was the least qualified to do so.

I wondered if she guessed my connection to Amber was more complex than the transient kind of friendship that springs up during a limited run. One way or another, I had to find out.

"You can trust me, Rose. Let me buy you a cup of coffee. Or a drink. Your choice." I took her arm. "The Fremont Hotel is down the block. We can sit in their lobby and pretend we're guests."

She let me lead her into the hotel, and we sat at the bar. While she engaged the bartender in a discussion about which exotic cocktail best suited her mood, I did a quick calculation. Unless Rose spilled her guts in sixty minutes or less, I'd have to either postpone my dinner with Bryan or show up at one of the hottest restaurants in Manhattan dressed in a puffy jacket, worn jeans, and a sweater that only a family of moths could love. We had to speed things up.

Rose ordered an espresso martini, which sounded so delicious it made me forget about the time The number of calories in that drink wasn't in my vast mental database, and I had to check what the damages might be before getting one for myself. The numbers were appalling, and I ordered a white wine spritzer instead. Sixty calories, which I knew without checking.

Watching the bartender mix her cocktail, I said, "Whoever thought of putting coffee and vodka together was a genius. I'm talking Nobel-Prize-type brains."

She laughed, and two quick drinks later, we were best buds. For some people, buying them a drink is the grownup equivalent of pricking your finger and declaring you're blood sisters.

Encouraged by her change in attitude, I said, "Why were you crying? And why on earth did you run away from me?"

She toyed with the stem of her glass. "Maybe you know that, um, Sam Flannery and I have been seeing each other?"

"Of course. That information doesn't rise to the level of a state secret. Is that why you ran away from me?"

Rose ordered a plate of truffle oil parmesan french fries and picked at the snack with long, delicate fingers. I ignored the intoxicating scent of fat and carbs. Eating fried potatoes with extra oil and cheese wasn't an option for me unless an asteroid was going to hit the Earth, and humanity had less than one week before the world-annihilating impact.

She waved a seductive slice of potato and said, "There was a lot of mean gossip making the rounds. People said I wouldn't have gotten the job with *Mad Music* if I wasn't having sex with Sam."

Like the first one she'd offered, this revelation didn't qualify as ground-breaking. "I heard that too. But don't feel bad. They're saying the same thing about me and Bryan."

She didn't deny it. "Yeah. But you're a great dancer, so it doesn't matter if that's what people think. I'm not. I'm a really good singer and actress, though. I'm waiting for the chance to show what I can do."

She sounded like Natalie. And she resembled my friend in other ways as well. *Mad Music* had four cast members who were uncommonly beautiful, with showgirl legs and killer smiles, but they lacked the perfect technique and elegant bearing of the more gifted dancers. I wondered if the under-performing quartet had secured their jobs, at union-scale wages, via the casting couch.

Rose's aggrieved expression irritated me in spite of myself. Too many dancers, far better than she, were waitressing at places like the Fremont Hotel and hoping to get a Broadway gig. She got the job a more talented woman had lost, a job that legions of dancers sweated for and wept for.

Though maybe I was being too judgmental. It's not as if she didn't pay for it. One way or another, we all did.

I forced myself to see the situation from her perspective. "I suppose we're even, because the rumors about both of us are the same. Except I'm not in a relationship with Bryan, but you are with Sam."

Her eyes got red, and her mouth trembled. "Not anymore. I can't compete with Amber. Even though she's ancient. She's gotta be ten years older than him."

This additional piece of information, similar to the other two nuggets she passed my way, didn't qualify as a news flash. It was also rather sexist, since the age gap between her and Sam was easily ten years, if not more. "No one can compete with Amber. Not at any age. Did Sam dump you for her?"

She finished the potatoes and started eating from a bowl of nuts. "He denied it, although I don't know whether or not I can believe him. It all happened while I was out with that stupid injury. Sam sent piles of flowers, but by the time I got back to work, she had her claws in him."

I bent my head over the wine spritzer and watched her from the corner of my eye. "If you ask me, you're well out of it. Sam's girlfriends seem to have had a run of bad luck. First you, then Amber."

She ducked her head, as if embarrassed. "I-it was an accident. Typical me. The one day we got to rehearse in the theater, I tripped over a loose cable. It wasn't anyone's fault, other than mine. I'm a klutz."

I was still unsure if Rose was as innocent as she seemed. Half the time, she reminded me of a trusting kid. But underneath that childlike charm, she might have a more cunning side to her personality. Did she not know about the rumors, still in circulation, that speculated the loose cable was intended to trip up Amber and not her?

"Don't be so down on yourself. Dancers can't be trusted to put one foot in front of the other if they're outside the studio or the stage. I've been known to trip over invisible objects or my own feet." I waited a beat and then added, "Although when I fell during rehearsal, that wasn't my fault. Any idea who could have booby trapped my exit?"

She skipped past my question in favor of the topic that interested her. "Sam said he wants us to take a break until after the show opens and that he's hanging with Amber because he thinks it'll make for good PR. Do you think he'll come back to me?"

If she could avoid uncomfortable questions, so could I. "You haven't explained why you ran away from me. That was, um, kind of a surprise."

Unexpectedly, she dimpled. "I didn't want you to know all the stuff I just told you. But you won't tell anyone, will you?"

After promising to keep her secret until death, torture, or a really bad hair day forced it out of me, I made a mental note to tell Jonah. And that's when I remembered I had two dates at the same time, with different men. In less than an hour.

I didn't want to offend Rose with a hasty exit, but as soon as I stood up, a guy who looked like he belonged in a magazine ad for a Rolex watch immediately took my place. He even paid the bill before I could, which was a good thing, given the price of those drinks and fries.

On the subway home, I texted Jonah. **Ok to meet later? Bryan invited me to dinner-business/not pleasure.**

He texted back, **Need pleasure/not business**

I laughed, but not loud enough or long enough to make the other riders vacate the car to avoid a potentially unstable person in their midst.

I sent a last text as the train pulled into my station. **Later? My place?**

He answered with a like. Jonah knew all about my history with Bryan, which had never been romantic, and I was relieved not to have to deal with a jealous response.

When the subway doors opened, I fought against a crush of people determined to enter the car before the exiting straphangers could leave. I climbed the stairs to the street level and, for the second time that day, sprinted down the length of a city block, although this time, I was in pursuit of time and not an emotionally wounded starlet.

This fifty-yard dash was followed by the daily mountain climb up five steep flights of stairs to my apartment. My leg muscles joined my knees in a heated protest against the abuse, but I had no time to baby them with a massage or cool compress. I showered off the dirt and perspiration of the day, reapplied makeup, and contemplated the limited contents of my closet.

If Bryan hadn't been willing to foot the bill, I wouldn't have accepted his invitation. Paradox was the kind of chic and expensive restaurant my former boyfriend and his current wife would have loved. Jonah, who lived on a cop's salary, was more likely to suggest a hot dog at a Mets game or spaghetti at a red-sauce dive in Little Italy. Paradox wasn't simply expensive. It was also famously exclusive, and even if I had sufficient income to purchase so pricey a meal, I still couldn't have gotten a reservation for months, possibly ever. Bryan's star was certainly rising.

I possessed leotards and tights in abundance but few items sophisticated enough to pass muster at Paradox. Choosing a color, however, was easy. Nearly every item in my closet was black, since I'm not confident enough to wear bright colors unless I'm in costume. I picked out a pair of skinny black pants, a clingy black lace shirt with a high neck and bare back, and the stiletto boots with red soles my mother bought me from her favorite thrift shop.

The boots were my first tactical error of the evening. In the eternal fight between vanity and comfort, I was a sucker for good looks over good sense. By the time I got to the bottom of the stairs, my bunions were furious with their unexpected and unreasonable confinement. Instead of changing shoes, I splurged on a taxi.

The cost of a ride from the Upper West Side to Chelsea would easily be offset by the free dinner. That's what I told myself, and I'm sticking to it.

Chapter Eleven

Part of the joy of dancing is conversation.
Trouble is, some men can't dance and talk at the same time.
—Ginger Rogers

Double-parked cars lined the street in front of Paradox, and diners hoping to capitalize on a last-minute cancellation jammed the sidewalk. The restaurant had two levels of seating, and I climbed a circular staircase to where Bryan was waiting at a balcony table that provided us with a view of the rich and famous customers below. He rose and kissed me on both cheeks. I wasn't expecting the debonair double smooch, since his usual greeting was a grunt and a light shoulder punch.

Bryan settled into his chair and said, "Thanks for coming, Leah. I wanted to meet away from the theater or rehearsals, where we could have some privacy."

I didn't question his choice of a meeting place, although, like Amber, he'd selected a very public space for an intimate conversation. Maybe that was how Broadway people did things. The last time Bryan and I met, we went to the Aband-Inn, which was located on a desolate strip in the Far West Village. The only movers and shakers at that place were cab drivers and truckers.

The server uncorked a bottle of Bordeaux and handed us two menus so beautiful they should have been hanging in an art gallery instead of subjected to fingerprints and water stains. There were four options: Omni, Pesci, Veggie, and Vegan. The descriptions identified the farm-to-table source of the food but omitted a clear explanation of what we'd be eating.

When I questioned Bryan about the menu, which outdid Hemingway in brevity, he said, as if it were common knowledge, "You're supposed to give yourself over to the experience and not bring preconceptions to the meal."

If given the choice, I would have been wearing sweatpants and eating a grilled cheese or tuna melt. Since neither of those items was on the menu, I ordered the Veggie and hoped for the best. As soon as the waiter left, I asked Bryan to give me a rundown of events that took place before I arrived for my first rehearsal. So much had happened, it was hard to believe I'd come onto the scene a mere three days earlier.

He mistook my query for an invitation to discuss our personal relationship, but what I wanted to know had nothing to do with our history. Clinking his raised glass against mine, he said, "I was delighted when you agreed to join *Mad Music* not only because you're perfect for the role, but because I want this to be a new start for us. We used to be friends, good friends, but the last time we were together, it was under super stressful circumstances. Let's go back to being a great team. So, no hard feelings, right?"

If Bryan had made his plea with a less complacent expression, I might have answered with greater forbearance. His assumption that I would overlook his previous ill treatment of me was infuriating. Did he think he was so powerful he could get away with any transgression? Or was that his version of an apology? The less emotional side of my brain argued it was reasonable of him to assume I didn't hold a grudge. As far as he knew, I'd taken a leave of absence from American Ballet Company because I couldn't resist the opportunity to dance with him again.

I leaned back and crossed my arms. "How much retroactive forgiveness did you have in mind?"

His smile lost some of its toothy confidence. "Uh, I totally get it if you're still mad, but it all worked out okay in the end. I was under a lot of pressure at the time. I was choreographing my first piece for the company. And the murder devastated me."

Our food arrived, which gave me time to craft a reply that was kinder than the one he deserved. The server, with a flourish worthy of Houdini, placed before me an assortment of vegetables that had been tortured into fantastical shapes that bore no relation to their humble beginnings. A spaceship made of string beans floated on a cloud of asparagus fronds, which sat next to a pyramid built from tiny carrot bricks that were held together with a mashed pea mortar. A chunky avocado river meandered around a brown mountain range of...mushrooms? Turnips? It looked too pretty and precious to taste good, but it smelled like veggie heaven: sweet, savory, and salty.

I picked up my fork but had to swallow my anger before I could get anything more tangible down my throat. Bryan, in his typical self-serving fashion, left out several salient details in his review of our last collaboration. Most notably, he failed to mention that during his period of artistic stress, I was the one who'd been falsely accused of murder.

He reached across the table and took my hand. "I hope we can be friends."

Someday, I'd tell him how I felt when he cut me in favor of a younger dancer, but that time had yet to come. I agreed to meet him for dinner because I was investigating threats against Amber Castle, and I needed him on my side. Dredging up the past wouldn't further those goals.

I kept to my version of the script and returned his smile. "I've always been your friend, Bryan. I think your choreography is going to be the hit of the show." The second part, at least, was true.

He gnawed on the last piece of bread in the basket. "Obviously, my choreography is going to be great. The problem is the advance ticket sales, which are way below expectations for a show like this. If *Mad Music* closes in two days, it could be a good long while, maybe forever, before I get another shot at Broadway. That's my main concern."

I stared at the table to avoid staring at him. Two people left the previous day's rehearsal in an ambulance, and one was still in the intensive care unit. Bryan's self-absorption was annoying and appalling, but it also, perhaps, made him vulnerable to manipulation.

I mimicked his narcissism. "I'm right with you on that. I thought I was signing up for a smash hit that would help my career, not a flop that'll bury it."

"Exactly. There is some good news, though. After the PR release that announced you joined the cast, there was a definite spike in sales. We need to keep the ball rolling. Show up at a few high-profile events together as, er, as a couple." He had the grace to look embarrassed.

Bryan's proposal sounded suspiciously like the one Rose told me about, in relation to Sam and Amber. I didn't know if the romance between the director and the star of his show was real, but the prospect of faking a relationship with Bryan made me queasy. Or maybe it was the onion jam that disagreed with me.

"There has to be some other way to promote the show. The cast thinks I was hired because we're hooking up. Let's not give that rumor legs."

He pushed back his chair. "I don't care what the cast thinks. Broadway hoofers are a dime a dozen. It's the producers, the press, and the industry insiders who concern me."

How soon they forget. It wasn't long ago that he was a dime-a-dozen, insecure member of the ABC corps de ballet.

Bryan beckoned to a passing server and handed her his phone. He lifted his wine glass and told me to do the same, and we smiled for the camera. He muttered a distracted thank you and then framed and edited the photo. The Sistine Chapel didn't get as much attention from Michelangelo as Bryan's social media posts got from him.

I switched from wine to water and waited until Bryan emptied most of the bottle before inviting further confidences.

"What did you and Sam talk about this afternoon? Did it have anything to do with Amber?"

He pushed a tiny stack of matchstick potatoes around his plate. "Uh, no. He's very upbeat. Loves Amber and the choreography."

I put my hand on his arm to prevent him from further deconstruction of his food, a transparent attempt to avoid a direct answer. "C'mon, Bryan. It's late, and I'm tired. Don't hold out on me."

He responded by telling me what the entire theatrical world already knew. "Amber doesn't have the pull she did a few years ago. She got some brutal reviews after her last show, and she wasn't Sam's first choice. He wanted someone young and hot, but after Lily Ferrante backed out, he took what he could get. Sam wants to change the narrative, make it sexier, and give the gossips something positive to talk about. It was his idea that you and I appear together as a couple. He wants us to come with him and Amber to a big fundraising party she's hosting for her charity."

I wondered if it was Sam Flannery who'd secured us a prized table at Paradox, where our presence would be seen and noted by Important People. Famous directors got seats wherever and whenever they wanted them. I hoped the couple who'd been bumped to accommodate Bryan and me hadn't been forced to wait and that the unlucky twosome weren't tourists who'd booked a reservation six months in advance and were now sitting at the bar or eating at a makeshift table behind the swinging doors to the kitchen.

After a moment of complete non-suspense for both of us, I agreed to go with him to the fundraiser. I was motivated more by sympathy for Amber than any practical consideration. She wasn't the only one aging out of her profession.

As with Bryan's earlier assumptions about me, it was clear he expected me to acquiesce. "It's Friday night at some luxury event space in Tribeca. I'll pick you up at six-thirty. This is a major event, you know. Tickets start at five hundred bucks apiece, and that's just for cocktails. We've got a spot at the head table for dinner. Doesn't get more high profile than that."

"What else did you and Sam talk about?"

"Nothing. A few housekeeping items connected with the show."

"Bryan, I hope you're not a poker player. Quit lying and tell me what's going on."

A telltale pink flush bloomed around his ears. "You have to keep this secret, Leah. I swore to Sam I wouldn't tell anyone."

I rested my elbow on the table and put my chin in my hand to indicate complete attention and discretion.

He leaned close. "Someone is threatening Amber. Until yesterday, it was limited to online trolling. Sam thinks now it could be someone in the show."

"Bryan, everyone knows Amber's got a stalker. Some unknown person posts trash about her. A secondary group of trolls shares it, and then thousands defend her. It has all the reality of a wrestling tournament. If you want to share secrets, you'll have to do better than that. Start by telling me who you think could have spiked Amber's coffee. And while you're at it, I want to know who Sam thinks could have done it."

He picked up his wine glass and stared into its crystal depths as if it held the answer to the meaning of life. "I don't know. I'd tell you if I did."

"I'm not going to Amber's gala with you unless you quit lying and tell me everything you know. Now. Before I walk out."

The pink flush around his ears spread across the rest of his face. "I don't want to make false accusations, but since you're so interested, Lynne Heller had the best opportunity to spike both cups of coffee."

There's nothing like a double fake to make one's head spin. Sam told me that when Amber called for *lin* she was referring to insulin and not to the costume mistress. Bryan's theory brought me back to my first impression. Which was true?

"What possible motive could Lynne Heller have to hurt Amber? I know she was angry with Marty for flirting instead of working, but that's not a good enough reason to send him, let alone Amber, to the hospital."

Bryan peered at my pile of uneaten food. "If you're done, do you mind if I...?"

"Not at all." I exchanged my half-full plate for his empty one. His hunger was justified. Sometimes, the more you paid for a meal, the less food you got. On the other hand, I wasn't taken in by Bryan's attempt to change the topic.

"Bryan, this little ploy you have going, trying to distract me, won't work. Who, besides Lynne, had either the motive or the opportunity?"

He crunched on something green and stringy that wasn't a string bean. "You sound like you're investigating a murder."

I corrected him. "Attempted murder. I'm interested in who might have poisoned two people, because I don't want to be the next victim."

His mouth hung open as if he hadn't heard, nearly verbatim, the same complaint from Carly. Despite his choreographic talent, he was, perhaps, not the brightest light on Broadway.

Bryan spoke softly, although the noise level at Paradox was high enough to threaten future hearing loss. "I could be wrong about Lynne. She had the best opportunity to tamper with the drinks, but that doesn't mean she did it. If someone deliberately poured sugar into Amber's coffee, the most likely suspect is Natalie, possibly with Carly's help. If Natalie took over the role of Leading Lady, then Carly would end up dancing Dreamcatcher. The two of them don't look as much alike as you and Amber, but the resemblance is close enough." He brushed his palms as if washing his hands clean of blame. "No offense, Leah. That's the way it is. Easy come, easy go."

"No offense taken. At this point, I'd pay to get out of my contract."

Bryan dropped his cavalier attitude and gripped my arm with the same nervous energy that animated him at rehearsals. "Don't say that! I put Carly in your place yesterday because you walked out on me. We need some serious star power to lift this dead weight of a musical. Without advance ticket sales, we're sunk."

I unhooked his fingers from my arm. "Then think, Bryan. Is there anyone else, besides the obvious two who will benefit? The person who hurt Amber is likely to try again."

"I can't think of a single other person who would hurt Amber. She may not have been Sam's first choice, but everyone loves her."

"Amber's online stalker doesn't love her. The people who troll her don't love her. And she stands in the way of two ambitious women, both of whom have a huge social media following and are more popular with the cast than either of us."

He curled his lip in disdain. "I'm not running for office, and I don't care what the dancers think about me as long as they get the job done. As for the rest, you, of all people, should know you can't judge a person based on social media. Remember when you went through that? Plenty of people hated on you, but even more came to your defense. Eventually."

If he wasn't obtuse, he was still holding back.

As if sensing my doubt, he added, "You haven't had the chance to spend much time with Amber, but I'm telling you, she's the opposite of a diva. She treats everyone, from the custodians to the stagehands, like they're good friends, and she's known for helping other performers. On top of that, she's poured a lot of time and money into her charity. It's famous, although I can't remember the exact name of it."

I didn't know much about Amber's charity either, other than the name. "It's called Dress the Dream."

He snapped his fingers. "Right. She gets big designers to donate clothes, and she auctions them off to fund diabetes research."

Thinking of the thrift-store remnants in my closet, I said, "I hope no one will expect me to donate or bid on any clothes. I can't afford haute cuisine, let alone haute couture."

The server returned to our table with the dessert menu. Bryan ordered tiramisu, which was an unnecessarily harsh move on the part of the diet gods. Earlier, I'd had to resist an espresso martini when I was with Rose, and now I had to resist an espresso and chocolate dessert.

For the record, I had an espresso coffee. Bryan paired his dessert with a cappuccino topped with whipped cream. If I ate the way he did, they'd have to roll me out of the restaurant.

The rest of the meal passed with relative ease. We chatted about mutual friends from American Ballet Company until the waiter brought the check in a black silk folder that could have doubled as an evening clutch.

Although Bryan promised to treat me, after I saw the price of our meal, I offered to help pay for it. Dinner for two at Paradox cost more than my entire outfit, painful boots and cab fare included. He refused and withdrew a black AmEx card from his wallet.

I didn't inquire into his finances, as the NYPD was better equipped to investigate that part of his life than I was. His romantic bottom line, however, was my job. If his relationship with Tess Morgan—and yes, she was related to *those* Morgans—was over, his standard of living should have declined. And yet, he treated the cost of our meal the way I did the price of a microwave dinner.

Aside from my investigation, I was genuinely curious. "Have you and Tess broken up?"

He was untroubled by the question. "Why would you think that?"

I approached the matter tangentially. "If I were your girlfriend, I wouldn't be happy that you were taking me and not her to this super-pricey dinner.

What's Tess going to say when you also take me to Amber's fundraiser? Those big social events are her kind of stomping ground, not mine."

"Tess understands what's going on. And anyway, she's in London for a big meeting of banking and hedge fund minds." He tossed his napkin on the table. "While we're on the subject, how's your detective friend going to handle our new relationship?"

I wondered what took him so long to ask. Bryan was still with American Ballet Company when Jonah and I met. He knew more about my personal life than anyone else at *Mad Music*.

"You and I don't have a relationship. Even if we did, it wouldn't matter to Detective Sobol. He and I are good friends. Nothing more than that."

"I'm still tight with the ABC dancers, and they said you guys are seeing each other and that it's serious." He scraped the last bit of cream from the dessert plate.

Gossip. The dance world runs on it. "They're right, if by 'seeing each other' you mean giving him a statement yesterday afternoon. Otherwise, no. Though, like I say, we're friends."

Bryan seemed satisfied with this answer, which indicated he continued to underestimate me and overestimate his charm and powers of persuasion. I couldn't afford to make the same mistake about him.

Chapter Twelve

I don't keep my secrets or my knowledge to myself.
—Natalia Makarova

I didn't get home from my dinner with Bryan until midnight. For our fellow diners at Paradox, this time slot was the prelude to an evening spent clubbing, but for someone who had to take a ballet class in the morning, it was an exhausting end of a long day.

I called Jonah. "Are you awake?"

He mumbled something that sounded like *mslvyou*.

"I'll take that as a no. Let's meet tomorrow night."

Sounding more alert, he said, "That works. But no last-minute cancellations. You can't dump me for another guy two days in a row. I'll get a complex."

I rubbed my aching feet. "Deal. I'm off tomorrow. Or, technically, today."

"That makes one of us. I'll try to get to your place by seven. Eight at the latest."

I tossed my bunion-crushing boots into the back of the closet. "Detective Sobol, you've got yourself a dinner date. As long as I don't have to cook."

"I would never ask you to cook. My job is dangerous enough."

Working undercover was a lonely business. I was sworn to secrecy, but this didn't prevent me from consulting Gabriela Acevedo, because unburdening myself to Gabi was the same as keeping a secret, except better. We met on the first day of seventh grade, and while most kids our age obsessed over zits and slumber parties, we single-mindedly pursued our dream of becoming ballerinas. Gabi and I joined American Ballet Company the day after our high school graduation and advanced through the ranks at the same pace. In the cutthroat world of professional dance, where true friends were in short supply, we had each other. Until we didn't.

I tried not to feel betrayed when Gabi fell in love, got married, and gave birth to Lucie. Although many dancers returned to the stage after having a kid, she gave up performing and began a new career as a teacher.

Happily, the bond we forged as kids remained as strong as ever, and after Amber canceled our lunch date, I headed to my best friend's apartment. In her narrow kitchen, I spooned a repulsive-looking banana and yogurt mixture into Lucie's mouth as Gabi listened to my story.

"For heaven's sake, Sid, what were you thinking? You're totally alone and defenseless. At least at ABC, you had Madame M, Olivia, and Tex. Jonah is crazy to be sending you into a situation like that."

Gabi was the only person who called me Sid. After my parents divorced, my mother decided her maiden name, Siderova, would look better on a Playbill and on her books than my father's surname, Feldbaum. She wasn't wrong, but the change felt contrived and pretentious, as if I was one of those ballerinas from a century ago who altered their names to sound more Russian. That was how Alicia Marks became Alicia Markova, and Hilda Munnings became Lydia Sokolova. The fact that I came by my exotic name honestly didn't change how I felt. It wasn't until Gabi started calling me Sid that I was able to embrace my professional name as my own.

I wiped banana muck off Lucie's face, which she interpreted as an invitation to smear herself anew.

"I'm not completely alone. Bryan will watch out for me as a means of protecting his career. I don't think he's aware I'm investigating, but after what happened to Amber and Marty, he'll be on high alert."

Gabi paced the kitchen on long, thin legs. "*Querida amiga*, I hope you're not counting on Bryan to look out for you. Unless he undergoes a major personality transplant, he will never care about anyone as much as he cares about himself. This is the same guy who took advantage of you and treated you like dirt. Is he still living with Miss Trust Fund and bagging ballerinas on the side?"

I straightened my legs to relieve the pressure on my knees. "Last night was the first time we've gotten together outside the rehearsal studio since he left the company, and we didn't discuss his sex life. But centuries will pass before I forget how he treated me the last time we worked together."

Bryan broke faith with me professionally, not sexually. It was, nonetheless, a painful episode. Long before he secured his job at *Mad Music*, I danced for him for free. I performed on open-air stages and tiny basement spaces, ensuring through my greater fame that he'd get noticed. He rewarded me by choosing a much younger rival to star in his first major ballet. In the end, I was the one who danced the role, but that was a story for another day. There are many ways a choreographer can take advantage of a dancer, and Bryan's ill treatment of me wasn't unique.

My loyal friend couldn't let it go. "He betrayed you." She lifted Lucie out of her highchair, hugged her tightly, and told her, "Never trust a guy who's prettier than you. They're all selfish." She glanced at her wedding photo, which featured a luminously beautiful Gabi and the pleasant but plain guy she married.

I traveled so deeply into memories of the last time Bryan and I worked together it took me a moment to return to Gabi's kitchen. She tapped me on the shoulder. "I will repeat the question. Who's going to protect you while you're snooping around dark corners of the theater?"

"You know the answer. There isn't anyone. Madame M, Olivia, and Tex are all on tour. And you're teaching at NYU."

Gabi shifted Lucie to one hip and ate the rest of the baby's food. I averted my eyes.

She prodded me. "Call Olga. No one's going to mess with you if she's there to protect you."

Gabi had a point. Olga Shevchenko, our steadfast Ukrainian friend, was physically imposing. Her cheerful façade hid equally massive tech skills, which made her doubly effective. Few people would guess that behind her twinkling blue eyes and warm smile was a brain that could hack The Matrix.

If I could convince Amber to give me access to her social media, Olga would surely be able to point us in the right direction.

"I'll text her now. If she's not working another job, I can try to pass her off as a Russian investor who's interested in dumping excess cash into our sinking show."

Olga didn't answer my message, but a few moments later, I got a phone call from a number I didn't recognize. I usually let those calls go to voice mail but picked up this one, because Olga often used burner phones when she was working.

To my relief, it was indeed Olga and not a scammer in need of a new source of income. The connection wasn't good, and I struggled to understand what she was trying to tell me.

"This is Irina you have called. Not available right now. But your health, it is good?"

"I'm fine, er, Irina. When will you be free? Can we meet tomorrow?"

Static broke up much of what she said next, but Olga's booming voice ensured the words that did come through were loud enough for Gabi to hear without putting her on speakerphone. "First, I must find place where the dog is buried. Must pay bills! But if emergency, will leave the dog and come home."

Olga's idioms were difficult to parse, but her tone, despite the static, conveyed the need for caution. "I understand. I, um, I've got a tsar in my head, so there's no rush."

"*Tak*, dear friend. Better not to contact again until I—"

The call abruptly ended. Gabi said, "What was that all about? Did a dog die?"

"I don't think an actual canine was involved. Talking about buried dogs is her way of saying she's on the hunt and looking for something. It's an old Russian saying. Olga must be working on a case and can't discuss it or use her real name. Although, for all we know, Olga isn't her real name either. She'll be in touch when she gets back."

Gabi held Lucie and gently bounced her up and down. "Where is she?"

"No idea. But you know Olga. She could be anywhere from Moscow to

Dubai to a safe house in Brooklyn or Queens."

She patted Lucie, whose eyes were starting to close. "I've never known who Olga works for when she's not helping us out of a jam. And what did you mean by telling her you had a star in your head? Is this a secret code that you've kept from me, your best friend?"

"I would never hold anything back from you! That's another of Olga's expressions. Having a *tsar*—not a star—in your head means you know what you're doing, that you're not making a mistake or misjudging a situation."

Gabi put her finger to her lips. Lucie was fast asleep on her shoulder. I whispered, "Olga's never told me what she does when she's off on one of her jobs. All she's ever said is that she mostly works for good guys. I hope she's safe."

I tiptoed after my friend and watched her put the baby in her crib. The kid was adorable, even with drool coming out of her mouth.

We returned to the kitchen. Gabi wiped up the mess on Lucie's highchair and said, "With Olga out of the picture for the foreseeable future, who else can you count on to watch your back?"

"One of the first things Amber said to me was that she would watch my back if I did the same for her."

Gabi looked up from her scrubbing. "That won't work. She's more vulnerable than you are. Think, Leah. Who can spot a faked pirouette from the back of the theater and would kill to protect you?"

The answer to her question was easy, but the suggestion was impractical. "The Weird Sisters, of course. But how can I plausibly get them into closed rehearsals? Once we're in the theater, I might be able to sneak them in. They can pose as cleaning ladies, and during the performance, they can carry programs and usher people to their seats. That won't help for at least a few more days. I'm not sure we can wait that long for backup."

Although I'd nicknamed my three elderly friends after the trio of witches in *Macbeth*, the Weird Sisters weren't weird, they weren't sisters, and they were emphatically good, not evil. They also were accomplished amateur dancers who helped nail the notorious ABC killer during a most memorable performance. Unfortunately, there was no place for them to hide in the bare, cavernous practice room at the D'Anconia.

Gabi scooped a pile of toys into a basket. "Talk to Jonah about the Weird Sisters. Abigail, Izzy, and Audrey are your best bet. Maybe he can work something out on his end."

I retrieved my coat. "I think you're overestimating the danger to me. As long as I don't blow my cover, I won't be a target."

My friend had one more piece of advice. "Don't get too close to Amber. She can't go anywhere without being recognized, and if you're seen with her, you could end up in the crossfire."

I tugged big, clunky boots over my swollen feet. "I could have used this recommendation before I agreed to attend her big fundraiser."

Gabi grabbed my sleeve. "You're going to the Dress the Dream gala? Couldn't you find a higher-profile event?"

I pointed to Lucie's bedroom, and Gabi lowered her voice. "Don't go, Leah. I don't care how fancy and high-class a bash it is. Say you have other plans."

"I can't back out now. I agreed to go with Bryan as part of a grand plan to rev up positive PR for the show. We're going with Amber and Sam."

"Why? Was the President not available?"

I wished I had Gabi, instead of Amber, by my side. "Your sarcasm is duly noted and appreciated. And let's hope the President does make an appearance, because if he does, the Secret Service will be there too."

She followed me into the hall. "What's Jonah going to say about you going with Bryan?"

"I'll find out tonight."

Chapter Thirteen

There is obviously a truth in action that doesn't lie, which words easily can do.
—Twyla Tharp

When I left Gabi's apartment, the clouds parted, and an unexpectedly balmy end to the day inspired me to walk across Central Park to the West Side. The air had a springlike sweetness to it, and a few hardy crocuses responded by poking their heads through the mud. In New York City, the stores were a more reliable indicator of the seasons than the weather, and the shop windows along Columbus, Amsterdam, and Broadway were bright with pink and yellow bunnies and chicks. Snowstorms can blow through as late as April, but that late March day soothed my jangled nerves with its promise that winter was nearly over.

I picked up two dinners from a local Italian restaurant and a bunch of daffodils from the bodega on the corner. When I got home I swiped the floor with a mop and transferred the lineup of drying leotards and tights hanging in the bathroom to the oven. Since most of my cooking took place in the microwave or on the stove top, using the oven for storage made efficient use of the limited space in my apartment.

I unpacked cartons of takeout salad for me and pasta for Jonah and was in the middle of setting the table when the intercom buzzed. Ten minutes later, when Jonah didn't show up, I went down a flight of stairs to rescue him from Mrs. Pargiter's clutches. My neighbor kept a strict and disapproving eye on my comings and goings, and she was capable of interrogating Jonah for a good thirty minutes.

I liked to keep things interesting for her, so I called out, "Come on up. My husband's not home."

Jonah said, with mock gruffness, "This is the police. Come out with your hands up."

When he finally made it to the top of the stairs, he didn't waste time talking. He pulled me close and said, "Dinner can wait. I need dessert."

His touch, his lips, burned through me. I was starving, not for food, but for him.

Later, over my wilted salad and his lukewarm noodles, we discussed the recent turn of events at the *Mad Music* rehearsals. Jonah said, "We've gone over the statements of every person at the rehearsal and a few who weren't. I crosschecked each one against your report and put together a timeline, but so far, it's not helping much. There was a window of opportunity when nearly everyone had the chance to spike Marty's coffee. Same for Amber's."

I poured wine into Jonah's glass and sparkling water into mine. "Did you get the lab results? Amber said Marty's coffee was roofied but didn't specify what knocked him out."

"He got a hefty dose of ketamine, and Amber got coffee that was loaded with sugar. Separately, they wouldn't do much damage, but the combination of the two is deadly for a diabetic. That makes it even more likely that Marty was collateral damage in an attack that was meant for Amber."

I entered ketamine into my browser. "This is interesting. I knew ketamine was used for pain and depression but didn't know it was used for horses." I scrolled down. "There's also a bunch of websites that talk about addiction and abuse."

Jonah said, "It's not hard to come by off-label, and we see it a lot in date rape victims. Marty's a toothpick, and the dose hit him hard enough that he passed out. He would've been fine if he hadn't hit his head on the radiator at an unfortunate angle. But like I say, I don't think he was supposed to get the drug. If Amber had gotten the ketamine along with the sugar, the combination could have killed her. The doc said ketamine can worsen a condition called..." he stopped to consult his sheaf of papers, "It's called acidosis. So, a diabetic with high blood sugar who takes ketamine goes into diabetic ketoacidosis. DKA, for short." He showed me the doctor's report.

I remembered the medic saying much the same thing. "I'm surprised Amber didn't taste the sugar in her coffee. I would have."

"You drink your coffee black. She uses cream and a sugar substitute and couldn't tell the difference." He retrieved his backpack from the living room and withdrew a notebook. "The most plausible scenario is one in which the perp dumps sugar in Amber's drink, or maybe switches her cup with Marty's, but can't manage to drop the ketamine without someone noticing. Maybe the person leaves the table and then returns and hits the wrong cup. Who had the best chance of doing it? Or, is there anyone you can definitively exclude?"

I wished I hadn't allowed myself to get distracted by the wig fitting. "It must have happened when everyone was saying how much I looked like Amber, and—"

Jonah interrupted me, which was rare for him. He was too good an interviewer, whether he was inside an interrogation room or in my kitchen, to stop people from telling their stories.

"Hold, it, Leah. Your report said Natalie was the one who handed you the mirror. Maybe she created a distraction so the person she was working with could doctor the coffee." He snapped his fingers. "Or maybe she got everyone to look at you while she finished the job. She might not have had a partner."

I closed my eyes, trying to visualize the rehearsal room during the brief period we were on break. "I didn't witness anyone tampering with the drinks, but I remember Lynne was annoyed with Marty for taking so long to get to work. Marty said something to Natalie about the coffee tasting bitter, but she didn't touch anyone's drink except her own. You don't know Natalie, Jonah. She's a genuinely kind and good person and has gone out of her way to make me feel welcome."

His dark eyes bored into mine. "She might be more devious than you think, and if she suspects you're investigating her, she could go after you. You've got a good cover story, but a smart person, someone who's cautious and afraid of getting caught, isn't likely to forget your past exploits. Why would Natalie, of all the women in the cast, make it a point to get close to you, when the rest of the group was so resentful? Don't get taken in by her apparent friendliness."

I wasn't pleased Jonah thought me so naïve. I was similarly unhappy with the possibility he was right. "You're underestimating what a prize I am. Who wouldn't want to be my friend?"

"I want you, and I'm sure every man you meet wants you. That's beside the point."

His lips began a journey that started at my neck, moved south with teasing slowness, and ended in the bedroom after a mutual desire to postpone further commentary.

When our breathing returned to a normal rhythm, he continued the argument. "Natalie might have wanted to put Amber out of commission without killing her. And she might be leveraging contact with you to get close to Amber."

I searched for an alternate explanation. "Natalie offered me a friendly hand and good advice, and there are others who would benefit if Amber dropped out of the show. She's too talented to have to resort to that kind of scheme."

We returned to the kitchen table, where I picked at the salad, searching for any bits of avocado still hiding in the greens. "Carly has as much to gain as Natalie, maybe more. Natalie is young. She has plenty of time to make her mark, but Carly is looking down the barrel of forty. It's more likely that Carly is guilty. Natalie can't stand her, so I doubt they'd work together."

Unbidden, the memory of Natalie and Carly whispering together came to mind, as if to tell me nothing good would come of ignoring a possible collaboration between them. "The problem for me is I can't do much investigating while I'm dancing. I didn't realize how big a role I was going to play. I'm onstage for much of the show."

Jonah's tone was mild, but I now knew him well enough to read the emotion behind the deceptively calm exterior. "The fact that Amber's online threats turned into a real-life attack right after you joined the cast could be deliberate, or it could be coincidental. Focus on that."

A sense of foreboding, which sprang from my fear of again failing to protect Amber, chilled me. "Can you assign someone to be with us? She'd have a fit if she heard me propose this, but what about Francie Morelli?"

"As much as I'd like to, I can't. The investigation into the tampered drinks is ongoing, but we're not in the business of providing round-the-clock personal protection. Sam Flannery said he's going to hire a security detail. That'll help."

"I'm glad to hear it. I asked Amber why she hadn't hired someone, but she put me off."

I wasn't nearly as good as Jonah at hiding what I was thinking. He answered the question I didn't ask with as much understanding as if I'd articulated those painful regrets.

"You're not at fault for what happened to Amber. Your job was to investigate threats. No one wants or expects you to provide protection against an actual attack. At the same time, don't underestimate the value of what you're doing. People like to talk. Draw them out and write down what they tell you the same way you've been doing. We'll check every statement. Sooner or later, someone's going to make a mistake. We're not tracking a serial killer or confidence trickster, although even they get overconfident and sloppy."

I was too edgy to sit still and used the countertop to stretch my legs. "We're looking for a risk-taker. Those drinks were poisoned in full view of the cast, which is why I feel responsible. I should have been more vigilant."

"If two people were involved, that halved the risk. It wasn't as big a gamble as you might think. The paper cups had no lids. Easy enough to prepare coffee for yourself while doctoring someone else's. In the meantime, the days of free coffee and cake are over."

I tossed the salad into the fridge. "Speaking of free, Sam arranged for me and Bryan to attend Amber's Design the Dream fundraising gala. According to Bryan, the tickets for the cocktail hour alone are five hundred bucks apiece. Not many people I work with can afford that pricey a night out, but I might get some good intel from people who know Amber outside the show."

He held up his phone to show me his invitation. "I'll be there with Farrow and Morelli. I hate having to keep our relationship secret, but that's the way it has to be until this case is solved."

"Since you can't be my date, I'd rather go solo, but I'm stuck with Bryan. It'll be a good opportunity to pump him for information, but I'm not looking forward to spending another evening in his company."

Jonah looked at me from those dark, enigmatic eyes. I still couldn't read him when he chose to keep his thoughts private. "What's going on between the two of you? I know you have a good working relationship, but two dates in less than a week?"

"Bryan has this idea in his head that if we're seen together, people will think we're a couple, and it'll generate positive buzz for the play. I wouldn't agree to such a pointless charade if it weren't for our investigation."

"I don't like it. How is dating Bryan going to make *Mad Music* a success?"

Even to me, the plan sounded silly. "Marketing and public relations aren't part of my job description. All I know is that he and I are going as a couple, and Amber and Sam are doing the same. I suppose a double romance, one of them between the choreographer and his lead dancer and the other between a director and his lead actress, will make *Mad Music* a hot item. I don't see it happening, but if I have to go to one of these awful events, I'll milk it for whatever it's worth. I'm glad you'll be there."

He still didn't look happy. "All that publicity might make for a healthy bottom line, but you're supposed to be working undercover. The less attention, the better, because the press is inevitably going to bring up your past. I don't like it."

I teased him. "Are you jealous?"

Another inscrutable look. "Should I be?"

I outlined his mouth with my finger. "What do you think?"

His answer wasn't in words, but the text message that interrupted us was. It was from Amber, telling me she again was too busy to meet. **Sorry, gf! No can do- forgot about dr appt.**

Jonah said, "Ask her if she can meet you later. It was Sam Flannery who wanted you to investigate, not Amber, and I need her to trust you. Your best asset is your ability to put together random bits of information and make them into a coherent whole. You can't do that without her."

Getting Amber to trust me wasn't enough. "At ABC, I got to hear all kinds of gossip. At *Mad Music*, I don't have the same kind of access. Natalie might be able to help with getting the rest of the cast to accept me, even if she is involved."

He pulled away. "I don't trust Natalie. Neither does Amber."

"Amber is great at acting, but she's not as good at figuring out who her friends are."

Two lines, shaped like backward parentheses, creased the inside of Jonah's dark eyebrows. "Amber has one, possibly two people working against her. Do you think there are others who want her to go down?"

"I think they're all playing a part. For each other, for me, and definitely for you."

Chapter Fourteen

I knew it was possible because our masters died with their shoes on...
You dance until your nineties.
—Michelle Dorrance

Whenever I couldn't take Madame Maksimova's class at American Ballet Company, I went to Studio Dance. The daytime students were an eclectic mix of professional dancers, aspiring kids, and former ballerinas. In the evening, the place was packed with adult beginners. The one thing we all had in common was a deep love for the art of dance.

I arrived early at the Upper West Side studio, but the three women I'd privately dubbed the Weird Sisters were already there. When I entered the classroom, Abigail, Isabel, and Audrey rushed to greet me.

Izzy could barely contain her excitement. "We're so excited you're going to be dancing on Broadway!"

Abigail, the most reserved of the three, was mostly silent while I answered Izzy's eager questions. She tapped the side of her head. "You're fifteen minutes earlier than your usual time, which makes me think you've got something on your mind. A new investigation, perhaps? Life has been too predictable and much too boring since our collaboration. What gives?"

Before the newspapers reported on the bravery of this trio, few people at Studio Dance bothered to talk to them. They were far older than most of the other students, and although accomplished dancers, they'd never performed on a professional stage, which would have brought them a measure of respect.

They belonged to a subgroup of quirky balletomanes that younger people tended to ignore.

Every dance studio has a cluster of elderly practitioners who existed outside the barbed-wire margins of a society that prized youth as much as talent and beauty. Few people were interested in engaging with this outcast band of zealous fans, but I was. Their dedication moved me, and I protected, as best I could, the vulnerable women who provoked ire from those around them when they forgot which direction the choreographed steps were supposed to take them.

I became friends with the Weird Sisters after two disdainful dancers from the San Francisco Ballet refused to go across the floor with them. The teacher instructed the class to execute the combination of steps in groups of four or five, and my friends missed their cue when this pair of West Coast mean girls stepped away at the last minute. I rushed to join them, and that was the beginning of what turned out to be a most unusual partnership.

The ladies enjoyed a burst of fame and popularity after the apprehension of the ABC Killer, but it didn't last. Like me, many dancers took class at Studio Dance sporadically, and there was an ever-changing roster of people in attendance. My friends soon returned to obscurity.

I, however, was well known to all. When our animated conversation attracted attention, I drew them close. "If you're free after class, let's have lunch at the Lincoln Center Diner."

Audrey brushed back a few strands of fair hair that escaped her bun. "We're, um, we usually aren't hungry after class, but we'll keep you company."

My friends spent a good deal of their slender income on dance classes and tickets to the ballet, usually in a standing room. Lunch at a New York City restaurant, however modest, was probably not a line item in their budget.

I cast about for a credible excuse to pay for them. "I've got a gift certificate that's going to expire. I was hoping you gals would help me out with it. I'd hate for the money to go to waste."

They agreed to help me spend my nonexistent gift certificate, and we took our places at the barre. The room grew quiet when the instructor, whom I knew well, entered the room. Marco air-kissed me with an exaggerated *mwah* and said, "This is an unexpected pleasure, Leah. Why aren't you with ABC and wowing audiences in Tampa or Topeka? I hope your knees aren't the reason for your absence."

I smiled and said, "I signed onto a three-month stint with *Mad Music,* and I'm not missing our whistle-stop tour one bit. I hate being on the road. But without Madame M, I'm counting on you to keep me in shape."

Ever the teacher, he tapped my left shoulder, which, without my consent, had moved a fraction of an inch higher than the right. "Then, um, you and Bryan Leister are working together again."

I fixed my posture. "Yes, we are. If nothing else, the dance sequences will be a hit."

Marco opened his mouth to speak and then closed it, as if rethinking what he was going to say. After a moment, he said, "Meet me after class. We'll talk."

He signaled to the pianist, and the class began, as it always did, with deep knee bends called *pliés.* The outside world receded. What remained was the music, the mirror, and the movement.

Ninety minutes later, I was dripping with sweat and reveling in the euphoria that follows an exceptional workout. We cheered Marco, who seemed pleased at the impromptu, enthusiastic response. Every ballet class ends with a *reverence,* in which the dancers clap and bow to the pianist and the teacher. It's a respectful and polite ritual, but a great class will inspire us to the equivalent of a standing ovation. We didn't stop applauding until the students for the next class displaced us.

Marco whispered, "Come with me." He opened the door to the stairway, and I followed him to the deserted landing.

He was apologetic. "I don't want you to take this the wrong way, Leah."

Those were not words anyone wants to hear. They inevitably preceded bad news. "Spit it out, Marco. Whatever you want to tell me isn't as bad as what I'm imagining."

Marco's gaze shifted from me to an invisible point above my head. "How tight are you with Bryan Leister? I know you worked with him at ABC, but how well do you know him on a personal level?"

I let my dance bag slide to the floor and massaged the back of my neck. "Are you the last person on the planet not to know he shafted me? Bryan and I are working friends, which means he's using me, and I'm using him. There's nothing personal about it."

The muscles around his mouth relaxed. "That's what I thought, but there are rumors you guys are hooking up. I've been working in Amsterdam for the last two years and missed most of the gossip that was happening stateside."

Was everyone dishing dirt about me and Bryan? The pervasive rumors made me suspect Bryan himself was the source. "I'm unattached, and Bryan is living high above the High Line with Tess Morgan. But if you want me to give him a message, I'll deliver it at tomorrow's rehearsal."

Marco was bitter. "If you're asking me that, then you've also missed some timely gossip. My husband was supposed to be the choreographer for *Mad Music*. We made plans to return to the States when our contract in Europe was over, but Sam Flannery backed out and told us Bryan got the job. How did that happen? If Bryan is throwing shade about my husband to a big-time director like Sam, we have to set the record straight, or Garret won't get arrested, let alone hired, for any other job."

The wheeling and dealing never ends. "Did Garret talk to Sam about it?"

Marco's voice cracked with strain. "Of course. That's the weirdest part of the whole thing. Sam said it was out of his hands. He sent us a huge check as a wedding gift, but it felt like a payoff."

I wondered if Garret was the one who'd promised Carly the role of Dreamcatcher. The tangled web of broken promises and fraught relationships kept growing, but I couldn't connect the disparate strands.

The intensity of his gaze made my skin crawl. Seeking to reassure him I was innocent of any backstage intrigue, I said, "I didn't join the cast until a few days ago, and I know nothing about this. No one mentioned Garret's name, and as far as I knew, Bryan was in from the beginning. I wish I could help, but what can I do? It's too late now to make changes."

His breath quickened. "If it's true that Bryan trashed Garret, I want to know so that we can one day return the favor. Will you do that for me?"

Marco's request had me stumped. How many roles could I plausibly juggle, and how many parallel investigations could I successfully conduct? Unless they all tied together in a way that was as yet unknown, success was unlikely.

I offered him a sympathetic hug and a vague promise and left to meet the Weird Sisters.

The Lincoln Center Diner wasn't the restaurant's real name, but it might as well have been. It was how everyone in the surrounding area referred to it, for obvious reasons. The owners catered to neighborhood regulars, students at the surrounding schools, and legions of homegrown and visiting performers. It sat in stark contrast to the high-priced and high-traffic restaurants that bordered one of New York City's most iconic venues. Other than the sidewalk food vendors, it was the best place for good food that didn't set you back a month's worth of rent.

Rita, my favorite waitress, was on duty. She poured coffee and said, "I know ballerinas are always dieting, but that doesn't mean everyone should have to eat lettuce leaves. Lemme take care of your skinny friends before they starve to death."

She filled the table with an assortment of sandwiches and sides of french fries. I, of course, couldn't eat most of it, but I enjoyed watching my friends dig in.

Over a towering club sandwich, Abigail said, "I'm dying of curiosity. Does this lunch meeting have something to do with your role in *Mad Music*? Will we be working together on another investigation?"

I speared a pickle from the communal dish. "Maybe. But you have to keep it a secret. I'll tell you more after I talk to Detective Sobol."

I ignored their coy looks when I mentioned Jonah's name and asked, "Are you three still swing dancing? Most of *Mad Music* is set to big band tunes. I think you'll love it."

Izzy shyly pulled out a flier for their upcoming showcase. In tiny print on the back, she pointed out their names. "We didn't want you to feel obligated to come. We know how busy you are."

I took the flier. "I would never miss one of your performances. Of course,

I want to come."

Abigail winked. "Will you be bringing the handsome Detective Sobol with you?"

"I think I'm going to bring someone else." Their flier had given me the beginnings of a new idea.

Abigail wrinkled her nose. "Are you still dating that doctor? I liked him, but not as much as the detective."

"It's not a date. I'm going to invite Bryan Leister, the guy who's choreographing *Mad Music*. Maybe you could teach him a thing or two about swing dancing."

The three women were not impressed. Like Gabi, Jonah, and Marco, they reacted with reserve, if not outright dislike.

Audrey's curls escaped two dozen bobby pins that were unequal to the task of restraining her hair. "Mr. Leister is a good choreographer, but I've heard some not-very-nice things about his personal life. You can do better, Leah."

"Yes. Dating a snake would be better. But this isn't a date. I'm on a mission, and I could use your help."

Izzy dropped her fork. "Does it have anything to do with Amber Castle? People have been saying such awful things about her on social media. It reminded me of what you went through when Savannah Collier posted those terrible rumors." Izzy tapped at her phone. "Amber's getting trashed on Twitter, but she seems to have lots of support on Instagram."

Was there anything they didn't know? From ballet to pop culture to data on the latest NASA launch, their interests were as varied as their careers.

"You ladies don't miss much. And yes, this has everything to do with Amber. Tell me what you know, and I'll fill in the rest."

Audrey pushed back her flyaway hair. "Amber Castle is a beautiful and talented actress, although her last two shows flopped. She's also a hero to people like me. She's raised tens of thousands of dollars to support diabetes research."

"I'm so sorry, Audrey. I didn't know you had diabetes."

The three women exchanged glances in a silent conversation I couldn't decode.

After a moment, Audrey said, "I don't have diabetes. My husband does. Did. He died of a heart attack years ago from complications connected to the disease. It would make me very happy to help Amber and, by extension, her charity."

Abigail's eyes were bright with interest. "I'm a big fan as well, of course. What did you have in mind, and what does this have to do with our swing dancing?"

Now that the time had come to approach them with my plan, I hesitated. I wasn't yet sure of how it might work and didn't want their loyalty to put them in danger. Marco's revelations added to the feeling that I was in over my head.

"You can't share what I'm about to tell you with anyone. Someone at a *Mad Music* rehearsal spiked Amber's coffee with sugar, and she nearly went into shock. There was another victim as well, a young guy who is still in the hospital. I can give you the details later. In the meantime, I need to know if you'd be willing to help me keep her safe. Jonah doesn't have the manpower to do it, and I can't be on the lookout for suspicious behavior while I'm dancing."

Audrey said, "Have you spoken to Olga? We'd walk through fire for you, but when it comes to physical protection, we can't provide the muscle she can." She ate a few more bites and then seemed to reconsider. "Though my tech skills are still pretty good. Not up to Olga's level, but not too shabby either. I'll start that part of the investigation as soon as I get home and check in with her later."

"That's a good idea, but Olga is off on another job, and I don't know when she'll be back. You know Olga."

In unison, they recited one of Olga's favorite expressions, "Must pay bills!"

"Right. And we don't inquire too closely into how she goes about doing that."

As usual, Abigail was the spokesperson for all three. "We'll do it. But you still haven't explained how you're going to get us into closed rehearsals."

"It's a work in progress."

81

Chapter Fifteen

Minor things can become moments of great revelation
when encountered for the first time.
—Dame Margot Fonteyn

Abigail, Izzy, and Audrey packed what was left of their sandwiches in paper napkins. I paid the bill at the register, so they didn't see me using my bank card instead of a gift certificate. When I returned to the table, they broke off their animated conversation.

The unaccustomed reserve from my chatty friends disconcerted me. In the short time I was gone, it was clear they'd come to a group decision. Their closed faces suggested that once they realized the difficulty of the task I was proposing, they were loath to follow through.

I was quick to reassure them. "Let's take some time to think before going forward. I might not be able to find a plausible excuse to have you come to rehearsals, and you might not feel comfortable lurking in the shadows."

Abigail spoke with the authority of a woman who spent thirty years as a high school librarian. "You've misread us and misjudged us. I don't blame you. Most people do. What we want you to understand is that we can do a lot more than sit around and eavesdrop."

I had no idea where this conversation was going. "I would never underestimate you, but I also don't want to risk hurting you."

I searched for a persuasive reason that would allow them to gracefully excuse themselves from agreeing to my quixotic request. "The more I think about having you ladies attend rehearsals, the less I like it. What if someone at *Mad Music* puts two and two together and remembers that you were at ABC when the killer was apprehended? Your names and faces were in every newspaper. I'm supposed to be undercover, not reminding people of the last time I was involved in a murder investigation. You're too famous to work this job."

Audrey folded her napkin into a precise rectangle. "Three old ladies? No one's going to recognize us. No one pays attention to us. We can use fake names." Her eyes were bright with excitement. "I'll be Alana Turing. Or Ada Lovelace."

Izzy equaled her in enthusiasm. "And I'll be Bertha Skinner. Like a female version of the psychologist B. F. Skinner, but better looking."

Abigail rested her chin on clasped hands. "What Izzy and Audrey are trying to tell you, without sounding boastful, is that there's a lot more to us than you might think. Audrey was a computer scientist. Graduated from MIT. That's why she chose those two ridiculous names."

Audrey corrected her friend. "I graduated before they had a computer science major. So, I'm mostly self-taught. Plus, those names are fabulous."

Abigail conceded Audrey's point. "Izzy was a psychologist. You won't find a better profiler."

Izzy was pleased with her friend's praise. "I'm no math whiz like Audrey, but after a lifetime of listening to other people's problems, I'm pretty good at figuring out personality and motive."

Abigail lightly pounded on the table. "What you have sitting before you is the perfect team to help unmask a hidden threat. One techie, one psychologist, and," she held up her bony hand in a tight first, "one librarian. We're not afraid. If you recall what I said earlier, life has been boring lately. A case of attempted murder will keep us busy and keep us sharp."

I knew my friends had lived rich lives before we met, but my relationship with them had been predicated on a mutual love of ballet and abstract puzzle-solving. I'd underestimated their knowledge and their passion.

"It's true I didn't know much about your professional lives, but I never doubted your intelligence. Now that I know more about your skill set, I have to convince Bryan without revealing the real reason for your presence.

Are you sure you understand the risks involved?"

Izzy pulled two long, sharp, metallic objects from her bag. "We're all armed."

I wasn't sure how well a pair of number ten knitting needles would work against an assailant who used off-label drugs as a weapon, but I didn't argue with her. "Once we begin rehearsals in the theater, you'll be relatively safe. Sam Flannery is hiring a security detail."

I had yet to convince Bryan to allow the Weird Sisters into rehearsals without tipping him off to the double role I was playing. Assuming, of course, he didn't already know.

My knees ached from sitting too long. "You ladies should stay and have dessert. I'm going to work out some kinks."

Audrey looked up from her phone, where she was tapping an image of a chessboard. "Give me one minute. Not literally one minute. Thirty seconds should be sufficient. I'm in the middle of a game of bullet chess."

Izzy explained, "Bullet chess is like blitz chess, but faster. She says it clears her brain."

Audrey had a pleased look on her face. "I won. And yes, you're right. It does clear my brain. Leah, please send us a list of all the people who were in the room when the coffee was spiked, preferably with a photo and brief description. I'm a visual person, and I want to attach all the people involved in this puzzle to chess pieces. It helps me sort out patterns."

I eased out of the booth and said, "Sounds like a plan. I'll come backstage after your performance."

The Weird Sisters divided one slice of cheesecake into three neat portions. I hoped to spend the rest of the day resting my aching knees and relaxing with my mother's latest manuscript, but the person who contacted me from a blocked phone number had other ideas.

The message read **Lunch looks good. So do you.**

I dropped my phone, and it clattered across the table.

Abigail handed it to me without looking at the screen.

Izzy said, "Show us."

I didn't want the texter to know I'd confided in the Weird Sisters. "It's nothing. Just a reminder about tomorrow's rehearsal."

A second message came through. It was a photo of me and Bryan and said, **Wheres the boyfriend?**

I sat back down, removed a menu from its stand on the table and, from behind it, checked out the other customers. Three teenage boys hunched over hamburgers and fries. Two middle-aged women who looked like sisters bickered over the check, nearly ripping it in half. A line of guys sat at the counter, their backs to us, waiting for their to-go orders.

On the other side of the restaurant's plate glass windows, a mother ambled past us, pushing a stroller. A delivery guy illegally rode his electric bike on the sidewalk. Two lovers were locked in a passionate kiss. And a car with tinted windows was parked across the street.

It was broad daylight on a busy thoroughfare. Even a coward like me couldn't justify running away, but the presence of my elderly friends argued against making any rash moves.

I beckoned to Rita, who brought her coffee pot to the table.

I said, "Hypothetically speaking, if someone wanted her three friends to leave without anyone noticing, is there another way out?"

Rita was as matter-of-fact as if my request happened with the same frequency as demands for the Breakfast Special. "No problem. I suggest your three hypothetical friends walk past the ladies' room, where they'll find the emergency exit. Across the alley is the back entrance for a clothing store called The Collective. Go inside, but stay away from the windows in front. I'll arrange for a ride home and text you when the cab arrives."

"Rita, you're an amazing human being. Were you a double agent in your previous life?"

The waitress dropped her sarcastic armor. "My name wasn't always Rita." She grinned and resumed her usual humorous tone. "I'd tell you my real name, but then I'd have to kill you."

I assumed Abigail, Izzy, and Audrey would follow Rita's directions and leave the diner while I confronted whoever was in the parked car with tinted windows.

The motor was running, and the driver didn't wait for me to get close enough to see inside. With a screech of tires, the car took off and sped down the street and around the corner. I ran after it, but by the time I got to Columbus Ave., it was lost in a sea of moving traffic.

When I turned around, Rita was hot on my trail and waving a large metal spatula. The Weird Sisters brought up the rear. Abigail, Izzy, and Audrey all brought knitting needles, which they held in front of them like swords. Thankfully, none of them stumbled and ended up stabbing themselves or an innocent bystander.

So much for covert maneuvers. I might as well have had a marching band accompany me.

Out of breath, the waitress gasped, "Did you get the license plate?"

I had to admit defeat. "It was a black sedan. That's as far as I got." As if on cue, two cars of the same description rolled by, although neither had tinted windows.

When we returned to the diner, the manager peered over his glasses at Rita but didn't complain. The waitress pulled me behind the counter and asked, in a barely audible whisper, "Who are you protecting your friends against? Was it an ex-husband, jealous boyfriend, or bail bondsman?"

Taking a page out of her book, I said, "I'd tell you, but then I'd have to kill you."

My friends were thrilled after the excitement of the chase. I showed them the anonymous text messages, figuring the threats would dampen their zeal.

I was wrong. It fired them up even further. They did, however, consent to Rita's offer to have her cousin drive us home.

We waited by the door until Paulina pulled up in a shiny yellow cab. After we settled in and gave her the first address, she said, "Rita and me, we help out at the battered women's shelter. We seen all kinds, and we don't fool around." She stopped at a red light and turned around to look at me. "Do yourself a favor, girlie, and don't go back to him. A guy treats you bad, you got choices."

I accepted her advice and didn't bother explaining the true nature of our situation.

Paulina took each of the Weird Sisters home. Before pulling up to their buildings, she circled the block twice to make sure no one was following us. I handed her double the amount on the meter. It was the least I could do.

She tipped an imaginary hat and said, "My pleasure. You ever need help, gimme a call. Me and Rita, we go way back. I'm very discreet."

My apartment was as quiet as it ever got during the day. The sanitation trucks had long since completed their grinding, screeching path down my street, traffic was light, and the married couple next door, if they were home, had taken a break from their incessant quarrels. The anonymous, threatening texts shattered what should have been a peaceful respite from work, and I paced in uneasy anticipation of another scary message. I feared the words were literally true and that even after a secret taxi ride and in the privacy of my home, someone was watching me.

I closed the curtains, lowered the blinds, and forwarded the messages to Jonah. Beyond that, I didn't have a plan.

Jonah called seconds after I sent the text. "I don't want you to be alone. Call a cab, wait inside until it arrives, and go to your mother's place. Let me know if you get another text."

Shortly after he hung up, Barbara's maternal ESP kicked in. "Leah, darling! I want you to come over for dinner."

I found her jovial tone suspicious. "Is there something you're not telling me?"

"Don't be absurd. Is it so crazy for a mother to want to see her daughter?" A slight cough escaped her. "You might as well bring that detective with you since I've given up all hope of you marrying Zach."

"You know perfectly well that detective's name is Jonah. Did he call you?"

Her indignant answer sounded genuine, but with Barbara, it was hard to tell. "I have no idea what you're talking about. I simply want to know how you are and how rehearsals are going. I know so little about your new show."

Although Barbara wrote fiction, she had the soul of an investigative journalist. The odds of her not knowing what was trending on social media were the same as the odds of me climbing Mount Everest. In a bikini.

Chapter Sixteen

The only thing worse than a flop is a hit.
—Michael Bennett

M y mother retained the apartment where I grew up as part of her amicable divorce from my father. Although many things stayed the same over the years, including Gerald, the now-elderly doorman, the interior of Barbara's apartment was in the process of radical renewal.

I walked into the scent of coffee, which was one of the things about my childhood home that hadn't changed. I wasn't expecting a home-cooked meal, as Barbara was no more likely to fire up the oven than I was, but she was on a first-name basis with every restaurateur on the Upper West Side. Monsieur Babineaux, the owner of Café Cassis, adored her, and I hoped to find one of his signature dishes waiting for me. As far as my nose could tell, however, caffeine was the only item on the menu.

Barbara took my puffy down jacket and made a fuss over how much room it took up in her closet. "Really, Leah? If I'd known you were still wearing that sleeping bag as a coat, I could have met you at Rafe's. They're having a winter sale. Fifty percent off everything."

"I can't afford Rafe's, even on sale. And I don't want you to buy me a coat. You've given me half the clothes I own."

She pecked my cheek. "Let me spoil you. You're one of my top two daughters." She took my hand and drew me into the living room. "Look at my new furniture! Do you love it?"

The couch with faded pillows was gone, as was my favorite comfy chair. Barbara had replaced them with pieces so spare they wouldn't have been out of place in an operating room.

I scratched my head, hoping the external stimuli would enable my brain to come up with a credible compliment. The white upholstered sofa, with its too-wide seat, was less comfortable than a bus stop bench. The metal and glass coffee table, with its squared edges and six spiny legs, resembled a futuristic predator.

"Yes, this is all, um, so different. Very neat. Neat and tidy. And sleek. It looks sleek."

If she noticed my lack of enthusiasm, it wasn't apparent from her expression. "I knew you'd love it. I was sick to death of that clunky furniture. This is so much cleaner. More sophisticated." She smiled. "Like me."

There was no argument about that claim. My mother dressed far better than I did, and her level of grooming was magazine-shoot perfect. She poured wine into two glasses. "I invited you here so we could talk about *Mad Music.* I heard Amber Castle and some other guy ended up in the hospital. What's going on, Leah? You've been so cagey about your decision to ditch the ABC tour. What are you not telling me?"

I sipped the wine to buy time. My mother wrote crime fiction novels, and she fancied herself an amateur sleuth. I had my hands full keeping Amber safe, and I didn't relish the prospect of having Barbara insert herself into the investigation.

"The police are looking into the matter. That's all I can say." I stood up. "I'm starving. Where's dinner?"

We entered the kitchen, the one room in the house that survived alteration. Gleaming, rarely used copper pots hung over the counter, and the scratched wooden table where I'd eaten a thousand meals was still in place. Barbara took a plastic bowl of salad out of the refrigerator, spilled its contents onto two plates, and carefully apportioned salad dressing from a separate container.

She motioned with her wineglass. "Dig in. The whole meal, including wine, will come to four hundred calories apiece."

I was two forkfuls into my meal and regretting there was so little of it when the buzzer rang. My mother murmured what sounded like a reluctant consent, and a few moments later, Aunt Rachel entered.

She carried a large shopping bag, from which she withdrew a baking pan redolent with the scent of tomato and fresh basil. "I hope you don't mind me barging in, Leah. Barbara said you were coming to dinner, and I have to get rid of this lasagna. It would be a shame to let it go to waste."

My mother's tone was drier than the wine. "I notice you didn't ask me if I minded."

Rachel was unperturbed by Barbara's rebuke. "You're my sister. I knew you'd be happy to see me." She cut a large, cheesy square of lasagna and buried my salad under it. "The price of everything in New York City is so high, it's enough to make me think about going back to Minneapolis."

Unlike the lasagna, this news met with my mother's approval. "Sounds like a good plan to me. I'm sure you'd live more comfortably there. Although, of course, I'd miss you."

Rachel got herself a plate and slid an acre of lasagna onto it. "Just kidding. You're not getting rid of me so easily. I've got a job interview! I'll bet you can't guess what it is."

I'd never seen her so happy, other than when she was needling Barbara. "That's fantastic news, Aunt Rachel. Will you be teaching ballet?"

Rachel, after a short and mostly unsuccessful career as a dancer, got married and relocated to Minneapolis. After many years, her ballet school, like her marriage, went belly up, and she moved back to New York. Except for Melissa, my happily married sister, the Siderova women weren't winners in the marriage sweepstakes.

She spoke over a mouthful of food. "The new job doesn't require me to teach ballet, although knowing dance will be a definite plus. You can think of it as a job that's dance adjacent. I'm meeting with Lynne Heller, the wardrobe mistress at *Mad Music*. She's looking for an assistant. I gave your name as a reference. Won't that be amazing? We could be working together!"

Barbara froze, her fork halfway to her mouth. "What makes you qualified to work in the wardrobe department of a Broadway show?"

Rachel poured herself a glass of wine. "I made all the costumes for my ballet school. You can learn a lot on YouTube."

I lost my appetite as completely as if the lasagna had transformed into toxic sludge. Working undercover would be infinitely more difficult with Rachel lurking in the shadows of the theater. Not for a moment did I consider taking her into my confidence. My aunt had many sterling qualities, but discretion was not one of them.

Rachel lost some of her earlier assurance. "You don't mind, Leah, do you? I thought you'd be pleased."

I swallowed my distress with a forkful of pasta. "Of course not. I'm delighted for you."

Barbara was less forgiving. "You've put Leah in a very awkward position."

Rachel flexed her fingers. "Not if I turn out to be the best wardrobe assistant on the whole Great White Way!"

My mother thought she had the last word when she said, "Your *if* is too large a leap for me. Just make sure that while you're sewing hems and gluing sequins, you don't distract Leah."

My aunt was unfazed by Barbara's disapproval, so I tossed out a few arguments of my own. I didn't have to embellish the truth to make my point. "Rachel, you can't do this. The reason there's a job opening is because the previous assistant is in the hospital. Somebody spiked his coffee. He passed out, hit his head when he went down, and is in the intensive care unit. We don't know who did it, and it's too risky for you to take his place."

Rachel mowed through her pasta, her appetite undiminished. "I know all about what happened to Marty, Leah. It was a freak accident and had nothing to do with the threats against Amber Castle."

In response to my open-mouthed reaction, she added, "Yeah, I know all about that, too. I'm on Instagram now. You should follow me. But don't get all worked up about it. I'll be fine."

I couldn't tell Rachel about the anonymous texts I'd gotten without simultaneously alarming Barbara. Minus that ammunition, I had few resources in my arsenal of persuasive bullets.

I opened with warm flattery, "I have no doubt you'd be great, Aunt Rachel," and concluded with a dose of cold reality, "But Lynne would never hire a newbie if she could find a single qualified person willing to step in. She's an exacting, impatient boss."

Rachel incinerated any hope I had of extinguishing her ambition. "The budget is so tight at *Mad Music* they're hiring me as an apprentice, so they don't have to pay union scale wages. It's part of a new pilot program to help seniors find work in the arts. You wouldn't believe how hard it is to get a job once you're past sixty. People act like getting old is a contagious disease. I can't deny I'm inexperienced, but I'm cheap, and I'm willing to learn. Can you tell that to Lynne? Tell her how great I am."

There were many things I could tell the wardrobe mistress about Rachel. Extolling her willingness to learn wasn't on the list.

Barbara drilled me with a look that could cut a diamond. "How is it, my dear daughter, that your aunt has information about Amber and Marty and I do not?" She huffed a bit and then smiled. The smile was worse than the diamond-cutting look. "If Rachel is going to work at *Mad Music,* then I will too."

As she often did, my mother used her own books to bolster judgments that might meet with resistance. "In *The Merry Knives of Windsor*, there's an accidental poisoning that turns out to be premeditated murder. So you see, I've got plenty of experience and I can help you investigate. Maybe the directors, or the producers, need a script doctor. Unlike your aunt, I'm a professional."

Added to the distress I felt at the possibility that my aunt and my mother would attend *Mad Music* rehearsals was a growing suspicion about Barbara's impromptu invitation to dinner. Her reference to *The Merry Knives of Windsor* hit the mark a little too precisely to be completely unrehearsed. "You knew about this all along, didn't you?"

"Of course. Elementary, my dear daughter. I did expect, however, that you, and not Rachel, would be the one to confide in me. And I meant what I said about working on the *Mad Music* script. People are saying the show is cursed. I have experience, and I can help, in more ways than one."

Barbara looked showily at her watch and then at Rachel. "You'd better get a good night's sleep so you can begin preparing for your big interview."

My aunt interpreted this comment as tacit approval, which it was not. She divided the remaining food into three equal portions, put one of them into her shopping bag, and kissed us goodbye. "You have a big day tomorrow, too, Leah. Don't stay up too late. If you want, I can wait for you, and we can—"

Barbara cut in. "Leah is spending the night. Goodbye, Rachel."

After fifteen more minutes of saying goodbye, she left.

Barbara took the remaining lasagna and was about to toss it in the garbage when I stopped her.

In response to my complaint, she said, "Don't tell me I'm being wasteful. I'm saving us five thousand calories apiece. If I know Rachel, she used full-fat cheese and a gallon of olive oil."

"You shouldn't throw it out. What would Professor Romanova say?"

She wavered, not because I objected, but because she's obsessed with her fictional character, a literature-loving Russian expatriate.

Barbara held the lasagna over the garbage can but didn't commit to throwing it in. "Professor Romanova did suffer hunger as a child, before she emigrated from what used to be the Soviet Union. This is a tough call." She compromised by wrapping the lasagna in a sheet of aluminum foil. When she was sure Rachel had left the building, she delivered it to the doorman.

With the threat of incoming carbohydrates no longer imperiling her waistline, she appeared to relax. "Let's get back to where we were before we were so rudely interrupted. What's the real reason you're doing this show?"

"I thought it would be fun to do something different."

She eyed me with the same look she employed when I was a teenager and broke curfew. "That may be true. But it's not the whole story. Does that detective friend of yours have anything to do with your decision to spend the spring season dancing on Broadway instead of going on tour with American Ballet Company?"

I stretched my aching legs straight out in front of me and bent double over them. This felt good and also allowed me to address my answer to my knees instead of to her face. "Career-wise, it's a smart move. ABC's spring schedule is a killer. The new management company booked a twenty-city tour that's going to be a nightmare of one-night stands. You know what it's like. The dancers will be spending as much time traveling as dancing, which will destroy my joints."

She took out a broom and swept invisible crumbs from around my feet, poking under the table as if searching for dropped clues. "You've given me two plausible reasons for this ill-considered decision. What's behind door number three? Professor Romanova thinks it might be a dead body. Or, perhaps, the threat of one."

Resistance was futile. When my mother starts identifying with Professor Romanova, her intuition gets even more prescient than usual. Nonetheless, I attempted one more diversion. "Why do you persist in referring to Jonah as 'that detective'? You remind me of Nana, who pretends she can't remember the title of cheesy TV shows she doesn't want to admit she's watched."

Undeterred, Barbara said, "I'm proud of you for that noble effort. Using distraction is an excellent ploy, but it won't work with me."

I relented to the point of confirming my involvement. "I joined the cast because the online threats against Amber Castle terrified her, and she wanted someone with her she could trust. Insiders knew Bryan wanted me to dance Dreamcatcher, which gave us the perfect cover story. Initially, my job was to investigate the possibility that the danger would spill over from the virtual world to the real one." I paused. "But that's already happened. Not sure what the next step is."

"The next step is to stop Rachel from taking a job with the show."

If only it were that simple. "What do you want me to do? Trash her?"

She closed the door of the broom closet and said, "Yes. Difficult, but necessary. Rachel will blow your cover in ten seconds." She refilled her wine glass but not mine. "I suppose I could get a job there as well. I refuse to stay on the sidelines if she's in the middle of all the action."

My mother's lifelong competition with my aunt was a frequent source of amusement for my sister and me. This latest manifestation of the rivalry between them, however, had not a jot of humor in it. My relationship with my sister was very different. Melissa and I didn't vie with each other for supremacy, partly because we'd chosen different lives and partly because she was as perfect as human beings get.

Logic never helps resolve emotional disputes, but it couldn't hurt to point out to my mother the problem with her suggestion. "Even you must realize this is an impossible situation. How am I supposed to investigate if I'm tripping over my mother and my aunt? Did you think the presence of three Siderova women would go unmarked?"

Barbara patted my arm. "We can help. You're a star. Everyone's always going to be looking at you. I, on the other hand, can be invisible."

In theory, she wasn't wrong. The Weird Sisters had made a similar argument. I could have explained that I'd tapped them for the role she wanted but didn't want to hazard another jealous response.

"As far as I know, the job openings at *Mad Music* are for a wardrobe assistant and a clarinet player. Unless you're prepared to sew or play, I don't see a way for you to get in."

My ever-resourceful mother remained optimistic. "Trust me. I'll find a way. I wrote about a similar situation in *The Taming of the Clue*. If I can't get them to use me as a script doctor, I'll have my agent talk to their PR department about doing an article on them."

I checked my phone to see if I'd missed any threatening messages. For the moment, I appeared to be beyond my stalker's view. "Yeah, that's a great idea. What could possibly go wrong?"

Chapter Seventeen

My mother's flexible relationship with the truth enabled her, without hesitation or compunction, to tell Rachel I was spending the night in my childhood bedroom. Although the fib was morally questionable, I was nonetheless grateful. I was quite fond of Rachel in small doses, but our conversation regarding her potential employment in the wardrobe department of *Mad Music* wasn't a topic I wanted to pursue with her.

I did my best thinking while walking and looked forward to a solitary trip home. My knees were stiff from sitting too long, and the gentle exercise would do them good. Despite the recent warm spell, the sidewalks were still edged in dirty, melting snow, and a few slick patches of ice remained. Filthy puddles, made iridescent by drops of leaked gasoline, lined the gutter, and a dense fog blanketed the city. The street was quiet enough that I could hear the sound of footsteps coming closer.

I told myself that this was New York City, where people were in a perpetual rush to either get to a location or escape from one. The intuitive part of my brain, however, remained unconvinced by logical reasoning. The air was cool, but hot prickles crawled across the back of my neck, like a warning that something wasn't right. I peered over my shoulder and, through the mist, saw a figure in a trench coat, scarf, and hat, the face shrouded in darkness, gaining ground.

There was no reason to think I was being followed, but the lone walker's posture was too purposeful, the gait too quick, for me to ignore the voice in my head telling me to flee. I gripped my keys, which I held in the defensive pose Jonah taught me.

My first thought was to run, but my left knee, the really fragile one, clicked faintly with each step. That click, which was more a feeling than a sound, was one I couldn't ignore. If I started running without first manipulating the joint to its proper position, it would fail me.

In the city that famously never sleeps, the residential street I was on was completely deserted.

My second impulse was to take refuge inside the lobby of a nearby building, but my mother's apartment house was the only one with a doorman. The road ahead had a shuttered nursery school, an empty playground, and private townhouses with no lights in the windows. If anyone was home, the best I could hope for, from the residents of those pricey, heavily secured houses was that after banging on the door, the people inside would think I was a criminal and would call nine-one-one.

There was a third choice: the element of surprise. If someone was after me, the logical move would be to run away. I went toward my stalker. A face-to-face confrontation, however, was too much to ask of my cowardly self. I circled back from behind a row of parked cars that were lined up along the curb. They formed a barricade between the sidewalk and the street.

I inched my way closer to the person in the trench coat, which had the added benefit of bringing me nearer to Barbara's building. I could hear very little, other than the sound of my own breathing. Thinking I'd outwitted the stalker, I peered over the hood of the car I was hiding behind. Pointed at me was an object in the shape of a gun.

I hurled my keys at the attacker, and the scarf-wrapped head ducked. I missed my target, but the key toss threw off the stalker's aim and kept a stream of fluid aimed at my face from completely blinding me.

A sticky, wet substance burned my left eye. Wild fears of an acid burn that would disfigure me and end my career drove me to react as I never had before. Using words that would appall my mother, I went on the attack. If my face was ruined, I wanted to know who did it. And, in the process, inflict some damage of my own.

The stalker ran away. Despite my blurred vision, I followed as fast as I could but couldn't close the gap. Yelling and waving my arms, I didn't stop until I reached Broadway, where a few wary passersby crossed the street to avoid me. Trench Coat disappeared, either down the stairs to the subway station or into a passing cab.

I touched my face and was relieved to find the skin smooth and unbroken. My eye throbbed, and I couldn't see clearly through it, but counted myself lucky to have escaped worse damage. I retraced my steps and returned to Barbara's apartment house. Gerald was at his desk, surreptitiously eating Aunt Rachel's lasagna and dabbing his mouth with the napkin Barbara had thoughtfully provided.

When he caught sight of my face, he toppled off his chair. "What happened? Who did this to you?"

I was too out of breath to answer and dashed to the mirror that hung on the far wall of the lobby. My left eye was swollen, and my face had red, slimy streaks across it that smelled like tomato.

It was ketchup. My stalker attacked me with a condiment.

Gerald wrung his hands and said, "I'm calling the police. And I'll let Mrs. Siderova know you're, uh, you came back."

"No police. And please don't call my mother. It's nothing. Just a stupid prank. All I need is a few of those napkins and a cab."

He took a whistle from his pocket. "No problem, Leah. Wait here. I'll get one for you." Noting my stiff gait, he said, "Sit down. You shouldn't be standing if your knees are hurting."

Grateful for the perpetual excuse of bad knees, I leaned against the wall and let my shoulders slump. Gerald knew all about my surgeries, since I stayed with Barbara after each operation. Despite his injunction to wait in the lobby, I followed him into the street.

It was too dark and foggy to see faces. A teenager in a hoodie turned the corner and sped by on a skateboard. A woman in a chador got out of a car and stopped to talk on her phone. A black sedan pulled out from the curb across the street and sped off.

I remembered to retrieve my keys and was safely back in my apartment when my phone pinged, again from a blocked number. No words. Just a picture of me, standing in front of my mother's building, entering a taxi.

I called Jonah and told him what happened.

He said, "I'm on my way. Don't answer the door, and don't leave the apartment."

I sat in the kitchen with the curtains closed and the blinds down. My brain was frozen, but my body couldn't stay seated, and I ended up pacing the length of my tiny living space dozens of times until he arrived. The buzzer startled me, although I'd been expecting it. Jonah's voice, over the staticky intercom, said, "It's me."

He took the stairs at a record pace and without stopping, as it was too late in the evening for Mrs. Pargiter to indulge in her usual interrogation. I opened the door, and he wrapped me in his arms. His familiar scent, a little bitter and a little sweet, inspired very different imaginings than the ones that had me so scared.

Jonah's words were less soothing than his embrace. Shaking me gently, he said, "How could you let me in? All I said was that it was me. It could have been anyone."

Nettled at his tone, I tried to pull away. "I recognized your voice. I'm not a child."

His muscles tensed. "The sound quality from your intercom is so bad, I doubt you could tell if it was me or Mrs. Pargiter. From now on, you don't let anyone in without checking. If someone rings the bell, tell them to step into the street and look out the window to make a positive ID."

"Why not a secret code? Or maybe you could send me messages that self-destruct after I read them."

He laughed and loosened his grip. "The next time I show up, ask me to text you. If it's me, I'll send a text that says ICAY."

"What's that supposed to mean?"

"It's short for I'm Crazy About You."

The tight band of tension around my throat eased. "I'm crazy about you too. About this phantom texter, however, not so much. Every day, there's some new and inexplicable event that turns on its head everything I thought I knew. Do you think the person threatening me is the same one who's going after Amber? What did I do to tip them off? And, not that I'm complaining, but who uses ketchup as a weapon?"

Jonah stroked my hair. "I think you're a secondary target, and the attacker's motive is to isolate Amber by scaring you off." He heaved an exasperated sigh. "You didn't do anything wrong. It was Amber who put you in the spotlight. She posted pictures of the two of you, saying what a great pal you are and showing off how much you resemble each other. I don't see it myself, but the picture of you in the red wig helps."

I was stunned. "How could she be so reckless? She knows it's critical that I stay undercover and under the radar. The last thing we need is a concrete link between us."

He went to the sink and poured a glass of water, which he finished in one go. "It's too late for that now. Focus on what happened today. Did the guy following you look familiar? Anything about the shape of his face, or the set of his body you recognized?"

I shut my eyes, but no clear image emerged. "It was dark, and I didn't get close enough to see his face, although there was something about his posture that was familiar. Maybe a dancer?"

Dissatisfied with this conclusion, I banged my fist against the wall. "I can't say for sure what he looked like. When I went back into the street to see if he was still there—"

Jonah opened his mouth, but I didn't let him say any of the angry things he was so clearly thinking. "Give me some credit. I didn't go back outside by myself. I was with Gerald."

His voice was like ice. "Gerald is unarmed and eighty years old."

"He's very spry. And he has a whistle loud enough to summon cabs from either cross street."

"We can discuss Gerald's ability to fight off an assailant later. I need a description, Leah."

"The person following me wore a trench coat and hat and had a scarf wrapped around his face. He was short and slim. I'm not sure it was a guy. It was foggy and dark, but something about the walk and posture looked female to me. Maybe it was the shape of the coat."

Jonah refilled his glass. "Could it have been Carly? Or Natalie? If they got rid of you and Amber, they'd be the stars on opening night."

The lump in my throat returned, but for a different reason. "They're both ambitious, I'll give you that. They might gossip, strategize, or, in a pinch, hold out a foot for someone to trip over. Maybe they'd even attack me with a squirt gun filled with ketchup. But a physical attack that could have killed Amber? No."

"I need more than that to cross them off the list." Jonah glanced up at the clock and groaned when he saw how late it was. "We both need some rest." He pulled me toward the bedroom. "Or at least go to bed. We can talk in the morning."

I held back. "There's one more thing you need to know. I met an old friend of mine today at Studio Dance. His name is Marco, and his husband, Garret, is a choreographer. Garret was supposed to choreograph *Mad Music*, but Sam Flannery reneged on his promise to hire him and chose Bryan instead. Sam gave them a ton of cash as a wedding present, which Marco said felt like a payoff."

Jonah rubbed his bloodshot eyes. "Do you think Marco or Garret is implicated in the threats against you and Amber?" Before I could say anything, he answered his own question. "Maybe they're attacking Sam and Bryan indirectly by going after Amber and now you. When did you get the first threatening text?"

"One hour after talking to Marco."

Jonah took out his notebook and paged through it. "What happened to you tonight is part of a pattern of intimidation. If you quit *Mad Music*, it would hurt the show and, at the same time, would make the director and the choreographer look bad. Revenge is a powerful motive, and the use of ketchup as a weapon isn't that different from the sugar and ketamine-spiked drinks. I've been rethinking what happened with Marty. Maybe the person who spiked the drinks wasn't trying to kill Amber and purposely put the ketamine in a different cup of coffee, knowing we'd assume both were meant for Amber. The person who's doing this might not want to inflict serious damage but is willing to go to great lengths to scare off both of you."

Jonah might be correct in the motive but not the person. "Do you think Marco and Garret are guilty, as opposed to Natalie and Carly?"

Jonah didn't seem to hear me. "Is there any way for you to break your contract with *Mad Music* and join ABC for the remainder of the tour? You've been rehearsing such a short time, it's not as if they've invested months of practice. Your job is done. Let me take it from here. It would be foolish to assume the situation won't get more dangerous the closer you get to opening night."

"It's not that simple. I can't walk out without giving notice. They're counting on me."

We'd been together for too long, and he knew too much about my world, for him to fall for that excuse. "We both know Carly can take your place. Let her. The audience isn't going to care that she's taller than Amber."

"You don't care, but Bryan does. I'm not sure about Sam. All they'd have to do is rewrite a few lines in the script, and anyone could dance the part. Unfortunately, Amber's made such a big deal over how much we look alike."

It was clear I hadn't yet persuaded him, so I kept going. "I have a few other reasons, though, as to why I don't want to quit. The first one is selfish. I can't break my contract without doing some serious damage to my career. I might never get another shot at Broadway. The other reason, the thing that's stopping me from packing my bags and taking the first flight out, is that I can't bring myself to abandon Amber. She's in such a vulnerable position."

Those inverted parentheses I'd come to know well appeared inside his eyebrows, a mute expression of concern. "You're as exposed as she is. Don't you understand what those text messages mean? Your cover is blown." He lifted my chin and gazed into my eyes. "Listen, Leah, I made a mistake in dragging you into this. I thought the Broadway gig would give us some time together while ABC was on tour. I miscalculated the threat, but it's time to cut our losses. Things may escalate beyond what either of us can control.

Time to get out of Dodge."

Leaving *Mad Music* had its appeal, but more as a wish than an achievable goal. "This mysterious texter scares me so much, I can't wait to get back to my old life. But I can't leave. Amber is depending on me to help her."

"And who's going to help you? I'm afraid to let you out of my sight."

Since I didn't think the presence of the Weird Sisters, Aunt Rachel, or my mother was quite what he had in mind, I reminded him of Sam's promise to hire security guards.

He seized on my argument and used it against me. "In that case, you can step back and let the pros protect Amber and you. If you can't bring yourself to leave the show, you can still drop the investigation."

"That's no longer possible. Short of entering the Witness Protection Program, there's no assurance of safety until we find the person who's found me."

Chapter Eighteen

There's something about live theater that hits you in the heart.
—Susan Stroman

Jonah slept soundly, his chest rising and falling in a regular, uninterrupted rhythm. I tried to follow his example, but it took much longer for me to unwind. When I finally fell asleep, visions of being pursued by a shadowy killer haunted me. My nightmare self, who had to drag two heavy, unconscious bodies to safety, didn't make it. She fell off a cliff.

I didn't need Izzy's knowledge of psychology to interpret those uneasy dreams. The two bodies dragging me down were my mother and aunt. My subconscious was telling me that if my well-meaning relatives finagled their way into the *Mad Music* rehearsals, they might suffer a similar fate.

The face of the monster that haunted me was no clearer when I woke than when I was asleep, but a teasing resemblance, like a forgotten name, poked at me. The monster was someone I knew well. I corrected myself: Someone I *thought* I knew well.

Barbara and Rachel were dissimilar in their disposition and style, but they shared a razor-sharp intelligence and a taste for snooping. Under other circumstances, their skills would have been an asset to an investigation. But not now. Whoever taunted me had followed me to my mother's house. I couldn't risk making her and Rachel a target. It was bad enough I'd become one myself.

Striking a preemptive blow by preventing Lynne from hiring Rachel would keep them safe. Despite Barbara's endorsement of a clandestine action against my aunt, my inconvenient conscience, which sounded a lot like my father, refused to shut up.

My philosophy professor father and crime-fiction-writing mother had different ideas regarding ethical behavior. There was nothing my parents loved more than examining abstract problems, and they were capable of turning the most innocuous, mundane decision into a debate on morality. These arguments usually ended with my father quoting Aristotle and my mother countering with a pointed reference to Miss Marple. Their divorce, however, was most amicable, and they remained friends as well as sparring partners.

I weighed the evidence and decided Rachel's physical safety was more important than her career aspirations. With that ethical conundrum resolved, all that remained was to decide upon an appropriate strategy.

If I was going to thwart my aunt's job application, I needed more knowledge about Lynne Heller's character and personality. My sole interaction with the wardrobe mistress occurred during the brief period of time while she was fitting me with the wig. On that occasion, she was all business: scolding Marty, jotting copious notes, and snapping photos to document her work.

Natalie, who had been with the show since its workshop phase, might be able to help. She had the added advantage of being one of the few people who was willing to spend unpaid time with me. Her positive qualities included a love of gossip, and she was on good terms with everyone in the cast, other than Amber, who resented Natalie's poorly hidden desire to take her place.

I planned to torpedo Rachel's job application with well-placed backhanded compliments, and for that, I needed to know the wardrobe mistress's work habits, her likes, and her dislikes. Other than Lynne's fury over Marty's cigarette breaks, I was in the dark.

I was impatient for morning to come and distracted myself with a detective show I'd watched twice, from its cliched opening to the improbable conclusion. After the most unlikely suspect admitted to the crime without claiming her right to a lawyer, I watched the credits roll by. Eventually, I fell back asleep and didn't get up again until Jonah's footsteps woke me at dawn. Without sufficient time to relitigate the previous night's argument, we postponed further discussion. After two cups of coffee he left for work and I waited another restless hour before texting Natalie.

I tapped out an invitation to meet at a nearby café but didn't send it.

Instead, I fixed upon Rose as a more promising source. The young actress's romance with Sam Flannery might be over, but she'd been by the director's side for many weeks and might have inside information. An added incentive was the opportunity to use Rose to verify Natalie's statements.

Seconds after sending the invitation to Rose, she answered with seven hearts. I was pleased her initial reluctance to talk to me, which she'd subtly indicated by fleeing down the steep stairs of the D'Anconia while I pursued her, was definitely over. After sharing several drinks, one plate of truffled french fries, and enough heartbroken tears to fill an orchestra pit, she'd trusted me with her most personal hopes and fears. Sometimes, the purchase of that type of confidence had a boomerang effect and ended in resentment rather than friendship. Rose, however, based on the number of hearts, held onto the warm, alcohol-fueled closeness of our previous meeting.

I met Rose at Café Noisette, a French bakery located five blocks from the D'Anconia. It was close enough to be convenient and far enough away that we were unlikely to be interrupted by anyone from *Mad Music*.

I was prepared to fork over an obscene amount of money for one black coffee, one latte, one croissant, and two bottles of vitamin-enriched water, but Rose grabbed the bill and insisted on paying. "I owe you, girlfriend."

Strictly speaking, she didn't owe me anything, since Mr. Hedge Fund had picked up our check at the hotel bar. I thanked her and said, "Not at all, er, girlfriend. Your admirer was the one who paid our bar tab. How did that go?"

Rose was dismissive. "Nothing special. Just your average rich guy looking to hook up with an actress."

Although she didn't strike me as an intellectual giant, I appreciated her ability to size up and reject a preening, overage frat boy when she saw one.

Her name was a good match for her delicate beauty and long-stemmed legs. When I told her so, she laughed. "My real name is Connie Eckstein. I changed it to Rose Summerson when I got my Equity card. What about you? Have you always been Leah Siderova?"

I was pleased to find something meaningful we had in common. It was the surest way to gain further confidence. "Like you, I didn't start life with my stage name, but I didn't wait until I was eligible to join the union before I changed it. My mother decided Siderova was a better fit for a ballerina than Feldbaum. Siderova is her maiden name, so it's not a complete departure, but it took a while before I got used to it."

Without changing my tone or expression, I said, "Too bad the guy you met last night was such a disappointment. I know it came on top of a tough day for you."

Without warning, her babyish, bland features hardened, and her voice changed so dramatically, she reminded me of a character in a horror movie, the kind whose multiple personalities resulted in actions too scary for me to watch.

Her carefully coached, accent-less speech turned harsh and nasal. "There's something you need to know about me, Leah Feldbaum Siderova. I've got more street smarts than almost anyone else in this business. And I'm not the type who's going to be taken in by some rich guy who thinks he can buy himself a good time with a few drinks and a plate of potatoes."

Rose's anger was understandable. No one wants to be thought a fool. I toasted her with my coffee and said, "Good for you. You're better than that. I'm glad you put him in his place." To redirect her raw emotion to a topic more in keeping with my goals, I asked her about Marty as a prelude to getting information about Lynne.

She remained fixated on the guy who tried to pick her up. "Marty's okay. For sure, he's nothing like Mr. Rich Guy. I thought I'd die of boredom listening to him talk about his family's horse farm and his vacations on a ranch in Idaho. I mean, someday, I'll probably settle down and marry a guy like him, but I'm not ready to give up on my shot at fame and fortune. I'm not like The Castle. Amber has no idea what it's like to struggle. Everything she's ever gotten has been handed to her by her fancy family."

This was news to me. "I didn't know Amber was rich. I thought she grew up in Brooklyn."

Her round blue eyes narrowed. "She likes people to think she's hardcore and came from the projects, but she grew up in Brooklyn Heights. Big difference, as far as I'm concerned."

I understood Rose's resentment. Brooklyn Heights was famous for its elegant brownstones that sold for millions of dollars; the grittier side of the borough was known more for public housing projects than pricey real estate. For people like Rose, who grew up on meaner streets, it was bad form to pretend you've got street cred when you went to private school and summered at the Vineyard.

My companion's bitterness made further inroads into her enunciation and grammar, and her accent thickened. "Amber didn't go to no public school, neither. Miss Too-Lucky-to-Live went to Yale Drama School. The Castle family has real castles, didja know that? And Amber, she was a dresser."

Unsure of what she meant, I stopped her aggrieved recitation of Amber's material advantages. "What kind of dresser?"

She pulled the corners of her mouth down. "You know. Like a horse dresser."

I finally understood what Rose was telling me. The star of *Mad Music* had been a dressage rider, which meant her family was indeed far wealthier than she let on. Dressage horses were as pricey as luxury cars. My knowledge of this rarified sport was courtesy of my mother, who, in one of her crime fiction novels, killed off a rider. Her original plotline included the death of the horse, but Barbara's agent forbade the killing of animals. According to her, readers wouldn't care if the posh horsewoman kicked the bucket, but if her prize-winning horse died, they'd revolt at the cruelty of it all.

Rose's anger probably had more to do with Sam Flannery than with her rival's privileged upbringing. I felt sorry for her and her disappointments, both professional and personal, but I felt sorrier for Amber. My famous friend thought everyone, except for Natalie, loved her. She clung to this fiction despite considerable evidence that demonstrated the opposite was true, and I wondered if this was a form of emotional protection. Despite my lesser claim to fame, I'd had many painful experiences as a consequence of a life lived in the spotlight. It made us vulnerable in ways the outside world can't imagine.

I didn't adequately question Amber's faith in her friends and fans until after the spiked coffee sent her to the hospital. Thanks to Rose, I had a better understanding of how the actress might have inspired less kindly feelings. Amber appeared to live a charmed existence. Beautiful, talented, and rich, she must have ignited more envy and jealousy than either she or I realized.

As useful as Rose's information about Amber might prove to be at some future point, my immediate need was to learn more about the costume mistress.

The time for subtlety was over. "Rose, how long have Lynne and Marty worked together?"

Her face was a perfect blank. "Hunh? I have no idea."

"What kind of person is Lynne? Do you know anything about her?"

She didn't question my interest or the abrupt shift in our conversation. "I know Marty better than I know Lynne. They worked together on a show I did last year, which closed almost as fast as it opened. She was always yelling at him, but he never seemed to mind. Lynne's a neat freak, and Marty was, well, you know."

"I don't know. This is my first show. What did Marty do to annoy her?"

"Let's start with what Lynne did to annoy Marty. He said Lynne didn't want an assistant. She wanted a slave. When he went outside for a cigarette break, she would run after him if he was one minute late. And every time he so much as looked at his phone, she would freak out. Lynne's kind of a weirdo that way. She totally didn't respect Marty, who's got a bazillion followers. The guy might not look like much, but he's a bigger influencer than Lynne will ever be. I should be so lucky."

Rose's definition of a cruel taskmaster wasn't mine, but I had a lot more experience than she did. I'd worked with choreographers who made fanatical dictators look like exemplars of gentle reason. According to my young friend, the wardrobe mistress's crimes were an aversion to smoking, social media, and tardiness.

In other words, Lynne's preferences matched Rachel's. I hoped Rose had other insights that would enable me to lay waste to my aunt's chances at a job with *Mad Music*. "Is there anything else you can tell me about her? Any quirks or pet peeves?"

Rose licked her finger and pressed it against the plate, removing the last crumbs of croissant. "Why do you care so much about Lynne? She's a nobody. A legend in her own mind if you ask me."

For once, I was able to speak candidly. "My aunt has an interview with Lynne. She's hoping to get Marty's job, at least temporarily, while he recovers. I wanted to help her out."

Admittedly, that last sentence wasn't strictly true, but it was close enough to the truth to appease some forms of moral philosophy.

Rose stood up and grabbed her bag. "That sounds super bizarre. If my aunt wanted the job, I'd scratch that in a heartbeat."

"We've got more in common than I thought. Girlfriend."

Chapter Nineteen

Sex is a dance in the eyes of the beholder.
—Gwen Verdon

Bryan exploded after watching the less-skillful dancers clunk their way through the finale. "If you overstuffed, undertalented wannabes can't do better, don't show up tomorrow. Sign up for unemployment and pray you get a job hauling dirty dishes."

Performers are used to abuse. The imbalance of power practically ensured it, and in the ballet world, Bryan's tirade was commonplace. Ballerinas would have responded to his insults with blank expressions and respectful poses, but the *Mad Music* dancers stood with their hands on their hips and sneers on their faces. Their anger at his outburst was understandable, but so was his frustration with them.

Bryan was more forgiving of the actors. They didn't need exceptional skill, because the choreography for them suited their different strengths. Amber, however, continued to struggle with the simplified routine he'd created for her. As the star of the show, she was exempt from his ire but not from her peers' derision. Bryan reworked her sections to make them easier, but the process was painful to watch.

Bryan's considerate treatment of Amber exacerbated his irritation with the weaker dancers, who labored to meet his exacting standards. The men were all gifted technicians, but the women exhibited a broad range of expertise. The gap between the beauty queens and the hoofers threatened the integrity of the whole, but they were united in their antipathy toward Bryan.

Natalie whispered, "Too bad it was Marty who got the poisoned drink."

Carly hushed her, and Natalie said, in an innocent voice, "What? Too soon?"

The muffled titters reached Bryan. He opened his mouth, but Carly cut him off and brokered a fragile peace. "I get it, Boss. But you have to get where we're coming from, too. Why don't you leave the rest of this rehearsal to me? That's what I'm here for. And don't forget about those Tonys. We'll make it happen."

The dance captain's conciliatory response caught our panicked choreographer off guard. Through clenched teeth, he said, "Thanks, Carly. I hope you're as good as you claim."

I checked my phone at every opportunity, but hours passed, and neither Lynne nor my phantom texter contacted me. I interpreted silence on both ends as a good sign. Rachel must not have advanced to a second interview.

The lack of communication from the trolling texter, however, didn't mean I wasn't being watched. My nervousness was very much like the stage fright I felt before every performance. I escaped as I always did, by throwing myself into dancing. Bryan had to remind me to scale back my efforts to avoid overstressing my muscles.

The remainder of the day unfolded without a renewal of hostilities. Bryan called us together before dismissing us to give us his notes. He smiled with his mouth.

"You're all doing better, but it's still not good enough." He ticked off sections that needed improvement and then invited Amber to join him in the front of the room. "And now, the star of our show has an announcement I know you'll like."

Amber opened her arms the same way she did after her stint in the hospital. "You're all invited to my Design the Dream gala! You're family, and I want you there."

The unexpected invitation broke barriers, as she must have known it would. She exclaimed, "Don't thank me! It was Sam and Bryan who suggested it."

Excited chatter replaced sour criticism, and the tension of the day disappeared in a flurry of goodwill that extended to Bryan.

I drew Amber aside and said, "Did you plan this all along?"

She winked. "What do you think?"

"I think you're a genius. The cast needed something to bring us together."

I lingered in the back of the room and waited for each person to leave. Although I hadn't gotten a good look at the person who'd followed me, I remembered the stalker's posture and gait. I watched the male dancers and actors pick up their bags and walk toward the door, checking their body language and silhouettes against my memory of the trench-coated stalker. There weren't as many men as there were women in the cast, and they were all too tall. Maybe Mr. Trench Coat was female. All I saw was the coat, a hat, and a scarf.

Amber remained by my side. "What's on your mind, Leah? You should get some rest."

I showed her the previous day's texts. Her eyes grew wide, and the pupils dilated. Without comment, she held up her phone. The same text I got appeared on the screen. She flicked to the next message, a picture of her leaving the hospital.

I felt sick. "Why didn't you tell me? We're supposed to be working together."

Patches of red stained her cheeks. "I feel terrible about this. I-I thought, well, to tell you the truth, I was scared you'd leave the show. I know that's what Jonah wants, and he's right. You don't owe me, or Bryan, anything. The smart thing to do would be to bail. It would make my life easier if you did, because I feel so guilty about getting you involved."

I'd met many famous and influential people from fields as diverse as art, architecture, finance, and the law. Very few had the courage to admit to their vulnerability.

"I'm not going anywhere. We're in this together. But don't keep secrets from me."

"I won't. You can trust me. But promise you'll consider my advice. The best thing for both of us would be for you to exit this mess." The actress brought her face closer to mine. "What happened to your eye?"

Getting pranked with a spray of ketchup was so absurd it didn't bear repeating. "I poked myself in the eye this morning. Who knew mascara could be so deadly?"

"I once did that right before a performance!" Looking more relaxed, she left me and took shelter under Sam's protective arm.

I tossed a sweatshirt and a pair of jeans over my leotard and tights and headed toward the elevator. In the lobby, Natalie was waiting for me.

"Let's drink."

Chapter Twenty

Broadway is so defeating...it doesn't encourage people to be as tenacious as they should be.
—Ann Reinking

Natalie and I bypassed the bars, restaurants, and hotels that catered to theater people and settled on a shabby Irish pub. She ordered a dark beer that smelled smoky and sweet. I had a flat Diet Coke that a large lemon slice was unable to resuscitate.

She flicked back her many braids. "What's going on with your boyfriend? Is he trying to ruin the show?"

For one stunned moment, I thought she was talking about Jonah. I choked a bit and then realized she was referring to our unpopular choreographer.

I was weary of having to defend my relationship with Bryan. "I worked with him for years at ABC, and yes, Bryan is tough. You're never going to get rainbows and puppy dogs from him, at least not during the rehearsal period. Away from the studio, he can be quite charming. But what do you care? You're a pro, and you've probably dealt with a lot worse. What's important is that he's a great choreographer. If we can pull it off, the dance sequences will bring down the house."

Natalie swirled the foamy beer. "I can deal with a Broadway diva, but I can't stand Bryan. He's a typical ballet nerd. So snooty. Thinks he's all that."

I fluttered my arms, reminding her that I, too, was a ballet nerd. I meant it as a joke, but she was mortified. "I didn't mean you, of course. You're not like that at all."

"No apologies necessary, Natalie. I live in that world, and I've worked with a ton of snooty dancers who'd cut your heart out for a role. Did I ever tell you about the time I danced on a program with Zarina Devereaux from the Rive Gauche Ballet? She thought her boyfriend was cheating on her with me and ended up smashing everything that wasn't nailed down. But life is too short in our business to hold grudges. Nothing is certain, least of all our careers."

Her shoulders relaxed from their tense position around her ears. "Did you know Bryan wasn't Sam Flannery's first choice?"

There was no benefit in feigning ignorance. "Yes, I know a little of what happened, but not much. I took a ballet class with Marco at Studio Dance, and he told me his husband got cut. He thinks Bryan shafted Garret, but he has no proof."

She stared at our reflection in the foggy mirror behind the bar. "I know you're friends with Bryan, but the facts are the facts. Marco and Garret left Amsterdam to join *Mad Music*. It's common knowledge that Bryan convinced Sam to hire him instead of Garret. I don't know the details of how he did it." She nudged me. "But I bet you do."

"Bryan doesn't have to scheme. He's a great choreographer. You have to admit, his work for *Mad Music* is fabulous. He might not be the most likable guy, but he's not the lowlife you think he is."

Her look was speculative. "And yet, he double-crossed you. Don't you find it strange that as good as he is, he hasn't done much lately?"

I tried to laugh off her brutal, if accurate, observation. "I admire your willingness to go for the frontal assault. Most people prefer to stick the knife in my back. Despite what you think, though, it was more complicated than that."

Natalie used one foot to swivel her barstool from left to right. I wished Izzy were there to see her. My psychologist friend, who represented one-third of the Weird Sisters' expertise, knew a lot more about body language than I did. It seemed to me that Natalie's side-to-side movement indicated she was trying to choose between two answers. Or between two people.

She stopped twirling with an abrupt click of her heel on the metal railing.

"I wasn't attacking you, Leah. I'm your friend."

I wanted to believe her. "You're also friends with Carly, who's no friend of mine."

She winced as if wounded. "Ouch. We're even now. But you're friends with Amber, who's no friend of mine. As for Carly, you have to understand that if Garret ended up choreographing the show, Carly would have been the Dreamcatcher. You can't blame her for resenting you."

"Actually, I can. As for Garret, if Sam or the producers wanted Bryan instead, he had every right to accept. You shouldn't hate him for taking the job. Anyone in his position would have done the same thing."

Natalie drank off most of her beer in one long, thirsty swallow. "If the rumors are true, and Bryan got his job by trashing Garret, I have plenty of reason to hate him. He ended up screwing over Carly and possibly me as well. We were all doing fine until he came along."

I sipped at my fizz-less soda to keep her company. "Let's make a deal. I'm going to Amber's big party with Bryan—"

She banged her glass against the bar, but I stopped her protest. "I'm not going as his date. Or even as his friend. Bryan thinks it'd be good PR if people saw us together. I'd rather go with a dead fish than with him."

She turned up her nose. "The fish would stink less."

I patted her shoulder. "That may be. My point, however, is that I can ask him, diplomatically, of course, what went down when he was hired. And if you keep me posted on whatever gossip is going around, I'll do the same for you."

She held out her long, strong hand. "Deal."

I took it, and her fingers tightened around mine. With a more cheerful expression, she said, "I'm starving. You?"

We moved to a booth, and a waiter followed to take our order. My stomach was empty, but an insistent buzz from my phone stopped me in the middle of a mathematical calculation of the number of calories in two different salads. By the time I extracted the phone from the bottomless depths of my bag, it stopped ringing. The call was from Lynne, who left a voice message.

I didn't want to talk to the wardrobe mistress about Aunt Rachel in front of Natalie, so I texted instead. **Can I call you back later?**

Three dots danced across the screen, disappeared, and then reappeared, which made me feel as if I could hear her thinking. Eventually, she messaged, **No. Meet me tomorrow- 30 min b4 rehearsal.**

I texted my assent and tucked the phone back in my bag. Natalie ate bread while we waited for our food, and I sat on my hands to keep them from reaching for a thick slice of carbohydrates. We both had the Caesar salad and spent the next hour exchanging stories about our families and our boyfriends.

She said with a grimace, "It took me a while, but I'm now out of a totally toxic relationship. Why do I do this to myself? I knew he wasn't the right guy. I should have broken up with him instead of waiting for the humiliation of having him do it first. He's married now, but I, of course, am still single. Not that there's anything wrong with that."

This was a theme I knew well. "Tell me about it. My last boyfriend was divorced, but half the time we were together, he was on the phone with his ex-wife. And the guy before him? He broke up with me while I was on tour with ABC. Talk about humiliation. You'd think he could have waited until we were on the same continent. At least he didn't post any pictures of himself and his new girlfriend, who's now his wife, until I changed my relationship status."

She laughed. "Breakups are so much worse when your exes find happiness with someone who's not you."

I picked croutons out of my salad and moved them to a small plate. "Who was your ex? Anyone I might know?"

Natalie worked at the last slice of bread until it broke into crumbs. "Um, no. I don't think you do."

The hesitation in her answer told me she was lying. I wondered who, among our mutual acquaintances, had broken her heart. Possible candidates included our amorous director and faithless choreographer. Perhaps Natalie's dislike of Bryan was more personal than she'd let on. She was a good actress, but not that good.

Chapter Twenty-One

Dance is not an exercise. Dance is an art.
—Alicia Alonso

My beloved aunt's presence in the fraught atmosphere at a Broadway rehearsal, even if it posed no danger to her or me, was not an agreeable prospect. Dancing is tough enough without having an unsubtle relative hanging over your shoulder like an overeager parent at a baseball game, the kind that yells embarrassing encouragement while the kid quakes in his cleats. Worse, I feared Rachel would intuit my double role and end up blowing my cover to whoever hadn't already figured it out.

I had less than twelve hours to fix upon a tactful way to scuttle my aunt's ambition to work in the *Mad Music* costume department. The challenge was to execute that delicate maneuver without making myself look like Benedict Arnold and Rachel look like George Washington.

Additional queries about Lynne confirmed my first impression. The wardrobe mistress was dedicated, reserved, impatient, and fastidious. Good news for me and bad news for my loud, extroverted, and talkative relative. The unadorned truth about Rachel should prove sufficient to bury her ambitions. By the time I finished praising her, Lynne would welcome my aunt with the same warmth as a dinner party host who's stuck with a guest sporting a rash and a hacking cough.

I planned to artfully describe Rachel's most objectionable qualities as strengths. Maybe a few compliments like *You won't be bored with Rachel. She*

never stops talking—the woman is a laugh a minute! Or *Rachel is very skillful.
Hardly any of her costumes came apart at the seams!*

Lynne was in the lobby of the D'Anconia when I arrived. If this had
been our first meeting, I probably would have passed her by and waited
for someone who better fit the stereotypical image of a wardrobe mistress.
Backstage people are paid to be invisible, but Lynne was a striking presence.
She was tall and broad, with sharp features and bright gray hair, which
hung in long, untidy, frizzled curls. Two-inch earrings that dangled with
stars and crescent moons peeked from behind the curtain of hair, and
a matching pattern of intergalactic-inspired embroidery decorated the
bottom of wide-leg pants. Her lips were a vivid red, and her eyelashes
long and unapologetically fake. Broadway performers often had outsized
personalities that soaked up the spotlight and vacuumed out all the air in
the room, but Lynne was a match for any of them.

She didn't bother with a greeting. "Rachel is your aunt, yes? Can you
vouch for her? I don't have much time."

I pressed the button for the elevator. "Yes, but I'd rather talk upstairs. It's
freezing here."

She stared at me with slightly protruding eyes. "Let's not. I prefer the
lobby."

Flustered by her abrupt manner, my prepared speech took flight and
landed in parts unknown. "What do you want to know about Rachel, other
than the fact that she's my aunt?"

Lynne drilled me with an unwavering stare. "I want to know if she's got
the work ethic to do the job and do it right. Can she handle long hours for
low pay and without complaining?"

I couldn't manage a blatant lie. Not about Rachel. She'd always been so
good to me. "Rachel is a hard worker. About that, there's no doubt."

"Can she follow directions? Stay off her cell phone? She swore she didn't
smoke, but I was positive I smelled tobacco."

I didn't need the analytical skills of Sherlock Holmes to conclude Rachel
met my mother in advance of her interview with Lynne. Barbara had mostly
given up cigarettes for a vape pen, but she resorted to the real thing in times

of stress. The source of that stress was likely to have been her fear that Rachel would secure employment on a Broadway show and lord it over her until the end of time. They still hadn't settled a decades-long debate over which of them their deceased father loved more.

Lynne's prolonged scrutiny of my face redirected me from those unsatisfying reflections, but my tiresome conscience continued its dominance over my actions.

She spoke with staccato impatience. "Well? Does she or doesn't she smoke?"

I sighed. "Rachel was telling the truth. She hates cigarettes."

With a closer adherence to my main goal, which was to keep my aunt from getting the job, I added, "You probably know she has no experience, although she's very enthusiastic. She made my first costume, and hardly any of the sequins fell off, even though she did break the glue gun. On the plus side, the smoke from the burning fabric set off the fire alarm, so no one was hurt."

Lynne chewed the inside of her cheek. "Experience isn't as important as you might think. I'd rather work with an older woman who's willing to learn than a mansplaining guy who thinks he knows everything."

The wardrobe mistress's flippant allusion to Marty as a nameless guy struck me as heartless. His hospital stay would have—should have—evoked a more sympathetic attitude. A slight break in Lynne's voice, however, made me wonder if she was as unmoved by Marty's plight as her words indicated. Or, maybe Marty wasn't the mansplaining guy she disliked.

Perhaps Lynne's reserved and aloof nature would prove better targets. "Rachel is very friendly, and she loves to talk. The family calls her Miss Congeniality."

The lines across her forehead relaxed. "Give me Miss Congeniality over Miss America any day of the week. She can yap all she wants, as long as she doesn't reveal any of my trade secrets."

Finally, something I could use. "She's so excited about working on a Broadway show, I can't promise she'll stay quiet about it. Discretion isn't her strong suit, but she's so nice I'm sure that won't be a problem."

If the imaginary conversation I had last night matched the one I was having in real life, Lynne would have long since rejected Rachel. Instead, the elements of my aunt's personality I thought most likely to ruin her chances had no effect at all.

Lynne scratched her head. "She's not like anyone else I interviewed, but she made a good first impression. I liked her, and she seemed trustworthy. Maybe you don't know your aunt as well as you think you do." She stabbed the elevator button. "I'm a good judge of character. And if hiring her turns out to be a mistake, that's easily fixed, since she's not a member of the union. That can be a real pain."

I wondered if she was still talking about Marty. He was a union member and not a powerless apprentice. Lynne appeared fierce enough to have poisoned his drink, but if she wanted a new assistant, murder was too extreme a solution. Perhaps Jonah was right, and whoever dosed him with ketamine hadn't meant to hurt him so grievously. The drug, by itself, wouldn't have put him in the hospital. It was the unlucky nature of his fall, in which he hit his head against a metal radiator, that did the real harm.

Except Marty probably wasn't the target. I shuddered to think of what might have happened if the ketamine and the sugar ended up in Amber's drink.

We entered the musty elevator, which smelled like rotting wood and wet dog. The doors were halfway closed when Amber dashed into the lobby and called out, "Wait for me!"

I pressed the button to keep the doors open, but this didn't stop them from closing. Those buttons never worked, at least not in buildings of the D'Anconia's vintage, and I sometimes wondered if they were there simply to make the person inside feel useful. I didn't attempt to muscle the doors back open, as I knew from experience I was unequal to the job.

As we made our slow ascent, I racked my brains to come up with some scrap of information that would cause Lynne to rethink her estimation of Rachel. I'd yet to use my aunt's failure to remember scheduled appointments or her habit of arriving well past the time she was expected. Rachel's shortcomings in this regard were mostly limited to activities my mother made for her at the hair, nail, and skin salons, but Lynne didn't have to know that.

My aunt preferred what my mother called the Janis Joplin approach to grooming, and Barbara frequently chided Rachel for her hippie-era clothing. With this thought in mind, I reevaluated Lynne's dramatic outfit and realized it was pure Woodstock, circa 1969. Rachel probably had the same pants and earrings. No wonder Lynne trusted her. There's nothing like a shared love of vintage bell-bottom pants to bring people together.

The elevator stopped on the fourth floor before resuming its journey. No one got on, and I said to Lynne, "I bet whoever was waiting gave up. It's lucky Rachel made it in time to meet you."

Lynne clutched her capacious bag, which was large enough to double as a steamer trunk. "Rachel arrived exactly on time. She seems a very responsible person."

"My aunt tends to get flustered in new situations, and she's still figuring out the subway after spending over twenty years in Minnesota. Eventually, she'll adjust. Though she did say she was thinking about moving back to Minneapolis." I peeked at Lynne to see if this had any effect.

Once again, the things I hoped would prejudice Lynne against Rachel failed to work. Lynne jingled her earrings in an unconcerned manner. "Nothing wrong with the Midwest. I'm from Michigan, myself."

I gave up. She and Rachel must have had quite the bonding session. If I didn't know better, I'd think Lynne had an ulterior motive in making sure my aunt joined the crew.

The doors opened on the eleventh floor, and we walked together to the rehearsal room. It was still empty, and I asked, "Whom are you fitting today?"

She grunted. "Two twitchy nitwits."

Time for some bonding of my own. "Bobbie York, the wardrobe mistress at American Ballet Company, pokes dancers with her needle when they won't cooperate. She has no patience for people who can't stand still."

Her stern manner softened, and she stopped looking at me as if I were trying to sell her shares in the Brooklyn Bridge. "I think Bobbie and I would get along just fine. Tell her I appreciate the tip."

"I'll give Bobbie your message, as long as you don't stab me." With a rueful tone, I said, "I hope you won't find me too heartless if I confess it wouldn't bother me if you used a bunch of our cast members as a pin cushion. It hasn't been easy cozying up to that group. Very cliquish."

The comment was a random stab at sisterhood and worked better than I anticipated.

She clenched her fists. "Why do you care what a bunch of mean girls say? They're nothing and no one. Half of them couldn't dance or act their way out of a paper bag. You're a star."

After trying so hard to lie to Lynne, it was a relief to tell the unvarnished truth. "That's how Sam is promoting me, but at American Ballet Company, I'm what they call a workhorse. Nerdy balletomanes love me. But I don't have the pull of glamerinas like Marina Devereaux or Mavis Ferris. And at *Mad Music*, I don't feel like a star. I feel like an outcast."

Lynne paused to watch Amber and five dancers enter the room. The wardrobe mistress stepped back and leaned against the wall, scrutinizing them with the care of a jeweler examining a handful of gems, looking for the fakes. "When you're on top, there's never any shortage of people who want to push you off. If you don't believe me, ask Amber."

I closed the gap between us. "Do you know who poisoned her drink?"

Lynne bent down and whispered hoarsely. "Not yet. I'm counting on Marty to answer that question."

I wondered again about Lynne's feelings about her former assistant. She'd sent a bewildering array of mixed signals.

Natalie and Carly entered together and joined the group that held itself apart from us. Lynne used her thumb to jab twice in the direction of the empty refreshment table. "Marty has the attention span of a flea when he's around pretty girls. He could hardly keep his eyes off them, which was a definite problem when I needed him to concentrate. But that also means that more than anyone, he had the best chance to have seen who dropped the ketamine."

"I don't get it. Why would he have drunk from coffee he knew might have been roofied?"

Her face crumpled for a brief moment before she regained control. "I think, with his usual bad timing, he turned away just long enough to miss seeing who spiked his drink, but he might remember who interfered with Amber's. Somebody's got it in for Amber. And I think I know who."

I kept as still as if Bobbie was doing a costume fitting, knowing the tiniest movement would end with a spiteful pinprick. "Who?"

Lynne turned her uncompromising gaze on me. "I'm not sure. Not yet. But since you, like Amber, aren't winning any popularity contests around here, maybe it's not such a bad idea to have your aunt looking out for you."

I longed to tell her it was more likely I'd have to rescue my aunt than the other way around but refrained from further disparagement of Rachel. "Have you talked to Marty?"

She went back to chewing her cheek. "Still no visitors. His parents said he's drifting in and out of consciousness, which doesn't sound good, but he's making progress. The doctors said the recovery could go fast, slow, or not at all. He may get all of his memory back, but so far, it's not happening."

The chills that coursed down my back were from fear and not the room's inadequate insulation. "I suggest you keep information about Marty to yourself, for his sake as well as yours. And I wouldn't advertise the fact that you went to see him, either."

"It's a little late for that advice. Half the chorus was there, all of them dripping crocodile tears and acting up a storm."

The wardrobe mistress had so theatrical a manner I wondered if her resume included any stints as an actress. "Have you ever been onstage instead of backstage? My aunt was a dancer before she opened her ballet school. Maybe you have that in common with her? I know she'd do anything to revisit those days."

Lynne recoiled as if shot. "I hope you're wrong about that. I knew about Rachel's attempts to go pro when she was a kid. But she better not have any dreams of stardom on my watch."

Who knew? The one thing about Rachel that could have swayed Lynne's decision came too late to persuade her. I prodded her again. "You didn't answer the question. Were you, are you, an actress?"

CHAPTER TWENTY-ONE

"Honey, we're all onstage, one way or another."

Chapter Twenty-Two

There's an innate feeling when I choreograph in juxtaposition to how I feel as a dancer.
—Justin Peck

After a long rehearsal that left my legs shaking with stress, I had a second date with Bryan, this one at my request. My Weird Sisters were performing that evening in their swing dance showcase, and I wanted him to see them.

He proposed a brisk crosstown walk, which I vetoed. We shared a cab instead and arrived in time for him to snag a glass of wine and a packet of peanuts from the concession stand.

Bryan was not pleased when he saw the program, which included dancers from a half dozen schools and amateur companies. "There are seventeen individual performances. And your buddies are the last ones. If I conk out halfway through, don't bother me unless I'm drooling or snoring. I wish I'd seen the rules before I signed up for the game."

There was no curtain, but as the lights dimmed over the audience and brightened on the stage, I whispered, "It's a showcase. What did you expect? You'll thank me later. The Weird Sisters are amazing."

He didn't have to struggle to stay awake. A series of short, inventive dances, all very different from each other, succeeded each other at a rapid pace. Many of the performers had body types that didn't conform to the usual balletic silhouette, which delighted me. Bryan was noncommittal regarding the choreography, but I was both fascinated and inspired. I'd always been the instrument of someone else's artistic vision. Would I ever have the courage to take the lead myself?

As the evening wore on, the audience thinned, and at the end of the second intermission, there was a mass movement toward the exit doors. Sadly, the people who came to see the dancers in the first sections didn't feel obligated to cheer on the ones in the last act, and I feared my friends would be performing in a half-empty theater.

I whispered my concern to Bryan, who was indifferent. "I don't blame them for leaving. If it wasn't for you, I would've booked an hour ago."

As the lights rose on Abigail, Izzy, and Audrey, I was as nervous for them as I was before my performances. They wore heeled, t-strap shoes, swingy skirts, and jaunty ponytails, and their graceful poses told me I had nothing to worry about. When the irresistible drumbeat of Benny Goodman's "Sing, Sing, Sing" began, my body wanted to climb onto the stage and dance with them.

The trio stayed in place, tapping their feet for the opening beats, and then, as the familiar melody filled the theater, they each took a solo before beckoning three men onto the stage and swinging away. Each pair took turns as the featured couple, and for the finale, the women executed a series of spins that ended when they stretched backward over their partners' arms. Not bad for a bunch of grandmas.

Two of the men were young and looked like pros, but Abigail's partner was her age and an amateur. He was short and stocky, and although he gamely tried to keep pace with Abigail, he wasn't up to the level of the others. With a start, I realized why his face looked so familiar. It was Solly Greenfield, my Uncle Morty's friend and occasional accomplice.

The dance was short, but it brought down the house. Abigail, Izzy, and Audrey curtsied to loud applause and several wolf whistles. At the last minute, a large group of people had entered the theater, which made up for those who'd left early.

I turned to Bryan. "Admit I was right."

He shook my hand. "We've got a deal. I'll give them a cameo in the third act. It'll be great PR for the show."

"I told you so!"

Bryan rechecked the program. "What do they call themselves? The Weird Sisters?"

I wished I hadn't shared my secret nickname with him. "Don't call them that! It's how I first thought of them, but they're nothing like the witches in *Macbeth*."

"I'll try to remember, but it's you who put the name in my head. I kind of like it."

I blocked the aisle to keep him from leaving. "You should tell everyone you're the one who discovered them. It will reinforce your status as a creative genius. Also, I don't want my friends to start off on the wrong foot with Carly, who will give them a hard time if she thinks it was my idea."

He gazed at me longer than was comfortable, and I wondered how much he knew, or how much he'd guessed, about my clandestine investigation. Bryan was still working with American Ballet Company when I solved the murder of a fellow dancer, and he might have also been aware of my behind-the-scenes investigations when a second violent event occurred. If he did suspect I was investigating threats against Amber, it was information he kept to himself.

He took my arm. "Can we go now?"

I didn't let him pull me with him. "Don't you want to talk to them? They're such huge fans of yours."

"Tempting, but no. I'll go over the rehearsal schedule and text you when to bring them."

I went backstage to congratulate my friends on their performance. The two men who'd partnered Izzy and Audrey left, but Solly remained, his arm draped across Abigail's frail shoulders.

Solly pinched my cheek the way he did when I was a kid. His fingers still smelled like cigars. He pointed to Abigail and said, "What did you think of my lady?"

Abigail's cheeks were pink. "Leah, you remember Solly, don't you?"

"Of course I do. Solly's been a friend of the family for a long time."

Solly wasn't the kind of guy one forgets. Growing up, I knew him as one of my Uncle Morty's more colorful buddies. Years passed before I learned some of the shadier aspects of the Greenfields' line of work, which Morty euphemistically called "the family business."

In Brooklyn, neighborhood ties don't fray with time. About a year earlier, when I needed protection and had nowhere else to turn, Uncle Morty called in a favor, and Solly and his many sons kept me safe. In doing so, they ended up on the right side of the law, which was not always their fallback position.

Solly had a car waiting. Abigail, Izzy, and Audrey climbed into the limousine, and we headed to Mott Street in Chinatown. We stopped in front of a modest, nondescript tenement building with a faded sign that had a few Chinese characters and a chicken painted on it. The waiters hailed him as an old friend.

We settled into a booth with cracked vinyl seats and studied the menu, which was printed in Chinese, with tiny English translations underneath. Solly said, "You're in for a real treat. You ever want to eat great food, tell them Solly sent you."

Abigail giggled. "You make it sound like a speakeasy."

Solly squeezed her hand. "You wanna have a good time in this city? Solly Greenfield's your man." He winked at the rest of us. "Yo, Miss Leah Ballerina. Did you ever think a guy like me was gonna be on a dance floor?"

I laughed. "I can't say I have, but you were pretty smooth out there."

The talk became more general as the waiters brought steaming bowls and platters piled high with spicy food. I sipped the broth from a cup of wonton soup and ate the inside of three dumplings, picking apart the dough. Resisting the sweet and salty scent of fried rice, I ate the vegetables from a peppery dish showered in peanuts and chiles.

Abigail, Izzy, and Audrey ate almost as sparingly as I did, but Solly dug into each dish with unabashed gusto. He regaled us with colorful tales of his childhood, some of which featured my grandmother. In none of Nana's recollections to me had she ever mentioned cutting French class or smoking behind the high school, but he assured me she hadn't been nearly as straitlaced as a teenager as she was as a mother and grandmother.

Solly piled more food onto Abigail's nearly full plate. "I can't believe your

Nana left the old neighborhood. How does she like Florida?"

"You can take the gal out of Brooklyn, but you can't take the Brooklyn out of the gal. She still misses her old apartment."

Although I enjoyed Solly's stories, I didn't want to delay talking to my friends about *Mad Music*. The ladies were simultaneously terrified at the thought of auditioning for a Broadway show and elated at the possibility they'd be performing in one.

Audrey was so excited she needed two rounds of one-minute bullet chess to calm herself. "I had no idea this is what you planned! I thought you were going to get us a pass into some of the rehearsals."

Izzy's blue eyes sparkled. "We would have been thrilled to be ushers and get to see the show for free. I can't believe we might be on a Broadway stage."

I didn't want to promise more than I could deliver. "The final decision is Bryan's. But he loved your performance tonight. I think it's going to happen. I have no idea what role he's envisioned for you, and it's possible he doesn't yet know himself. We'll have to see."

Solly tapped the side of his nose. "Something tells me there's more to this offer than you're telling us. I remember the last time you got these gals onstage. What gives?"

There was a reason Solly was so good at his family business. Nothing escaped him. "You're right, Solly. It's a complicated situation, which I've explained to Abigail, Isabel, and Audrey. I've been working in an unofficial capacity with the police on a rather delicate matter. My first brief was to determine if the person threatening Amber Castle online presented a real risk. She's been dealing with some very unwelcome attention."

Solly snorted. "She's an actress, so she could have done it herself as some kind of crazy publicity stunt."

"That's what the police thought until someone tampered with her coffee, and she ended up in the hospital."

He put down his fork. "I don't like the sound of this. Too risky for them and too risky for you. My advice is to get out of it before you're in too deep. Know when to fold, Leah. You don't owe her nothing."

"You're right on both counts, but I'm in too deep to leave. Abigail, Izzy, and Audrey, however, aren't. They can take part in the play, but I'm no longer comfortable with involving them in the investigation. I promise you, they won't have to execute anything riskier than a few jazz turns. Bryan is going to take credit for finding and hiring them, so they'll have no obvious connection to me."

I spoke over their protests. "Please, ladies, let's think this through. Someone tried to kill Amber. And now I'm also getting threats." I swallowed hard to get my voice under control. "You have to respect how I feel. My assignment was to guard Amber. I think we all know how well that went."

Solly appeared lost in thought, but I kept talking, trying to justify my earlier, hasty offer. "I admit, at first, I hoped that by getting Abigail, Izzy, and Audrey into the show, they could help me with surveillance. But I've changed my mind. Hopefully, they'll get the chance to perform, but that will be the extent of their involvement."

With the precision of a mathematician, Audrey said, "You can't escape notice, Leah, even when you're not onstage. That's how we can help. You're exaggerating the risk we'd face. No one will suspect us."

Abigail nodded. "Audrey is right. You're a star, but the three of us are invisible. No one pays attention to women our age."

Solly kissed her hand. "Then they're crazy. You're beautiful."

Izzy cut in. "That's very romantic, but at the moment, not helpful. What you need to understand, Solly, is that we can help protect Leah, as well as Amber."

I agreed with Solly. "Once you're a part of the show, you'll be in the same position as the one limiting me. I can't escape notice, even when I'm not onstage."

Izzy said, "Precisely right. But you have a major role. Since we're unlikely to spend more than two minutes onstage, we can be watching from the wings while everyone else is performing. I'm worried about the gal who doesn't like you. Can't remember her name. Was it Carly or Natalie?"

"Natalie is my friend. I think I can trust her. Carly is the dance captain, and she despises me, but it's not personal. She wants the role I got."

As often happened when she was excited, Audrey's silvery hair came loose.

She combed it back with her fingers and said, "Don't forget about our skills. We're tougher than you think."

Solly held up his hand. "Leah's not debating your skills. Neither am I, but you can't enter a lion's den armed with knitting needles. I might know a few people who can pack some heat." He turned to me. "Your grandma would never forgive me if I let anything happen to you. Tell your friend Bryan it's a package deal. If he wants Abigail, Izzy, and Audrey, he's gotta take me too. Business is slow right now, and my boys can handle anything that comes up."

This was a complication I didn't expect. "With all due respect, Solly, Bryan isn't going to allow you into the show. He doesn't know about my investigation. I convinced him to audition Abigail, Izzy, and Audrey by telling him they would boost ticket sales. The average age of Broadway audiences is ten years younger than the one for ballet or opera. These ladies can help attract an older demographic. That's also my appeal."

With thick, roughened fingers, Solly caressed Abigail's cheek. "I can't let anything happen to this lady. She's the best thing that's happened to me in years. So it's all or nothing, Leah. I don't wanna dance. I'm not looking for a job. All I need is a pass for when my ladies are in the theater, which I can manage on my own." He gave me a crooked smile. "I've got a few friends who'll arrange for me to be there."

He spooned some fried rice onto his empty plate and said, "Tell me about the show."

I hadn't tagged Solly as a Broadway buff, but I also hadn't expected to see him twirl Abigail onstage. I gave him a short overview of *Mad Music* and said, "There isn't much of a storyline. It's about a woman who devotes her life to caring for her family but dreams of being onstage. It's practically a one-woman show, although I have several solo turns. It takes place in 1940s Brooklyn."

"Today's your lucky day. I was born in 1940s Brooklyn." He shoveled a tangle of lo mein onto my plate. "Eat up. You need your strength."

I ate a few forkfuls to please him. "You win, Solly. I'll talk to Bryan tomorrow. And I'll text all of you after I speak with him."

He said, "On second thought, let's both leave Bryan out of it. I'll get things done the way I do them."

I left my friends to finish their meal and went home, where I tossed and turned for hours, worried about making my Broadway debut accompanied by three elderly ladies, one mobster, two dozen resentful cast members, a malevolent dance captain, and Aunt Rachel.

Chapter Twenty-Three

Every dancer lives on the threshold of chucking it.
—Judith Jameson

An early morning phone call from Jonah roused me from a fitful slumber. "Are you awake, ballerina girl?"

I opened one sleep-deprived eye. "I am now. Where have you been?"

His voice was cheerful. "Since you were once again out on the town, I met Amber for dinner. Are you up for breakfast? We can go out. Or if you're feeling lazy, I'll bring breakfast to you."

I limped out of bed. "Yes. Bring breakfast, but not too soon. Maybe forty minutes?"

"Make it thirty."

My hair looked like a flock of agitated blackbirds had used it for a nest, and my skin was chalky, except for dark shadows under my eyes. Despite Jonah's imminent arrival, no personal grooming was possible without coffee.

The apartment, with its rattling windows, let puffs of frigid air in. I boiled pots of water on the stove to take off the chill. Although fatigued from the exertions of the last few days, I remembered to remove my leotards and tights before turning on the oven.

I drank half a cup of burning hot coffee and, with little time to spare, ran a brush through my hair and did a drive-by job of making up my face. Sweatpants and tee shirt got swapped out with stretchy yoga pants and a turtleneck. My relationship with Jonah hadn't progressed to the point where

I could allow him to see me at my worst, and my appearance that morning would have been a strong candidate for the top (bottom?) slot.

The intercom beeped, and Jonah announced himself through a storm of static. He texted his secret code, and I buzzed him in and waited. He usually made quick work of the five-story climb, but after ten minutes, I opened the door and peered over the railing to make sure he hadn't expired from exhaustion. When I heard the scratchy voice of Mrs. Pargiter, I resigned myself to further delay.

The tenants in my small building led quiet, private lives, which vexed my lonely neighbor, who delighted in gossip and kept a vigilant eye on all comings and goings. I provided some thrills for her a few months earlier when a team of police officers stormed through the halls and arrested a killer I'd thoughtfully invited into my apartment, but that wasn't the kind of entertainment I was able to deliver on a regular basis.

I leaned over the railing to eavesdrop but couldn't hear their murmured discussion. Overcome with curiosity, I went downstairs. Jonah was inside Mrs. Pargiter's apartment, and the door was half open.

He said, "You can't do better than this deadbolt. I've got the same one on my apartment door."

Mrs. Pargiter spoke with such warmth and friendliness, I almost didn't recognize her voice. "Detective, I can't thank you enough. What do you think about these smart things? Those cameras. Do I need one of them?"

Jonah said, "Let me look into it for you. I'll be back in a few days to let you know."

Jonah emerged with a plate of cookies. I met him on the landing, but he waited until we were inside my apartment before sweeping me into his arms. This put a serious dent in my attempt to treat him with reserve, a decision I made after he told me about his dinner date with Amber.

I struggled to break free. "Nice of you to stop by."

He held me at arm's length. "Don't be jealous of Mrs. Pargiter, although I gotta say, those cookies smell delicious."

His amused tone irked me. "Don't flatter yourself. I'm not the jealous type."

This was mostly true. If Jonah wanted to wine and dine a brilliantly talented and successful actress with a classically perfect profile surrounded by red-gold ringleted hair, I knew from bitter experience there was nothing I could do to stop him.

My previous boyfriend dumped me and remarried his ex-wife. The one before him got married shortly after telling me he couldn't commit to a long-term relationship. My track record, as my mother often pointed out, wasn't good, although it was excellent for women who dated my exes.

Jonah let me go. "Busy week, but let's make the most of the time we have together. While we eat, you can fill me in on what you've learned."

Without comment, I poured him a cup of coffee and peeked inside the bag to find my favorite breakfast: bagels, lox, and cream cheese. Thanks to a lifetime of dieting, I was adept at adding three-digit numbers in my head, but I didn't need those math skills for this meal. The sum total of calories and carbohydrates was burned into my brain.

I ate half anyway, figuring I could make up the calories by skipping lunch and dinner. Or not. One of the unexpected benefits of dancing on Broadway was that it freed me from having to maintain the general proportions of an undernourished pre-adolescent. The dancers in *Mad Music* were lean, but muscled and fit and not nearly as fixated on half-pound fluctuations as my ballerina buddies.

Jonah tore hungrily into his bagel and drank his coffee in quick gulps. "I needed that. Farrow and I have been putting in so much overtime, between the *Mad Music* case and two others, it's been pizza and not much else all week."

I prepared a second carafe of coffee. "Is that where you and Amber had dinner? A pizzeria?"

He grinned. "I suggested pizza, but she preferred Joe Allen's."

I shrugged to indicate my complete lack of interest. "Joe Allen's again? I'm starting to worry that Amber is going to end up on their wall of shame. It's famous for signed photos of epic Broadway flops, and I fear *Mad Music* is destined to add its name to the list."

Jonah put a finger to his forehead as if trying to unravel a riddle. "I feel as if you're trying to send me an important message. Does it have anything to do with the fact that you're madly in love with me?"

I copied his pose and said, "What I'm trying to find out is whether you accomplished anything last night other than eating, drinking, and partying with a Broadway legend."

"I prefer ballerinas." With a look that made my breath catch, he said, "You're the one for me. Never doubt that."

Fatigue eroded my usual self-control. I rarely succumbed to tears, but for some inexplicable reason, I couldn't speak without making a sentimental fool of myself. Jonah's caress told me that he heard what I didn't say. We didn't always need to talk.

At the end of a prolonged session of not talking, we got dressed and returned to our breakfast. Jonah picked up the conversation where we left off, before things got more interesting than a discussion of possible suspects.

"To answer your main question, Amber and I talked about the sequence of events that preceded your arrival. She's used to being in the public eye and had been trolled before. She said this felt different, even before the ketamine coffee and the menacing texts. On the surface, the threats seem to be coming from multiple sources, but I suspect a single person is behind them."

Memories of when a former dancer trolled me were still as fresh and painful as the day I found myself trending on social media as the prime suspect in a murder case. "Why do you think it's one person? What begins as a single online troll can quickly turn into an all-out hate campaign. Or, there could be a copycat stalker out there."

Jonah clasped my hand. "I know what you're thinking, and I haven't forgotten what you went through. But Amber's case is different. She's getting specific threats that mention the rehearsal studio, her gym, and where she picks up her morning coffee. Last night, she said someone tried to shove her into traffic. As far as you know, do any of the dancers seem capable of doing any of those things? Or, at the very least, of posting those kinds of things?"

"The only person mean enough is Carly Messina, the dance captain, but there's one good reason to eliminate her from the list of suspects. Her career is her life, and she has a vested interest in making *Mad Music* a hit. Losing Amber at this late date could doom the show before it opens, although I've seen Natalie perform the role, and she's terrific."

He took out a second bagel and ate it with the blithe disregard for calories genetically favored people took for granted. "I questioned Amber about each cast member. She mentioned a few suspects, but Carly wasn't one of them. No apparent rivalry or ill will between those two. Natalie is still her number one suspect. Rose Summerson is a close second."

Thinking about Carly made me nervous, and I started pacing. Ballet had mostly tamed my need for constant movement, but physical activity continued to be a source of comfort in stressful moments.

"Carly is furious about getting demoted to make room for me. You and I know the real reason I joined the cast, but she thinks Bryan gave me the role because we're sleeping together. She's been a nightmare to work with. Now that I think of it, maybe she is capable of a virtual attack followed by one in real life."

Jonah patted his pocket and took out a small notebook. "If Carly resents you and is jealous of you, work around her. Make friends with her friends. If they all think you got the job because you have an in with Bryan, so much the better. I'm willing to bet that behind Carly's back, they'll be happy to get an inside track to an up-and-coming Broadway choreographer. Instead of playing down your friendship with Bryan, lean into it at rehearsals and at the Design the Dream party."

Jonah didn't understand how difficult it had been to make friends among the dancers, but his idea had merit. "I'll do my best, although it's not going to be easy. Luckily, I will soon have a quite subtle and secret weapon to help me out."

He greeted the news without enthusiasm. "You should have told me about this before setting it up. The Weird Sisters are old and frail and could be a security risk. Call them off, Leah."

I held up my phone to show him Bryan's text confirming their audition. "It's too late. If you answered your phone when I called last night, I would have told you earlier. This is the first chance I got. It would break their heart if they couldn't dance in the show. They're really good, Jonah. They're not as frail as you think, and they have skills you don't know anything about."

He took my hand. "I didn't ignore you, Leah. I didn't answer your call because we don't want anyone, including Amber, to know about us. I suggest you tell your friends you changed your mind. If you prefer, tell them Bryan changed his mind, or tell them I'm the one who refused to allow them access. That, at least, has the advantage of being true. I like the idea that you won't be alone, but three old ladies aren't my idea of protection."

"We'll have plenty of muscle. Solly Greenfield will be there as well."

He threw up his hands. "Are you telling me that you've enlisted a mobster to keep you safe?"

"That mobster and those old ladies are the best chance we have of investigating any backstage threat against Amber. Think it over."

"I'm not in the mood for thinking." Jonah put down his coffee and drew me to him.

With other lovers, a part of me always remained distant, but with him, the separation between body and brain vanished the way it did when I was performing. Except this wasn't a performance. Maybe it was love.

His phone rang several inopportune moments later. I couldn't hear what the caller said, but his end of the conversation was sufficient to communicate a change in plans.

Although his fingers traced the curve of my shoulder, his tone was as impersonal as a cop filling out a routine traffic report. "Sobol here. Yeah. No. No problem. On my way."

I propped myself up on one elbow. "What's going on? Who was on the phone?"

"Farrow. I can't tell you how sorry I am to say this, but I have to go."

"What's going on? Is it Amber?"

"Yes. Don't know when I'll be back. Amber's been swatted."

I sat up. "I don't know what that means."

His tone was grim. "In this case, it means an anonymous caller sent in a tip about a drug deal gone wrong. Whoever did it hung out long enough to video the police at her apartment, arresting her for a crime she didn't commit."

He kissed me and left. Less than an hour later, my phone flashed with clickbait news stories that rarely got my attention. Amber's arrest headed the list.

Chapter Twenty-Four

Learning to walk sets you free. Learning to dance gives you the greatest freedom of all: to express with your whole self the person you are.
—Melissa Hayden

The theater world buzzed with news of Amber's arrest. There was quite a lot of hand wringing on the part of police and politicians, and a cross-section of talking heads held forth on the perils of online pranks. Despite this distraction, the day's rehearsal started on time. Sam hired a security detail to escort us into the D'Anconia and to guard the entrance.

Inside the rehearsal studio, suspicion and fear separated us. I'd never trusted any of them. After Amber's swatting, that wariness became universal.

Natalie tried to break the icy silence in the room with an attempt at the usual chitchat. "Hey, Rose, how was your date last night?"

"Leave me alone."

Natalie tossed her braids back and laughed off the rude answer. "I'm guessing it didn't go well."

Rose didn't let up. "Your guess was correct. Nothing is going well, not for me, not for you, and not for this show. And I'm warning you all: If I see your camera pointed in my direction, I'm stomping on it."

Natalie wasn't impressed. "What makes you think anyone's interested in you? Amber's the one who's getting trolled."

Rose's voice got louder and shriller. "I'm afraid. And you should be, too. Didn't you see that mob outside? They can't wait for us to give them more scandal and drama. So don't ask me where I am or where I've been. That's my business."

Bryan's voice cut across the room. "And this show is my business. Make it yours, and get in place for Act I."

A sudden roar from the rubberneckers below penetrated the drafty windows, and we broke off to see what new horror occurred. Bryan was testy. "Places, please. There's nothing to see. Amber is downstairs, and the vultures can't wait to get a piece of her."

A tense, expectant half-hour elapsed before Amber made it through the door. She had her dog in her arms, Sam close beside her, and a security officer bringing up the rear. She looked fragile, but she spoke with confidence.

With a toss of her head, she said, "I have to thank all of you again for your beautiful texts and messages. I can't tell you how much your support means to me during this scary time. I also want to say that I'm not going to let today's setback get the best of me or the best of us. We're going to fight against this negativity, and we're going to win."

It all sounded very brave, but Amber's repressed tension caused her to squeeze Farley too tightly. With a yap and a wriggle, the dog got free and scampered across the room. I scooped him up in my arms, and he licked my chin. When I tried to hand him back to Amber, she whispered, "Could you hold onto him for a bit? I'm more nervous than I thought."

Bryan told us to take ten, and he and Sam withdrew to the hallway to talk. While Amber regaled the rest of the cast with the dramatic story of how she'd been swatted, falsely arrested, and set free, Natalie sat on the floor in the far corner and watched from a cynical distance.

I sat next to Natalie. She bent her head and ruffled the dog's fur. "Ms. Amber Castle is the sharpest publicity hound in the business. She'll do anything to stay relevant, up to and including manufacturing threats that cast her as an innocent victim."

She took out her phone and held up the video of Amber getting swatted. "Look at her! Dressed to kill and every hair in place. And check out the comments. People are falling over themselves to rally around our poor little rich girl. There's even a Facebook page for people who've bought tickets for specific performances to support her, which Sam is going to love. You can't buy that kind of publicity. You have to make it."

If Natalie was correct, I was wasting my time trying to protect our stressed-out and long-suffering star, but her analysis failed to persuade me. "I don't think what happened today was an act. She seems genuinely frightened, and I don't blame her. I fear someone's out to get her, and today's events confirm that those online threats are invading her real life."

Natalie's voice was hoarse with emotion. "Never forget that playing a role is what she does best. Her other talent is getting herself in the news, and that goes for her so-called charity work, too. I'm not saying I blame her. When I'm her age, I'll probably be as desperate as she is. What choice does she have? Her years as an ingenue are over. Women her age are usually cast as mothers of men who are older than she is. It's not fair, and it's not right, but we all know the score. Don't tell me it's any different at American Ballet Company."

My friend was wrong about Amber but correct about everything else. "It's worse in the ballet world, which you know. As an actress, you can work your whole life, even if it's in a supporting role. There's no such thing in ballet. There aren't many roles for older characters, and most of the time, they're danced by people about to get terminated or by kids made up to look like elderly kings or queens."

She worried one of the colorful bands that held her braids in place. "In a few short weeks, Amber managed to change the chatter from her being too old to play the part of the Leading Lady to her being the target of a jealous mob. The longer she stays in the news, the better off she is."

Natalie's theory sounded plausible, but it worked equally well in reverse. Someone could have threatened Amber and set up the swatting to discredit the star, and the plan ended up backfiring when Amber used the episode to drum up sympathy. If that was what happened, Natalie's bitterness was understandable.

I pointed out the glaring hole in her argument. "I can't speak to what happened today, but there's no doubt in my mind Amber is in danger. Have you forgotten what happened when she left here in an ambulance? She could have died."

Natalie threw up her hands. "How could I forget about it after what she told the police? Detective Farrow grilled me until I was burned to a crisp."

I held Farley close, taking comfort in the dog's warmth. "It's no secret you're ambitious, but it's also no crime. You're so talented, you deserve the chance to show it to the world. As for Amber, is there, um, any reason why she might think you tried to poison her?"

She patted Farley, who answered her with gentle tail-wagging. "No, no. No reason. But all those coffee cups, they looked so much alike. You could see how someone could make a mistake."

I was careful in my answer. "They did all look alike. Is there something you noticed, that, er, maybe you forgot about until now?"

She sprang to her feet. "Of course not. If I did, I would have told the police. What do you take me for?"

I still wasn't sure how to answer that question, which had plagued me since the day I arrived. Was she a trustworthy friend? A scheming colleague? A ruthless opponent? I wished I knew.

Like a trio of fairy godmothers, Abigail, Izzy, and Audrey entered to grant me that wish.

Carly clapped her hands to get their attention. She spoke slowly and loudly, as if she was speaking to young children with limited language skills. "Are you ladies lost? The Senior Center is on the main floor."

I stepped forward, but with a quick gesture, Izzy stopped me. She was afraid, perhaps, I'd reveal we knew each other.

Abigail looked nervous, but her voice was firm. "We're here to audition for Mr. Leister. He told us to wait for him here."

The dance captain dropped her pretense of friendliness. She winked at the rest of us, inviting us to share in her scorn. "I rather doubt that. If you're looking for autographs, you can stand outside like the rest of the fans. We're kind of busy right now."

Audrey put her hand on the barre and began warming up. "Thanks for your advice. We'll wait."

When Bryan returned, he greeted them with the name I'd asked him not to use. "Ladies and gentlemen, these are the Weird Sisters."

The room rang with my colleagues' laughter. I was furious with Bryan for forgetting my injunction against using that name and even more angry with myself for revealing it to him.

Abigail seemed as entertained as the rest. "Pleased to meet you all. Although we don't have the same power as the witches in The Scottish Play, we'll do our best to make some magic."

I breathed a sigh of relief at Abigail's knowing reference to *Macbeth* as the Scottish Play, because actors are quite superstitious about a direct reference to Shakespeare's bloody work. Saying "Macbeth" to actors while they were in the theater, or even in a rehearsal room, was as bad as telling a ballerina to break a leg.

Bryan was often pleasant when he wasn't working, but in the studio or the theater, he could be impatient to the point of cruelty. He eyed Abigail, Isabel, and Audrey, sizing them up with a critical gaze. Without emotion, he said, "Let's see what you can do."

He told my friends to get ready, counted *five-six-seven-eight,* and clicked on a recording of the same song they'd danced to in the showcase. They didn't have partners, but they made a credible showing. The real test was yet to come.

He put them through a complex, swing-inspired series of steps. I held my breath. Although they'd spent years in dance classes, they'd never danced professionally. In class, the teachers gave combinations of sixty-four counts. A three-minute dance is made up of many more steps than that. Unless they could summon sufficient mental fortitude, as well as physical strength, they wouldn't make it to the end of the hour, let alone the end of the day.

Well-schooled in the habits of dancers, they were silent, other than a few questions about arm placement. I longed to stay with them, but Carly took the rest of us into the adjacent practice room and put us through our paces.

I trailed behind the other cast members, unsure what to do with Farley. The dog obligingly sat on command, but he wasn't nearly as good at *stay*.

The moment I left him, he followed after me.

Amber peered through the window at the street below. "My spoiled little pet is waiting for his ride to the priciest dog hotel in the city."

She waved her phone and said, "Carly, my sweet, I can't face those reporters again. Would you mind if Leah took Farley to the lobby? I need the practice more than she does, and the driver is waiting."

With a curt nod, the dance captain dismissed me. I took the dog down the elevator and left him with the liveried driver. The interruptions distracted several dancers, but not Carly. She was an excellent dance captain, and her attention never flagged. Her example inspired the rest of us, and when Bryan checked in, he was well pleased with our progress.

At the end of the day, Sam had yet another surprise guest with him. No one, however, was quite as astonished as I was.

He said, "We were incredibly lucky to get Leah Siderova to dance with us, and now we have the equally talented and charming Barbara Siderova as well. She'll be working as a script doctor, but she wanted to be here for the rehearsals."

My mother took a bow.

Chapter Twenty-Five

I think it was important that I learned to love to dance... for its own sake, as opposed to wanting to be a ballerina.
—Suzanne Farrell

B arbara and I didn't talk to each other until the end of the day when a security guard in the lobby escorted us to a waiting cab. My mother, after giving the driver meticulous directions on her preferred route, said with a pleased smile, "Why are you so glum? I told you I was going to offer myself as a script doctor. My agent got me in to see Sam Flannery, and he was most receptive. What do you think?"

"What do I think? I think you ambushed me. I think you're doing this to get back at Rachel."

My complaint didn't dent her glee. "You should be happy. I can assist in your investigation, and I can help protect Amber."

"Who's going to protect you? Aunt Rachel?"

"Don't frown like that. It makes wrinkles." She pressed her fingers against my forehead. "Instead of worrying about me, use me. The three of us will catch this miserable human being, and we'll be heroes."

In two short days, I'd gone from zero allies to five. The roster included the Weird Sisters, my mother, and my aunt.

I didn't count Solly Greenfield in the mix. He promised to provide protection, but I knew Abigail was the real reason he wanted to help. I didn't blame him. The guy was in love. As for the women, it was an open question as to whether they'd end up functioning as my secret weapon or

Achilles' heel.

When we arrived at my mother's apartment, Rachel was waiting. Barbara threw open the double doors to her closet. "I have the perfect gown for you to wear to the gala." She took out a scarlet dress, slit to mid-thigh. "How about this one?" She pursed her lips. "Unless you think a red dress on the red carpet is too obvious?"

I fingered the silky fabric. "It's stunning, but for once, I know what I'm going to wear and I don't have to depend on you. Amber had Mac Rosen design two gold gowns, one for her and one for me. He's a big supporter of her Design the Dream foundation. So, I'm all set. What I'm missing is something to wear over the dress. There will be an actual red carpet, and I need something more elegant than my puffer jacket to keep me warm from the curb to the front door."

Rachel, who was slumped in a chair, said, "Why do you and Amber have to dress alike? That sounds stupid to me. You're not five years old. Isn't it bad taste to show up in the same outfit someone else is wearing?"

My aunt's response was the same as mine when Amber told me her designer had created two gowns in the same shiny fabric. "I think you're right, Aunt Rachel, but this wasn't my call. I play a sort of alter ego or mirror image to Amber in *Mad Music*, and she thinks if we play up our physical similarity at the party, it will pump up interest in the show. The gowns are going to be auctioned off to raise money for her diabetes foundation. Everyone, other than you and me, thinks it's a win-win."

Rachel plucked at the red dress. "Tell Ms. Amber Castle you don't want to play her games and you want to go to the party dressed as yourself. And while you're at it, take me with you."

My mother patted her sister on the back. "Cheer up, Rachel. You're not the only one who didn't get an invite. Maybe you'll get to go to the Tony Awards. That'll be much more exciting. We can go together if my script gets nominated."

My aunt refused to be comforted. "It's not your script. And I don't understand why Amber invited everyone else in the cast except for me.

Lynne is going. The stage manager is going. Why was I left out?"

I could have pointed out that Lynne was the wardrobe mistress, which was a very different position from the wardrobe assistant, and that the stagehands also weren't invited, but I didn't want to hurt her feelings. Rachel was proud of her role and couldn't imagine the entire theater world wasn't similarly impressed. She was jealous of Barbara's ascension to Sam's inner circle but consoled by my mother's failure to make it onto the guest list for the gala.

I murmured a general apology on behalf of the unfeeling universe and paged through a line of texts. Friends from ABC sent messages and photos from their performance in Des Moines; interspersed with these were a few from Amber, Gabi, Bryan, and Natalie, all of which were variations of **See you at the party!** Nothing, however, from Jonah.

I was halfway through scrolling when Barbara emerged from the depths of the closet with a black velvet cape. "Take this. You'll be the belle of the ball."

I put it on over my jeans and sweater and twirled. Barbara clapped, and Rachel said, "You look like Zorro. Or Batman."

My mother was impatient. "Don't be bitter, Rachel. It makes wrinkles." Upon seeing her sister's wounded reaction, she added, "And don't be mad at me. You should have let me treat you to some Botox." She examined Rachel's face. "A few fillers would work wonders."

I headed off my aunt's furious response by assuring her she wouldn't miss much. "These events are long, boring, and filled with congratulatory speeches. I'll probably fall asleep over dinner."

Rachel snatched the cape, placed it on her shoulders, and held one end across her face like a masked superhero. "I can come as your bodyguard. Or your spy. What if you need backup?" She let the cape fall, grabbed a hanger, and waved it like a weapon. "The poisoner might be there. I'll guard your food."

Tenacity and melodrama. They were signature traits of the Siderova women. I assured Rachel the police department would provide security, and she plopped back into her chair.

With an exasperated cry, my mother rescued the cape Rachel had crushed underneath her. Barbara then evaluated her extensive collection of shoes, although my bunions ruled out most of her elegantly narrow footwear. She handed me a pair of gold stilettos. "Who's your date? Is it still that detective?"

"I'm going to be the grownup in the room and, therefore, won't point out that you know Detective Jonah Sobol's name perfectly well. As it happens, however, I'm going with Bryan Leister."

Rachel said, "I don't like him. No one likes him. You should hear what people say about him when they think no one's listening."

"Bryan wouldn't be my first choice either, but I'm taking one for the team. It's all part of the PR promo in the week before opening night."

I squeezed one misshapen foot into the sparkly shoe, unable to resist its appeal. "Did Lynne tell you she doesn't like Bryan? Or was it someone else on the long list of people who want to knock him down a peg?"

Rachel wiggled her foot into the matching shoe before wincing and hastily removing it. "She doesn't have to say anything. Everyone hates him like poison."

Not a good choice of words, but I didn't object. It was the truth.

Chapter Twenty-Six

Dancing should be completely understandable. Every move should mean something.
—Michael Kidd

I took a cab back to my apartment to save my aching joints and muscles from the stress of a long walk or short subway ride. In honor of Amber's big event, we quit early, so theoretically, I shouldn't have been as achy as I was. Unfortunately, there was no arguing with two cranky knees.

The gown Amber sent me was beautiful, although it wasn't something I would have chosen for myself. I preferred muted colors, and most of the items in my closet wouldn't be out of place at a funeral. My reliance on black was a matter of both convenience and reticence. Everything matched, and none of it was conspicuous. The dress Mac Rosen designed for me dazzled against the drab background. The rich gold fabric was edged in shiny crystals that caught the light and sparkled with the message: *Look at me! I'm very expensive!*

The dress should have come with an instruction manual and a set of tools. Like a tutu, it was designed to be worn without underwear but was so tight I had to cave in my chest and suck in my breath to get the finicky closures fastened. The heavy fabric weighed me down, and the crystals made clacking sounds when I walked. If I needed to hide or make a quick getaway, I'd have to scissor myself out of it.

My phone chimed as I was stuffing a lipstick and comb into a jeweled evening bag that was one of Barbara's thrift store finds.

It was Bryan. "Hey, Leah. I'm in the lobby. Don't bother buzzing me in. I'll wait for you down here. I can't face all those stairs or the dragon who lives underneath you."

"I'll be down in a minute, although I know Mrs. Pargiter would love to chat." I descended at a slower pace than usual, mindful of the long dress that didn't belong to me and the hazards of sharp heels combined with a swirling cape.

Mrs. Pargiter stopped me. "Look at you. Hot date?"

"Hello, Mrs. Pargiter. Yes, and he's waiting downstairs."

She sniffed. "In my day, a gentleman picked up a lady at her door. I expected better of Detective Sobol."

I squeezed by her. "It's not Jonah. I'm going out with someone else."

She put one hand on her heart and the other over her mouth. "Does Jonah know you're cheating on him? Such a nice man. He deserves better."

A tangle of excuses tried to get out of my mouth. Annoyed at myself for falling into her manipulative trap, I admitted defeat. "Indeed he does. And Mrs. Pargiter? Don't wait up. I may be late."

I didn't have far to walk, as the limo Bryan hired was double parked in front of the house. Before we left, I looked up at the lighted windows on the fourth floor, where my neighbor watched in rapt attention. I waved, but she didn't wave back.

When we arrived at the party, the driver opened the car door and stood at attention as Bryan gave me his hand and escorted me down the carpet, which was, in fact, red. He kept me close to his side for the benefit of photographers waiting by the entrance. Before entering, he took my chin in his hand and kissed me on the mouth, which elicited cheers and whistles from behind the velvet rope. I drew back, smiled at him, and whispered, "Do that again, and I'll kick you so hard you'll be limping for a week."

He smiled lovingly and said, through his teeth, "Play the game and quit complaining. I don't like this any more than you do. Neither does my girlfriend."

Under other circumstances, or with a different man, I might have been offended at his equal distaste for intimacy with me, but I was relieved, if still perversely irritated. Two guys who looked like models opened the large, green glass inner doors and ushered us inside.

Bryan and I joined the queue of guests waiting to go through the metal detectors. Security guards inspected my purse, but they gave it a mere cursory glance. I wouldn't have minded if they'd been more thorough, although there was little chance anyone would try to bring a knife or a gun inside. So far, the attacker's modus operandi was poison and intimidation, neither of which would get flagged in a perfunctory handbag check.

I was momentarily dazzled by the flashing lights and earsplitting noise. The event space had a very different vibe from ABC's galas. Ballet fundraisers took place at Lincoln Center and were formal and elegant. The loft for Amber's gala leaned into a grittier downtown aesthetic. It was a sham, of course. The market price for the neighboring apartments, which once housed starving artists and factory workers, started at seven figures.

The walls of the huge room were draped in gold gauze that was spattered with paint, the tables sparkled with an assortment of mismatched silver candles, and the music was so loud I could feel it reverberating in my chest. No chamber music quartets for this crowd.

Bryan and I posed again for the influencers who'd avoided the red carpet in favor of vantage points that were warmer and drier than the ones outside. He ditched me as soon as the publicity wolves moved onto fresh prey. I knew Jonah was at the party, but I was too small, even in sky-high heels, to see much. He must have seen me, though, because my phone buzzed with the message, **You look beautiful, ballerina girl.**

Jonah's text failed to dispel a growing dread. My neck prickled with the sense of someone watching me, the same feeling I had when the trench-coated stalker sprang out of the shadows outside Barbara's apartment house. I told myself the only threat was to my self-esteem. Surviving a ketchup attack was funny, not heroic. It had the stamp of a mean girl, not a killer.

Despite this logical line of reasoning, I failed to convince myself of the harmlessness of the episode, because the squirt of red liquid was more likely to have been a warning than a prank. I feared the next time the attacker went after me, it would be blood and not ketchup that ran down my face. I rubbed the back of my neck, willing the forebodings to go away.

As if to confirm my worst fears, a photo popped up on my phone from an unknown number. It was a picture of me, taken as I entered the party. The message said, **Wanna play?**

I texted Jonah. **He's here.**

His answer was quick. **Of course.**

A loud wolf whistle, followed by the words, "Sid! Over here!" distracted me and got me breathing again, but the fear remained.

Only one person called me Sid. From across the room, Gabi waved me over. "Are you surprised?"

"I'm stunned. However did you finagle a ticket? And why didn't you tell me you'd be here?" After inspecting her dress and hair, I said, "You don't look as if this was a spur-of-the-moment decision."

She gave me a half wink and adjusted the neckline of a black lace gown I wished I was wearing. "I've got connections." She tapped the shoulder of a guy a few inches shorter than she, who was talking to a group of *Mad Music* cast members. "I couldn't get a babysitter for Lucie, so I had to make do with a backup. But I think you've already met my date?"

Another shock, this one less welcome. Garret was the last person I expected to find at Amber's gala. The generous impulse that inspired my friend to invite him struck me as misguided. If the ousted choreographer of *Mad Music* was half as bitter as his husband, Sam and Bryan were in for an unpleasant confrontation.

Garret didn't appear to notice my dismay. I clasped his outstretched hand and said, "I'm happy to see you. Is Marco here as well? Or will it be pistols at dawn for him and Sam?"

He puffed up his cheeks and let the air out in a quick snort. "If it weren't for Gabi, I wouldn't be here. She was kind enough to invite me. I'm hoping to rub shoulders with a few producers and directors to see if I can pick up a gig to take the place of the one I lost."

He gave Gabi an affectionate look. "Our friend here has offered to hook me up with her people at NYU, who might be able to offer a more stable teaching position than the ones we have now. The pickings have been slim since Marco and I got back to the States, but I have no desire to get into a fight with Sam. Marco blames him, but I don't."

I would have breathed a sigh of relief if my dress hadn't made inhalation so difficult. "I'm glad to hear it. I know times are tough, but that's all the more reason not to cut off future prospects."

Garret said, "Speaking of future prospects, I've heard you and Amber are best friends, now that you're performing together."

Gabi feigned outrage. "If anyone is Leah's BFF, it's me."

He hugged her. "You'd be my choice any day of the week, but the sister pics Amber posted of her and Leah are wild. People are going nuts over them, which is why, Leah, I hope you won't be offended if I tell you to be cautious about your new buddy. She comes on all nice and friendly, but don't let that act fool you."

Gabi's amused expression turned sober. "It turns out Amber isn't the suffering angel everyone thinks she is. She refused to work with Garret, and that's why Sam fired him. Bryan had nothing to do with it."

I wasn't as easily persuaded as Gabi, who didn't know Amber as well as I did. Also, if that were true, why was Garret's explanation different from Marco's? Both spouses had the same information.

Couples didn't always agree, but the discrepancy bothered me. "The real reason why it happened might be more complicated than we think. It takes a lot of moving parts to get a Broadway show from the planning stage to opening night."

"If you're unlucky enough to get to know Amber better, you'll see what I mean." Garret tugged at his tie to loosen it. "Is it possible Bryan had a hand in cutting me? I can't say for sure, but if I take a pop at anyone tonight, it'll be Amber."

I did a quick search of the room. If Garret was serious, I had to warn Amber. The terrible feeling that I'd missed something important, and that I was being watched, made me anxious to find her.

Garret was still talking. "The word on the street is that I'd have to wait my turn. She's trampled too many people too many times, and it's catching up to her. I'm not saying I agree with everything that's been said, but she's been flaming hot for weeks. No smoke without fire is what I say."

His logic, which was based on popular opinion and rumors, was hollow. If anything, Garret's reasoning strengthened my disbelief. Having been burned by social media lies the rest of the world accepted as true, I knew better than to accept what the Twitterers thought. "You might be right, but I'm going to wait for the facts before I credit the rumors."

Garret put up his fists, lightening the mood with a joking imitation of a boxer's stance. He brushed his thumb against his nose and said, "When it comes to fighting dirty, there's nothing Amber won't do to get back at me."

He dropped his arms and his smile. "I thought enough time had passed that we could work together. It wasn't the first mistake I've made where she's concerned. Take it from one who knows: My ex-wife would cut you without mercy if you crossed her."

Several awkward seconds passed before I was able to fill the silence that followed Garret's revelation. "I-I didn't know you used to be married to her. I mean, Amber and I, we're close. She told me she had an ex-husband, but I had no idea it was you."

"Don't be offended. The relationship ended years ago, before she made it big. We were working together on an off-off-Broadway play at the time, and we decided to keep our marriage, and later, our divorce, on the down low. Her reputation is everything to her. Would you want the world to know your husband dumped you after two months?"

"No, I wouldn't. But I can think of many people who'd stop at nothing to get their hands on that story and would use it to hurt Amber."

I didn't tell him that at least one of those people was at the party. Aside from Garret himself, of course.

Chapter Twenty-Seven

I don't mind being listed alphabetically. I do mind being treated alphabetically.
—Maria Tallchief

When I put together everything I knew, the result wasn't as straightforward as a puzzle with missing pieces. It was more like three different puzzles. Everyone involved in *Mad Music* seemed to have a stake in obscuring some part of the truth, although their self-serving stories might not have been a function of sinister motives.

The most recent example was Garret's failure to mention the lavish wedding gift Sam sent him and Marco. Was the cash a generous gesture? Or was the director of *Mad Music* paying them off, hoping no further bad publicity would hound the star of his show?

Of equal interest was how Amber managed to keep her brief marriage to Garret a secret in an age when the lives of famous people were picked over by legions of hungry internet gobblers. If Sam's gift was intended as hush money, it wasn't working. Garret didn't ask us to keep his brief union to Amber secret. He practically shouted it from the rooftop. I wondered why Marco didn't mention Amber when he unburdened himself, with such seeming sincerity, to me.

I hoped to question Garret further, but Natalie joined our threesome. I concealed my disappointment with a smile and complimented her on her gown. She wore a clingy red dress that showed off her long legs. It was similar to the one Barbara wanted me to wear, and uncomfortable as I was in my tight, gold prison, I was pleased to have dodged a major style faux pas.

It was bad enough to have to dress like Amber. It would have been worse if I'd ended up dressed like Natalie. I'm too small and slight to compete against a statuesque beauty with elegantly braided hair and killer shoes.

Natalie towered over Garret and poked him so hard he nearly lost his balance. "Who let you in? Or did you crash the party?"

Gabi drew Garret closer. "I don't know who you are, but Garret is here as my guest." She offered her hand. "I'm Gabi Acevedo, and I'm the one who invited him. Is there a problem with that?"

Natalie left my friend's hand hanging in midair. She tried to jab Garret again, but Gabi deflected the blow by positioning herself between them.

Natalie said, "Ask him what the problem is, but prepare yourself for a bunch of lies and pathetic excuses. Maybe you don't care about dating a married man who cheats the way other people eat and breathe, but I did." She flicked her hand as if swatting off a fly and stalked off. We watched her leave, but she didn't get far. With three quick steps, she returned. Pulling Garret by his tie, she said, "He's coming with me."

Actors. They love dramatic exits.

When Natalie and Garret left, Gabi said, "Natalie is acting like a woman scorned and most likely ghosted. I don't know Garret well, but it appears as if he was quite the player before he married Marco. I wonder if he has any other angry wives or girlfriends up his sleeve." After some reflection, she said, "Or guys or husbands. He seems to have cast a wide net."

I, too, was at a loss, but for a different reason. "I've never seen Natalie like that. She's always so easygoing."

Gabi rolled her eyes. "Jealousy will do that to you."

"That's true, whether it's romantic or professional. The last time Natalie and I were together, she told me about a boyfriend who dumped her and married someone else. She didn't tell me the boyfriend in question was Garret. Maybe she was hoping to rekindle an old flame, which could explain why she was so angry when she saw him with you."

My friend softened. "I get where Natalie is coming from. Maybe the humiliation of getting rejected is worse when the guy in question marries someone you know and compounds the insult by cheating on his spouse with someone else. It doesn't make sense, but when did love ever make sense?"

I eased my weight from one foot to the other, trying to relieve the pressure on my bunions. "That may be the truest thing anyone has said to me tonight. Emotions don't make sense. For me, getting cut from a ballet was worse than having my ex-boyfriend, the one who didn't want a long-term commitment, get married six months after he broke up with me."

Gabi, whose hips joints were as bad as my knees, winced in sympathetic pain. "Let's find someplace to sit. We've both been on our feet long enough."

I spied two open chairs, but we were interrupted in our quest by one of the biggest backers of *Mad Music,* who chose that moment to introduce himself. After a few minutes of pleasant conversation with the show's deep-pocketed supporter and multiple assurances to him about how well the rehearsals were going, I resorted to the timeworn but eternally useful excuse to get away.

Gabi obligingly followed me toward the bathroom, where we found a line longer than the one at Rockefeller Center when the Rockettes were in town. We needed privacy, which even a shared single stall wouldn't provide.

I cornered a busboy coming out of the kitchen. "Where's the back entrance?"

He jerked his thumb toward a corridor behind the bathrooms. "That way. Left, then right. You can't miss it. But make sure you don't get locked out. It doesn't open from the outside."

In the past, I'd proven myself adept at failing to find places that the people giving me directions insisted couldn't be missed. On that occasion, I succeeded, because after turning left, turning right was the only other option. The heavy steel door opened onto a concrete platform about eight feet above the ground. A bright light affixed above the door illuminated the loading dock but didn't extend beyond it.

I removed a bottle from the recycling bucket, using a tissue to protect my fingers. I wedged the bottle in the door to keep it open and hoped no pathogenic germs made the jump from the bottle to the tissue to me.

Below us was a foul-smelling dumpster. Rodents topped the list of things that scared me, and the filthy backyard was prime real estate for a rat in need of a comfy home and plenty of garbage to eat. Despite my resolution not to look down, a slithering, moving shadow made me jump.

Gabi stayed close to the door. "Let's find somewhere else to talk. This place gives me goosebumps."

The dank air and gloomy shadows tested the limits of my courage. "Give me five minutes, and then we'll go back. First, tell me why you brought Garret to the party. I almost fainted when I saw you with him. And why didn't you give me a heads-up that you were coming? We could have planned this out a lot better if I knew about it ahead of time."

She hugged herself to keep warm. "You must have missed my text, which ended up being a good thing, because you obviously weren't acting when you saw us. I wasn't the one who pulled strings to get us in. That was Garret. How he did it, I don't know, but he wanted it kept secret and asked me if I'd say I was the one who invited him."

I took out my cell phone and found Gabi's text, sandwiched between photos from our friends at ABC and **See you laters** from the rest.

"Sorry, Gabi. I did miss it. But now that we're here in this lovely outdoor space that's infested with my worst nightmares, we have to find people who can confirm all the stuff he told us. Let's start with whoever got him the tickets."

Her teeth were chattering. "There's nothing much to tell, Sid. We don't know each other all that well, but he said he wanted me to be his date so I could introduce him to the dean at Tisch. There's an opening in the dance division at NYU, and he wants me to put in a good word for him. Maybe he bought the tickets, thinking it would pay for itself if he got the job."

So much surprising information had emerged about Garret, I was prepared for another seismic jolt, but the explanation was both reasonable and ordinary. There was nothing in it to fuel suspicions about a dastardly plot unless he lied.

Garret could be hiding many secrets behind his apparent sincerity. "He fed me an awful lot of information in a very short time. But how would that benefit him? What good would it do him?"

A slight noise from beyond the ledge made me jump. "Let's get out of here. We can finish this conversation later. Or tomorrow."

I didn't hear Gabi's answer, because someone removed the bottle holding the door open. It shut with a menacing clang.

And then the overhead light went out.

Between the terror of encountering various species of vermin and the shock of finding myself in the dark with no way out, a moment of unthinking panic was inevitable. We pounded and yelled, but no one responded. The door was without a window, and the wall was solid brick.

Gabi flicked the flashlight on her phone and swept the beam across the platform. I followed her to the edge, but we couldn't see beyond a few feet. She gingerly walked to the far end and pointed to a handrail. "There's a ladder over there. And I think I see an alleyway ahead. Hopefully, it's not a dead end."

Residents of hell would be making snowballs before I agreed to climb down into the germ-filled, weed-choked, rat-swarming back lot. "I have a better idea."

I tapped the emergency contact on my phone and explained the situation. Although I didn't relish stories in which the brave prince rescues the damsel in distress, I was willing to make a one-time, personal exception.

Jonah said, "Be right there."

A text from a blocked number lit up the screen. Underneath a blurry photo of me and Gabi was a message that said, **Having fun?**

Shaking with pure terror, I looked up at the dark, second-story windows, one of which was open. The picture was of our backs, taken while we were leaning over the edge of the platform.

I showed it to Gabi. "Someone inside is watching us."

Gabi turned off the flashlight and hugged the wall to avoid being seen. I threw back my head and yelled at the blank, faceless windows, "We're not afraid of you." If I hadn't known Jonah was coming, I might not have been so brave.

Another text. **You should be.**

I lied. I was terrified. But our Peeping Tom didn't need to know that. I put my mouth close to Gabi's ear, although whoever lurked above was unlikely to be able to hear us. "Change of plans."

I texted Jonah. **Stalker is on 2nd floor above loading dock. Go there- We're ok.**

Gabi whispered, "This is not a good plan. What if the guy comes after us?"

As if to answer her question, a trash can fell from the window and hit a glancing blow to the side of my head.

I hissed, through the pain that shot through me, "If he comes after us he'll run into Jonah."

I motioned for her to remain flush against the wall so that when the door opened, she wouldn't be visible. "Stay here."

She resisted. "What's going on, Sid?"

"Trust me."

I walked back to the center of the platform, held my arms wide, and yelled, "Come down! It's time for us to meet in person."

There was no answer. I texted the same invitation to the blocked number, but the screen remained blank.

When the light on the loading dock snapped back on, I was ready. Although I didn't possess a weapon, one good spritz of perfume in an attacker's eyes, followed by a blow to the nose from my boxy evening bag, should give us time to escape.

The door opened, and Jonah rushed through. I got as far as spraying him with perfume before falling against him as my knees grew weak.

Jonah said to the police officer still inside, "I got this, Morelli. Meet me back at the place."

I called after her, "Good to see you, Francie."

She left. Jonah breathed in the flowery scent that hung in the damp, heavy air and said, "Best smelling garbage dump in New York City."

Chapter Twenty-Eight

When someone blunders, we say that he makes a misstep. Is it then not clear that all the ills of mankind, all the tragic misfortunes that fill our history books, all the political blunders, all the failures of the great leaders have arisen merely from a lack of skill in dancing.

—Moliere

Across the hall that led to the loading dock was an interior door to the stairway. A police officer stood at attention when we approached. He said, "All clear, Detective. We've secured the area. Detective Farrow is still upstairs."

Jonah nodded. "Thanks." Gesturing to Gabi and me, he said, "This is Leah Siderova and her friend Gabriela Acevedo. They called in the complaint." Turning back to us, he said, "By the time I got to the second floor, whoever followed you and Gabi was gone. Could you see anything from the loading dock? Any idea as to height, gender, body type?"

My voice was scratchy from yelling in the cold night air. "Not a thing. I knew he was above us from the angle of the photo he took, but the windows were dark, and there wasn't so much as a shadow visible from where we stood. Once again, he's blended into the background."

Jonah stopped me from touching the doorknob. "We keep calling this person 'he' out of habit, but we can't forget the possibility it's a she. Or them. As for disappearing into the background, don't be so sure of that. I've got a team on the way to dust for fingerprints and check for any other trace evidence left behind."

165

Gabi said, "What's up there?"

Jonah steered us toward the kitchen. "Stuff for the caterer and a room for the staff to change clothes."

This wasn't good news. "In other words, tons of fingerprints and fibers."

He held open the swinging door. "Right. We're focusing on the windows, windowsills, and the areas around and underneath."

We entered the kitchen, which was an inferno of activity. It was also filled with steam. Very few serendipitous events occurred up to that point, but I was relieved the gold net that held my hair in place would keep it from frizzing in the humid air. This disquiet about my appearance wasn't on par with the fear there was a killer in our midst, but people should reserve judgment. In less than an hour, I'd be walking the runway in front of the city's most fashionable and discerning tastemakers, and I wanted to look like I belonged there.

I was the only nonprofessional model, as Amber would be organizing the auction from backstage. I accepted her invitation, knowing I couldn't compete with those long, lanky beauties, but quailed at the thought of looking like a bedraggled mess next to their polished perfection. The audience's critical gaze didn't unnerve me as much as the one from my anonymous stalker, but it added another layer of insecurity to a night filled with anxiety.

For all these reasons, I was impatient to repair the ravages that my adventure on the loading dock inflicted on my face and hair. I started the overhaul process by wiping off a trickle of blood that slid down my neck and threatened to stain the gold dress.

Jonah led us to an alcove next to two double sinks. The shallow space afforded us some privacy from the hubbub of the kitchen, and the dishwasher was too busy to spare us more than a single curious glance.

Jonah's mouth tightened when he saw the bruise on my head. "Come with me. I'll clean that up for you."

I brushed his fingers away and was relieved to find that my hair and headpiece would cover the aching wound. "Later. It probably looks worse than it feels."

In a rush of nonsequiturs, I apprised Jonah of all that had occurred over the course of the evening. "Garret's connection to Natalie or one of the other cast members might be important. He wasn't at the D'Anconia when Amber and Marty were poisoned, but he could have coordinated the plan with someone who was. Did you know he and Amber used to be married?"

Jonah said, "Their marriage ended years ago. Why would Garret go after Amber now? He's long since moved on."

I leaned over the sink and dampened a few tissues to press against my wound. "That's what I thought, but Garret is convinced Amber put pressure on Sam Flannery to fire him, and he's furious about it. He could be right. Given the lengths to which Amber has gone to hide her marriage and divorce, who could blame her for not wanting to work with Garret? The central issue is that losing the job was devastating for Garret and Marco, his husband. They blew up the life they had in Amsterdam to come here, and they're struggling. That gives them a motive now they wouldn't have had before."

Jonah looked at Gabi. "Why did Garret ask you to be his date? What's your connection to all this?"

Gabi lifted her shoulders in a *Who knows?* shrug. "Until tonight, very little. We're friendly without being friends and mostly keep in touch on social media. When I asked him why he wanted me to be his plus one, he said he wanted me to introduce him to the dean at NYU. I've been working as an instructor in the dance department for the last two years, and the admin just posted an opening for next semester."

Jonah considered this new information. "That's a good excuse for him to show up."

I said, "It's such a good excuse, it might be true. All the big players in the theater world are here. Garret knows Gabi and I are good friends. Maybe he hoped I could give him an inside track with the producers and backers of *Mad Music*."

He spoke slowly, as if thinking this through. "Those are all reasonable motives, but there's no way to confirm any of them. You said the stalker who followed you was short, so Garret fits the physical profile. If he can't get at Amber, going after you would be the next best thing."

Gabi answered before I could. "Why would Garret hurt Leah? Or me? And why do it at the gala? He needs me to help him get an interview at the university, and he needs Leah to put in a good word for him. It doesn't add up."

Jonah doesn't rely on his excellent memory. He filled two pages of his notebook with neat, precise handwriting. "The advantage of committing a crime in a public space is that it's easy to blend in, and you can count on there being plenty of suspects. Eyewitnesses are notoriously unreliable, and Garret sounds like a clever guy. Where was he when the two of you took off?"

Gabi said, "Natalie—whom I do not like at all—cornered him and literally pulled him away from us. If they're in it together, they can alibi each other."

I wasn't ready to give up on Natalie, but I couldn't count her out, either. "Garret could be using her as a convenient cover. If they're conspiring together, though, their argument could have been a setup. If so, it convinced me."

Jonah added this information to his notes and said, "Be careful tonight. Someone followed you to the loading dock, locked you out, and tried to intimidate you. That person is still here."

Gabi's face paled. "Garret is going to be by my side all evening."

He closed his notebook. "Make up an excuse to ditch him early or wait for Leah and go home with her. Garret may be innocent, but you can't take that chance." Jonah walked toward the swinging door. "On second thought, I suggest you both make polite excuses and leave the party now without your dates. You've done enough for one day."

I lagged behind. "Why didn't the person who texted me attack us? He, or rather, they, followed us, trapped us in the dark, and threw a trash can. In retrospect, it seems a bit underwhelming. Why threaten us instead of finishing us off?"

Gabi trembled. "Maybe the texter's not dangerous. Maybe they want to scare us off but not hurt us."

Jonah revealed no emotion other than a slight tightening of his lips. "The stalker wants to intimidate you, but don't kid yourself. It's not going to end there. If you didn't get attacked, it was because they didn't have an effective weapon at hand. Everyone had to go through the metal detectors, so no knives and no guns. The texter was unprepared for you to turn yourselves into sitting ducks and had to improvise. Who would have thought a vulnerable target would decide to go to a dark and deserted spot to have a heart-to-heart chat with her ninety-pound friend?"

Gabi swallowed. "Why not shove us off the platform? We were so vulnerable."

Jonah was less sure. "Maybe. But shoving two people off the platform was risky. One person? No problem, although the loading dock wasn't high enough to ensure you'd die. More likely, you'd end up with an assortment of broken bones, along with the ability to make a positive identification. With two people, one of you would have had a decent chance to escape and sound the alarm. So don't think you're safe. You're not."

The chef yelled at us from behind a stove that flamed with a half dozen pots and pans. "This is a restricted area. Employees only. Get outta here before I call the cops."

Jonah withdrew his walkie-talkie from a back pocket. "I'll do it for you."

Chapter Twenty-Nine

The mirror is not you. The mirror is you looking at yourself.
—George Balanchine

After we exited the kitchen, Jonah returned to whatever command post kept him hidden from me. Gabi and I slipped past the still-growing line of women waiting for the bathroom and returned to the party, which was in full swing. She joined a group of *Mad Music* dancers while I stood by myself in a corner of the room, trying to identify the person behind the bizarre episode on the loading dock. There had to be a common thread that tied together the trolling, the stalking, and the poisoning. What, or who, was it?

I was so on edge after getting locked out of the party that when Bryan tapped me on the shoulder, I nearly fainted. He was unfairly annoyed. "No one is going to think we're in love if you spend the night avoiding me."

I tugged at the bodice of my dress, which, like an instrument of medieval torture, got tighter and more painful the longer I wore it. "Nice try, but you're the one who abandoned me. Where did you go?"

He held my arm with cold fingers. I was still jumpy, and it was a struggle not to push him away. Ever the pragmatist, he said, "We're together now, so try and look happy. Amber has been looking for you. She wants some good pictures to post of the *Mad Music* crowd before dinner."

The room was hot, but Bryan's hands were cold. As cold as if he'd been standing by an open window that overlooked the loading dock. Was he my stalker? I didn't expect a truthful answer if he was, but a lie would be of almost equal value.

"That explains your sudden desire for my company, but it doesn't explain where you've been."

A muscle in his jaw twitched. "I've been networking, as you should be." Annoyed at my failure to be perfect, he said, "What happened to your head? You've got blood trickling behind your ear. Not a good look."

A murmur and rustle from the partygoers who had congregated next to the curving zinc bar interrupted us. They opened a path for Amber and Sam, who slowly crossed the room. They were, of course, the stars of the show. Unlike my tightly boned dress, Amber's gown fell in graceful folds. A gold filigree hairnet that matched mine held her curls in place.

Sam, tall and dark, with those smoky gray eyes that made him so arresting a figure, had a painted gold rose pinned to his lapel. The king and queen of Broadway pretended they were unaware of the flashing cameras that followed them, although I knew this publicity was the reason they stayed glued to each other's side. He paused to brush his lips against hers, and the onlookers reacted with delighted oohs and aahs.

When the royal couple reached us, Bryan took Amber's hand and kissed it. I tried not to gag. She acknowledged her circle of admirers with a voice loud enough to reach the back row of a theater. "What do you all think of my twin?"

She curtsied to the applause that followed and linked her arm in mine. At the urging of her fans, we slowly pivoted to allow as many seemingly candid shots as possible. Several people got uncomfortably close to me, zooming in on my face and body. Amber and I were separated, and I found myself surrounded by an over-eager mob. She tried to protect me by drawing attention to herself, but they disregarded her.

I didn't know most of the faces that beamed back at us, but three stood out. One was Rose, whose gaze was fixed upon Sam. He touched the gold rose on his lapel and put his finger to his lips. Was that a signal to the young actress? If so, was he asking for silence or for some other favor? Poor Rose looked miserable. Losing a guy is never easy. Losing a famous director like Sam Flannery to a Broadway legend like Amber Castle must have been torture.

Lynne, with her cynical expression and colorful outfit, also caught my eye. The wardrobe mistress wore clothes Aunt Rachel would have loved. Her slim pants, topped with a tunic shot through with metallic threads and belted with a leather thong from which hung an assortment of peace signs, was an elegant riff on 1960s-era chic. She watched the proceedings with a skeptical eye.

The third face that emerged from the crowd was Garret's. His was a study in rage. If Amber took note of his presence, she hid it well.

When the popping and flashing of cameras and phones died down, Amber said, "I love you all madly, but I must fly. They need me at the front table. There's some problem with the seating." I followed her gaze to the raised dais, garlanded in orchids and lilies and twinkling with candles.

Sam tried to stop her. "You've been doing this disappearing act since we got here. Relax and have a drink with us."

She slid from his embrace. "That's very funny, coming from you. You've avoided me all night." Amber sweetened her criticism with a smile. "I'm not complaining, my darling, but I truly can't linger. It's the biggest night of the year for my foundation. I want every detail to be perfect. The A-listers expect no less. That's what they're paying for. Or did you think they were motivated by an intense desire to fund diabetes research?" She blew him a kiss and melted away.

With less grace, Garret pushed past Amber's admirers and followed his ex-wife. Alarmed, I tried to go after them, but Bryan grabbed my arm and held it so tightly I couldn't detach myself from his side. With many eyes still upon us, I refrained from kicking him, although his shins presented a tempting target.

Bryan said, "You wait here. I'm going to see if I can give Amber a hand."

I answered through gritted teeth. "Let me go. I'll help Amber."

Sam appeared unaware of the tension between us. He gave us both an affable smile and said, "Let Leah go, Bryan. I want to introduce you to a few people worth meeting. The producer of my last movie is here."

Bryan practically pushed me away in his eagerness to make a Hollywood connection. I sent Sam a grateful glance and texted Amber to warn her about Garret. She didn't answer. Keeping to the edges of the room, which were less choked with people than the middle, I approached the dais. She wasn't there.

I peeked inside the makeshift green room, which had been set up for the models before their catwalk. Racks of dresses and gift boxes wrapped in silver and black cluttered the small space. Amber and Garret reacted with fierce surprise when I pulled back the curtain. Neither was pleased to see me. I backed off and apologized for interrupting them but remained on the other side of the curtain in case he became violent.

Garret left first. He patted my arm and said, "You're a good friend, Leah. Amber doesn't deserve your kind of loyalty."

I debated whether or not to check up on Amber. I waited, wavered, and waited some more before deciding to respect her privacy.

The cocktail hour stretched beyond the sixty promised minutes, but dinner wouldn't start until after Amber's speech. If she began soon, we could all get home before midnight, and I could discuss what I'd observed with Jonah. One thing emerged from the brief time the four of us spent together: Bryan and Amber had, as yet, no witnesses who could verify their presence during the time Gabi and I were on the loading dock. Sam also had no alibi. He could have been following us while claiming to be looking for Amber.

Not one of them, however, had any reason to lock me out, threaten me, or wish me harm, and all three had a powerful reason to keep me safe. I was central to their collective ambitions. That's what they claimed, and it pleased me to believe it.

This illusion of self-importance passed quickly, replaced by the merciless reality of a dancer's life. The one thing you learn, whether you're performing in *The Nutcracker* or on Broadway, is that no one is irreplaceable. There's always someone in the wings, someone who's waiting for you to make one mistake, so she can push you aside and render you as relevant as last week's news. How could I have forgotten that eternal truth?

I needed someone on the inside whom I could trust, but my potential allies at *Mad Music* were also my suspects. Carly was strong, independent, and knowledgeable, but the dance captain was never going to forgive me for replacing her as Dreamcatcher. Rose also wasn't an option, because she was too in love with Sam and with her dreams of future stardom to function as a dependable source. I wished I could trust Natalie, but her shortcomings matched Rose's, except Natalie's attachment, I now suspected, was to Garret. And, like Rose and Carly, her ambition limited her usefulness.

With no better choices among the cast, I fixed upon Lynne as the most promising. The wardrobe mistress was intelligent and pragmatic, and she had no personal ties that might influence her. Her position backstage was another powerful asset, as it gave her access to the cast, the crew, and the directors. An added incentive was Aunt Rachel. Although I'd initially been wary regarding her position as Lynne's assistant, now that it was a done deal, Rachel would be ideally placed to verify whatever Lynne told me.

I felt as if I were alone, in the way one can be while surrounded by strangers, and I had to remind myself to resist the false sense of secure anonymity. Jonah had stationed officers at every exit, and the person who stalked me and Gabi was almost certainly still at the party. Whoever was tracking me was someplace close.

Jonah remained invisible, but his surveillance, presumably via closed-circuit cameras, comforted me. I wondered if Amber had gotten any threatening messages. I texted her with no expectation of a reply, but she answered immediately.

He's here. Watching me.

My mouth went dry. **Did you tell Jonah?**

She attached what was surely an ironic *haha* to my question and added, **Go home! Don't want him going after you.**

I should have told her about the photo and the message that was sent to me while I was trapped on the loading dock, but texts don't lend themselves well to layered meanings. That had to wait until we could speak privately. I contented myself with two words: **Too late.**

Chapter Thirty

No artist is ahead of his time. He is time; the others are just behind the times.
—Martha Graham

I didn't yield to Amber's kind suggestion that I leave the party, although there were many incentives, other than caution, to call it quits. I was tired, I was wearing a dress that threatened to cut off circulation to several vital organs, and my knees hurt. For me, galas were always work-related, performative, and without much intrinsic pleasure. They inevitably required my participation in ways that went far beyond making nice with the moneyed class.

This was very much the case at Amber's Design the Dream fundraiser, where I was modeling Mac Rosen's dress during the fashion show. More important than that obligation, however, was my reluctance to abandon Amber. Jonah and his team were there to provide security, but I was there to provide emotional support.

Beyond that, I hoped to unearth a clue that would reveal the identity of Amber's—and my—mysterious stalker. When Sam extricated himself from a large group that included the mayor, his wife, and a circle of sycophants, I made my move.

I was two feet from my target when a trio of golden-haired ladies outmaneuvered me, waving jeweled fingers and yoo-hooing as they approached.

The tallest of the willowy group spoke first. "Lovely to see you, Mr. Flannery." She craned her neck. "But I don't see the star of the show." She threw a knowing look at her two companions and said, "We've heard the two of you have been inseparable."

Sam reached around her and drew me into their circle. "If you're looking for the star of the show, here she is. Allow me to introduce Leah Siderova."

The woman inspected me. "So you're the twin sister Amber's been raving about, although now that we've met face to face, I don't see a strong resemblance. Maybe it's the generational difference."

She waited a beat before continuing to make sure her allusion to Amber's age penetrated. "I do admire the matching dresses and that over-the-top gold hairpiece of course. It was lovely of Mac Rosen to design the gown for Amber. And you. So clever of him, but you don't get to his position without knowing the right people."

I ignored the sensible part of my brain, the one that told me to ignore the woman's implicit digs at Amber and Mac. "Mr. Rosen designed the dresses to help raise money for Amber's charity, not for us. They've both donated their time and their talent. I, for one, am grateful."

They giggled at my naivete. "If you say so. I'm sure all this free publicity had nothing to do with their devotion to diabetes."

Sam tried a different focus, perhaps hoping they would invest in the show. "Leah is a star in her own right. She's a ballerina with American Ballet Company. We're lucky to have her as the lead dancer in *Mad Music*."

The tallest woman continued as the spokesperson for her group. "Well, isn't that nice. I think I remember reading something about her in the *Times*, although I don't remember that it was for ballet." She inspected me and, with a slightly less condescending air, said, "We should do lunch. I'm sure you have a million interesting stories to tell."

Her shorter companion said, "No offense, Leah, but ballet seems so nineteenth-century to me. I'm into modern art, modern theater, and modern music. You wouldn't catch me dead at the opera, either, other than at the annual gala." She turned a flirtatious smile at Sam. "But I love Broadway, and we all can't wait to see *Mad Music*."

I refrained from mentioning the brilliant modern choreography and compositions that illuminated the last two hundred-plus years of ballet. Perhaps they'd move onto a bigger fish if I refused to eat their bait.

The music changed to one with a percussive beat, and the anti-ballet woman said, "Why don't you dance for us?"

Her condescending invitation was one I'd heard before. It never failed to infuriate me, but I kept my smile locked in place. "If you want to see me dance, you'll have to pay for the privilege, although you might be too late to score tickets for *Mad Music*. I wish you luck with that."

The fear-of-missing-out exclamations that followed were highly gratifying. I took out my phone and looked at a nonexistent message. "It was lovely to meet you ladies, but Mr. Flannery and I are being summoned. If you'll excuse us?"

A speedy departure to the opposite side of the room was my primary goal. Sam, however, had a destination in mind. He took my elbow and steered me behind a large pillar in a relatively quiet corner of the room.

He rubbed his jaw. "Thanks for the get-out-of-jail-free card. My mouth literally hurts from smiling at people I don't know, but who have the cash to invest in my work. If I had my choice, I'd be drinking a beer, sitting in front of the TV, and watching the Manchester United game." He made a cross with his index fingers, as if warding off evil spirits. "If you know the final score, I beg of you, please don't tell me."

"Relax. I haven't watched a sporting event on TV since my second-to-last boyfriend broke up with me. And I didn't know you were a soccer fan. I thought you were going to say you wanted to watch *Hamilton*. Or *West Side Story*."

He said, "Your second-to-last boyfriend was crazy to let you go. I'm going to hold you hostage for the rest of the party or until Amber commands us to report to the head table."

This guy was too cool and self-confident. "If it makes you feel better, I'll let you believe the length of time we spend together is up to you. No hostage negotiations necessary."

He bent over me, in a way that felt too intimate. "I wouldn't let a woman like you go without a fight. So in the interest of keeping the peace, let's just hang here for a few minutes and enjoy each other's company."

The more time I spent with the charismatic Sam Flannery, the better I understood how the director left a trail of broken hearts behind him. I was in love with Jonah and therefore inoculated against Sam's charm, but even I wasn't completely immune.

He looked at his champagne, as if noticing it for the first time, and finished it off. "I'll let you in on a secret. Once upon a time, I dreamed of attending a party like this. Now, I can't wait for it to be over."

I took a tiny sip from my full glass. If I didn't pace myself, I'd be asleep before dessert. "I know what you mean. It's like you wait your whole life to get an invitation to the cool kids' table, only to find out they're boring and that having lunch with the nerds is a lot more fun."

His gray eyes sparkled. "I'd love to tell that to some of the society matrons who bankrolled this party."

I gasped in mock horror. "You can't do that. I'll lose my invitation to eat with the ladies who lunch, and you'll never get another last-minute reservation at Paradox."

He frowned. "Did Bryan tell you? He wasn't supposed to."

Hah. So I was right. "He didn't have to. There was no way he could've scored a table on such short notice, if at all. The last time Bryan and I went out for an impromptu meal, it was at the Aband-Inn. Only you or Amber could have made a last-minute call to Paradox and gotten balcony seats."

He laughed appreciatively. "Clever Leah. Tell me, what other insights have you picked up after..." he paused to think, "How long has it been? Less than two weeks on the set."

"That's how long since I joined the group, but Bryan taught me the tracks and got me up to speed before then. During that time, he managed quite well without my after-hours company or pricey meals."

Sam was a director of plays and movies. I suspected he was a similarly talented stage manager of real-life events. He had the gift of making whomever he was with feel special, which made people want to please him.

Uncomfortable with his lips' proximity to my face, I backed away until my spine was against the pillar. Sam again narrowed the space that separated us. With a move I learned while rehearsing the part of the Cowgirl in the ballet

178

Rodeo, I do-si-do-ed around him so that our positions reversed. I didn't like feeling trapped, even when the person doing the trapping was six feet of gorgeous. As a rule, I wasn't attracted to tall men, but I could see how someone like Sam could cause a woman to rethink her preferences.

The call to dinner was imminent, and I didn't want to lose this opportunity to talk to him privately. "As long as we're speaking of Bryan, maybe you could clear something up for me. He is, without a doubt, a gifted choreographer, but so is Garret. Why did you make the switch?"

If Sam was surprised by the change of topic, his only indication of it was mild curiosity. "I thought you and Bryan were a team. Is working with him a problem for you?" He crinkled his eyes at me. "I did notice some tension between you tonight."

My goal wasn't to diminish Bryan but to understand the tangled backstory of how the cast of *Mad Music* came together. Was it Sam, Amber, or someone else who wanted Garret out? And what, if anything, did that have to do with the threatening texts, the stalking, and the poisoning?

Sam was one of the few people who understood my double role, but I'd gotten into the habit of not trusting anyone. "Bryan and I work well together. Isn't that why you wanted me to dance in the show?" Appalled by a different possibility, I said, "I hope I wasn't the reason Garret got the ax."

He furrowed his brow, as if unsure of what I was asking him. "I wanted you to be the featured dancer from the start, but you turned us down."

This was true. Following *The Nutcracker* season, I'd been cast as the lead in the ballet *Romeo and Juliet* and was unwilling to give up that prized role for a stint on Broadway. It wasn't until Sam decided to wait until the end of American Ballet Company's winter season that I agreed to join the cast.

He said, "You were Bryan's first choice, and mine as well. Unlike our three blonde friends who fancy themselves too trendy for ballet, I'm a fan. I was in the audience on opening night when you starred in Bryan's ballet for ABC, and I knew then that someday I wanted you to work for me. I didn't think it would be under these circumstances. It must have been fate."

I'm as much a sucker for flattery as the next wildly insecure ballerina, but what Sam said didn't fit with what I thought I knew. "You went to the police."

"Right. I filed a report about the online threats against Amber. I didn't expect the cops to take action, because there wasn't much they could do. The messages she got were a nuisance but not a crime, and her only option was to hire an investigator to hunt him down and then sue him in civil court. No one, including me, thought the threats were credible. Luckily, the complaint landed on Detective Sobol's desk, and he said you might be willing to work unofficially and undercover. You'd turned down my offer a few months earlier, and I was happy you said yes, whatever the reason."

These interesting details didn't answer my first question. "Let's go back to why you hired Bryan."

He answered without hesitation. "I was ready to commit to Garret when Bryan came to me and made his pitch. I wasn't initially interested in signing him on, but he convinced me otherwise. Most people, they would've tried to wine and dine me. Bryan invited me to meet him at the D'Anconia, where he showed me his work. He found out which big band tunes we'd be using, and he had such good ideas about what to do with them. It didn't hurt that he came cheap. A couple of commissions fell through for him, and he needed the gig."

"And that's it? No one else had a hand in the decision?"

Sam didn't falter. "Garret was still in Amsterdam. He wasn't willing to sign on until his contract ended there, and another postponement risked alienating potential investors. He also insisted that Marco be part of the deal."

"What's the matter with Marco? He's a terrific dancer." From what I'd seen, the chorus could use more dancers of Marco's caliber.

Sam's face and voice cooled. "I don't make those kinds of deals. I don't have to. I told Garret I needed him sooner and that his boyfriend would have to audition like everyone else. I knew I was getting a star with you. I'd seen you dance. Marco's a nobody. A few regional companies and one Off-Broadway show that closed in two weeks."

I was baffled. If Sam was so concerned about the caliber of the dancers in the show that he refused to hire Marco sight unseen, how did so many weak dancers end up getting in? If the rumors about him were true, and women auditioned first in his bedroom, this didn't fully account for the presence of under-qualified performers. Although Rose and Natalie, two of the shakiest dancers in the chorus, were uncommonly lovely, with one wave of his hand, Sam could have hired fifty women of equal beauty and greater talent.

Most surprising to me was Sam's role in hiring dancers, which I'd assumed was at the sole discretion of the choreographer. It was another reminder of the difference between ballet and Broadway. Perhaps Sam was unusually controlling. Or, perhaps, a still-unseen hand was stage-managing us all.

Looking at the director's chiseled chin, which was so finely molded it defied Nature's tendency to avoid perfection, I remembered he was an actor before he became a director. He was an expert in using words and vocal inflections to play a part.

I had a different way of communicating, as well as obscuring, how I felt. When the gong sounded, calling us to dinner, I used movement to project the image I wanted him to see. I looked up from under my lashes, keeping my elbows by my side and stretching my forearms out to him with my palms up. The wordless pose conveyed meekness, vulnerability, and the desire to please.

With a smile, he grabbed my hands, thinking he'd come out on top. And he was right, although not in the way he thought. Sam was now high on my list of suspects.

His affection for Amber could be as fake as Bryan's for me. His lead actress had failed to deliver the kind of buzzy excitement that drove ticket sales, but Sam couldn't risk the bad publicity that would ensue if he fired her. He admitted he didn't think the police would act on the complaint, so going to them was the perfect cover. The means and opportunity were less clear, although he could have used Rose, who adored him, to execute the poisoning. Or Natalie.

Sam and Garret were the ones to watch.

Chapter Thirty-One

The Dance instills in you something that sets you apart. Something heroic and remote.
—Edgar Degas

A large poster, placed on an easel and hung in front of the same paint-spattered gold gauze that covered the walls, stood at the entrance to the dining hall. It listed the names of the guests and their table assignments. Weary of vainly hunting one person or another, I took a photo of the poster. For the next ninety minutes, I'd know who was present and where they were supposed to be.

Bryan and I were at the head table, which was on a raised platform, and where each place setting had a gold-inscribed nameplate in front of it. The chairs lined one side of the table and faced the audience. I felt like a zoo animal at feeding time, eating her meal for the amusement of peanut-throwing visitors.

Mac Rosen stood behind Amber's empty seat and examined a dozen models queued up for his inspection. They were dressed in metallic, silvery gowns, with glittery silver makeup and filigreed hairnets that shone with tiny sequins.

When he got to the end of the line of models, he clapped his hands. "Perfection. Now sell it!" They swanned off, circling the room and posing at each table to the admiration of the dress-buying crowd.

When Mac saw me, he showily assessed my body from every angle. "Your makeup could use a refresher, but the dress, if I do say so myself, is flawless.

Fabulously fab. And so are you. Do you adore it?"

"How could I not?" I spoke as if it were a rhetorical question, although the pressure of the tightly elasticized waist provided an excellent reason not to love the gown. "It was so generous of you to donate your time and talent to Design the Dream. It's such a worthy cause."

He declaimed, "Love it and you!" Mac pivoted so that we both faced the crowd. He held my arm high, as if in victory. Resigned to my role as one of the animated mannikins, I raised my other arm as if having a fabulously fab time at the Design the Dream gala.

When the moment passed, Mac sat down and fanned himself with the program. "Am I happy to support a good cause like this one? Of course. Will I be even happier when this night is over? Indeed, I will. Assuming I don't have a heart attack or nervous breakdown first. This has been a tragically stressful experience. My nerves are shot."

Juxtaposed against his mask of sunny optimism and with the memory of the stalker's taunting texts fresh in my mind, Mac's gloomy words carried a double dose of shock value.

A series of imaginary, terrifying scenarios flashed before me. "Why? Has anything gone wrong?"

"Darling girl, this charity event is a fashion show on Broadway-style steroids. The correct question isn't what's gone wrong. You should be asking if anything has gone right. Other than my gowns, of course. Those are perfect. But Lynne what's-her-name, the wardrobe mistress, was supposed to do a final check on my lovelies. Did she show up? No, she did not. I've had to do everything myself, with a few lowly assistants to help. Was that fair? No, it was not. It was total hell."

My mouth went dry. "How long has Lynne been missing?"

"How should I know? Amber forced her to run and fetch all night. I half-expected our hostess to demand that Lynne give her a paw before playing dead or begging for a treat. And then, when I needed her, Lynne was a no-show. She—" He cut short his complaint to greet the same trio of golden-haired ladies who'd crashed my conversation with Sam. Using our five-minute-long acquaintance as an excuse to breach the invisible velvet rope that separated the front table from the rest, they greeted Mac and me as if we were long lost, shipwrecked siblings.

With Mac distracted by his admirers, I canvassed the room. Lynne wasn't at her assigned table, but I hesitated to alert Jonah. Maybe she was waiting to use the bathroom, which would explain her lengthy absence. Or maybe she didn't want to be at Amber's beck and call and decided to ignore Mac's summons. Amber's generous invitation to the *Mad Music* cast came with strings, and although we didn't have to pay money to attend the gala, it wasn't without its price.

At Bryan's behest, I went to my seat, which was the second to last chair on the raised dais. He was on my right, at the very end of the table. On my other side sat a woman with gray hair and deep lines across her forehead and at the corner of her eyes. The nameplate in front of her said *Dr. Martina Hurtado*. She was one of the honorees.

Dr. Hurtado extended her hand. "It's a pleasure to meet you, Ms. Siderova. I took my granddaughters to see you dance in *The Nutcracker* ballet, and now they want to grow up to be like you."

I loved hearing those kinds of stories, which matched my own. "It's a pleasure to meet you as well. Tell your granddaughters that when I grow up, I want to be like you. What made you decide to focus on diabetes research? I've read a bit about your work, and I'm fascinated with all you've accomplished."

She straightened, with surgical precision, the silverware on either side of her plate. "Like a lot of doctors, I got interested because of a personal connection. Diabetes runs in my family. Does ballet run in yours?"

I didn't want to offend Dr. Hurtado by dividing my attention between my phone, my search for Lynne, and our conversation, but I was so concerned about the missing costume mistress, I found it difficult to concentrate. "My aunt studied dance, but I'm the only one who pursued a career onstage." With an apologetic smile, I added, "I have a friend who's not doing well, so I, uh, I'm keeping in touch with her."

Dr. Hurtado said, "I think you're being paged. Maybe it's a message from your friend."

The busboy who'd directed Gabi and me to the back exit to the loading dock handed me a package. "This is for you. I guess."

The box was wrapped in the same gold fabric that decorated the walls of the room. It was addressed to the Gold Lady. Dr. Hurtado said, "You look like the Gold Lady to me. Aren't you going to open it?"

A clanging alarm went off in my brain, reminding me of the last time I'd gotten an anonymous gift. Shaking off the paranoid response, I slipped the clumsily tied fabric off a rectangular box and opened the lid.

Inside was a knife with red stains that looked like blood.

Bryan peered into the box and then shoved his chair so far back he nearly toppled off the rear of the dais.

Dr. Hurtado raised her brows but maintained her composure. "What does the note say?"

I unfolded a paper cocktail napkin that bore the Design the Dream logo. Ink from the pen had bled into the fibers, but the words remained scarily legible. *Can't take my eyes off you.* A clumsily drawn heart, stabbed with an arrow and dripping with inked-on blood, was its only signature.

My breath came in short, sharp gasps that strained against the corset of my dress. The thing I feared most came next. A faint vibration from my phone with an incoming message.

With trembling fingers, I opened my handbag, shielding the screen from both Bryan and Dr. Hurtado. The text message was a photo of me, taken seconds earlier, with three smiley faces that had red hearts for eyes.

I stared at the sea of people in front of me.

It was of no use. I was exposed. On display. There was no way to tell which one of the selfie-taking partygoers had sent it.

I could, however, eliminate people who hadn't sent the picture, and that small group included everyone sitting at the head table. Bryan, Dr. Hurtado, and Mac were in the clear. Everyone else was guilty until proven innocent.

Chapter Thirty-Two

The process of our profession, and not its final achievement, is the heart and soul of dance.
—Jacques d'Amboise.

I forwarded the text and a photo of the threatening message to Jonah. Seconds later, he called and said, "Stay where you are. Don't go anywhere alone. Don't go anywhere, period."

My body jerked with irregular hiccups of fear. Dr. Hurtado took my arm and held two fingers against the inside of my wrist. "Steady there, Ms. Siderova." After taking my pulse, she put gentle pressure on my upper back. "Put your head between your knees and breathe slowly and deeply. Three counts in and three counts out." She tapped a slow rhythm on the table.

I refused to give my tormentor the satisfaction of seeing me surrender to intimidation. Instead of bending over, I sat straight up and laughed, as if what she said amused me. "Thanks, Doctor. I'm fine. Help is on the way."

Jonah walked up the steps to the dais. "Give it to me." He used a cloth napkin from the table to place the box in a plastic bag. "Where's the guy who delivered it to you?"

Furious at myself for having lost sight of him, I said, "I'll find him. Be out the lookout for a tall busboy or server, with short dark hair and wide shoulders."

He didn't chide me, perhaps intuiting I was doing an excellent job of self-flagellation without his help. "Meet me in the kitchen. Same spot, next to the sinks. Keep your eyes peeled, and if you see him, wave. Morelli will be trailing behind, and she'll nab him."

Bryan broke in. "I don't know what this is about, or why Leah received a prank gift. I do know she doesn't have much time. The speeches begin after the first course, and she has to be on the runway when they auction off the dress." He appeared to have more to say, but when his shallow blue eyes met Jonah's dark gaze, his voice trailed off.

With Bryan thoroughly silenced, Jonah said, "I'll tell Amber to hold off dinner and have her, or someone else, make a speech as a distraction. Morelli's got your back. Farrow's doing a sweep, and I've got a team on site."

Dr. Hurtado said, "If it's a distraction you want, I can help." She knocked a pitcher of ice water off the front of the table and stood in front of me as three servers rushed to clean up the mess. I slipped behind them and circled the room.

It was impossible to escape notice. Although the dining hall was filled with women wearing brilliant gowns and men dressed in every possible iteration of glamour, my shiny dress functioned like a moving spotlight. I traversed the room without apparent hurry, but as soon as I passed through the gauzy gold curtain in the rear, I ran as fast as a person can go whose torso is encased in a tightly, if stylishly, laced and boned gown. No wonder Victorian ladies were prone to fainting spells.

The clatter in the kitchen had increased to the point that a runaway train could have barreled through without attracting notice. I squeezed myself into the corner next to the dishwasher and didn't move until Jonah arrived. I wished for a better vantage point to locate the busboy but didn't want to risk getting trampled. Nor did I want to draw any more attention to myself than I'd already garnered.

Jonah entered the kitchen moments after I did, still holding the box with its bloody knife and menacing note. He wasted no time on sentiment. "I've got all the exits covered. If the busboy is really a busboy, he'll return to the kitchen sooner or later, and there are too many people in here for him to attempt to hurt you. In the meantime, no one's getting past security. They have orders to hold anyone trying to leave."

"Was that real blood on the knife?"

His stony expression softened. "No one got hurt, Leah. It was lipstick, not blood. You stay here and watch for the guy who delivered the package."

Sitting passively in the kitchen while the action took place elsewhere didn't appeal to me. "I have a better plan. I don't know why I didn't think of this immediately, but Gabi can help us find him. She's the only one, other than me, who knows what he looks like. That will double our chances of finding him."

I tried to reach her, but she didn't answer. Although the loud music that greeted me upon entering the party had segued to a less pounding volume, the din of two hundred people talking kept the room at a decibel level that remained in the unhealthy range, and she didn't respond to my text or phone call.

I returned to the dining area. Officer Morelli followed me at a distance, as I skirted past the last brigade of people making their way from the bar to the dining hall. Gabi and Garret sat at a table at the edge of the room, in the area known as Siberia. It was not a place for the fashionable to see and be seen, which made it perfect for my purpose.

I caught her eye and slowly shook my head from side to side, hoping she'd understand the need for caution. She looked at me for a scant second, nodding her head a fraction of an inch, before unconcernedly gazing past me. Garret was in an animated conversation with Carly and barely acknowledged Gabi's departure. My friend followed me to the back of the room. I held up my phone and tilted my head toward hers as if taking a selfie.

"Gabi! We have to find the busboy. The one who showed us the back exit. If you see him, don't approach him, but keep your eye on him and let me know immediately. Let Francie know. She's right behind us."

My friend smiled at the camera as if her only thought was to present a happy face for the picture. Under her breath, she said, "Francie? Do I know her?"

"Yes. She's the tall police officer, the one who was assigned the ABC detail last year. Francie Morelli. I'll share her contact with you. Text or call her, Jonah, or me. You have Jonah's number, don't you?"

"Yes. On it." She took out her phone and let out an exasperated sigh when she saw the missed messages. "Sorry, Sid. After my family text group sent twenty messages about the weather in Puerto Madero, I stopped paying close attention." She palmed the phone and eyed the stream of black-clad servers circling the tables. "I only saw the guy for a few seconds. I'm not sure I'll recognize him, but I'll try. It doesn't help that half the men here are wearing all black."

"Do your best. I'll explain later."

With the intuition that only the best of friends possess, Gabi needed no further information to understand how important it was to locate the busboy. She began a slow, circuitous walk, weaving in and around the narrow spaces between the diners. I was poised to return to the kitchen, figuring the busboy would eventually return to that location, when a movement from the dais caught my attention. The object of my search was standing next to Amber, holding a second gauze-wrapped box.

I waved wildly at Francie and raced back to the head table. I got there first but wasn't quick enough to grab the box before Amber opened it.

She looked inside, screamed, and pressed her hands against her heart. She tried to stand up when she saw Jonah but couldn't manage it and collapsed into his arms. When I saw the contents, I understood why.

A red-stained dog collar that had been hacked into two pieces sat inside the box. The name *Farley*, spelled out in purple rhinestones, was neatly divided, three letters on one side and three on the other.

Jonah cradled Amber in his arms. Crushed against his chest, tears streaming down her face, she looked so fragile. So vulnerable. I knew exactly how she felt.

Chapter Thirty-Three

If you think you can do better, then do better.
—Bob Fosse

Amber was too distraught to cover her fear and anguish with a practiced façade. A consummate actress, she nonetheless broke down in full view of the guests, dropping Farley's slashed dog collar and clutching her heart. Half the guests in the front row of tables stared open-mouthed. The rest rose to their feet, taking pictures and videos, as if the turn of events was part of the evening's program. When I first sat at the head table, I felt as if I were on exhibit at the zoo. After Amber collapsed, it felt more as if I were at the Roman Coliseum, waiting my turn to be fed to the lions.

Mac Rosen's voice pierced the growing commotion. "Ladies and gentlemen! We promised you an evening filled with excitement, and as you can see, we've delivered. We'll, er, we'll get to the fashion show and the auction shortly." He glanced to his left at Amber's now empty seat and added, "Ms. Castle is, that is, she'll be back soon."

While Mac attempted to quiet the uproar, Detective Farrow bagged the torn dog collar, the box, and the ripped fabric. Waves of people stood to gawk at Jonah, who carried a sobbing Amber down the center aisle. Close behind, Francie propelled the busboy toward the exit. When he twisted around, his face registered fear, shame, and confusion. He didn't fight against his forced exit from the ballroom, but few people could easily resist Francie Morelli's imposing height and strength.

With everyone looking at the detective, the actress, the police officer, and the busboy, my departure went unmarked.

Officer Diaz cleared the corridor between the dining hall and the kitchen and dragged two chairs into the hallway for Jonah and Amber. I wanted to stay with them, but Jonah refused my offer. "Go with Francie. I'll let you know when I'm done."

Francie led the busboy past the kitchen. His embarrassed docility gave way to anger. "Let go of me! What's going on?"

She pushed him, none too gently, through the door to the staircase. "Keep moving."

I followed them to the landing, where we waited for Jonah. When he arrived, he told the police officer, "I'll take it from here. You look after Ms. Castle."

Jonah faced the busboy and spoke in a tone that was mild, even friendly. "What's your name?"

He muttered, "Hugh Madden. Who wants to know?"

Jonah flashed his badge. "I'm Detective Jonah Sobol. How long have you been working here, Mr. Madden? Who employed you?"

"I'm with the catering company Command Performances. Ask anyone here. They can vouch for me." The red flush of embarrassed anger receded from Hugh's face. "I'm really an actor. I do odd jobs when I'm between gigs, and Command Performances hires a lot of out-of-work theater people." He swallowed. "I-I demand to know why I'm here. I can tell you right now, you've got the wrong guy. I've done nothing wrong."

Jonah maintained his easy, non-threatening approach. "Let's start at the beginning. Did you know what was inside the box you gave to Ms. Siderova?"

He pulled at his shirt collar. "The box? How should I know what was inside? We were told to go into the curtained room, get the gifts, and distribute them to the guests. Silver for the women. Black for the guys. There was an extra box that had a sticky note attached that said it went to the Gold Lady. So I gave it to her." He pointed at me.

191

Jonah's tone got more urgent. "Who set out the gifts? Who was in charge?"

Hugh's voice rose. "I don't know!" He glared at me as if his predicament were my fault. "Ask her. I got nothing to do with this. It's not what you think."

The busboy was angry, confused, and scared. But guilty? He didn't look like a violent or vengeful man, but by his admission, he was an actor. Hugh had the same good looks, careful coiffing, and gym-toned body as thousands of other would-be performers.

I went after the part of his story that didn't match the rest of his claim. "You said there was one extra box. But you just delivered a second box to Ms. Castle."

Hugh wiped beads of perspiration from his forehead. "You gotta believe me. When I went back to check, I saw that there was one box left, even though I could swear we'd divided all of them between us to deliver. It had Ms. Castle's name on it. Like I said, I was just following orders, and giving out goodie bags was the next item on our punch list. But I'm gonna lose this job if I don't get back to my post."

Jonah said, "One last thing. You directed Ms. Siderova and her friend to the loading dock earlier this evening. Did you lock her out?"

His voice rose to a shriek. "It wasn't me! I warned her she could get locked out. Happens all the time with smokers."

This was true. He had warned me, but that didn't mean he didn't remove the bottle that kept the door open.

Jonah said, "You can prove your innocence by showing me your phone."

His eyes darted to the doorway as if gauging the possibility of an escape.

Jonah remained relaxed. "Don't even think about it. Step through that door, and you'll find yourself in handcuffs and on your way to the station. Hand over your phone, please."

Hugh put his hand in his back pocket. "I know my rights. I'm not giving you the phone. It's private property."

Jonah said, "Your choice. You give me the phone for five minutes, or we get a warrant, and you lose it for as long as it takes the forensics people to crawl through the last six months of your life. Like I say, it's your call."

Muttering under his breath, he unlocked the phone and handed it to Jonah, who slowly scrolled through a line of texts and photos. His eyelids flickered once or twice, but he made no comment and handed it back to Hugh when he was done. "That's all for now. Give your contact information to the officer outside. We'll be in touch."

After the door closed on Hugh, I said to Jonah, "What's next? I'm guessing there weren't any texts or photos of me and Gabi out on the loading dock. But couldn't he have deleted them?"

"Yes. But I have no way of recovering them now. That's something for the techies, if and when I decide it's worth it. I imagine Hugh wasn't thrilled with having me see his sexts to someone named Honey Bunny, but that was as lurid as things got. We'll bring him for another questioning tomorrow."

I pulled a few pins out of my gold hairnet to ease the pain in my head. "I feel as if I've spent the entire night running around in circles. And now we've got two more clues that don't seem to lead anywhere. Why would the attacker send one package to me and another to Amber? Is there any reason behind these threats other than to scare us?"

He opened the door. "What makes you think the first package was meant for you? Amber could have been the intended recipient. The note said it was for the Gold Lady."

This was true, thanks to the fancy gold dress that I couldn't wait to take off. Good luck to whoever purchased it at the auction. "You could be right. But why would one package have Amber's name on it, and the other one be marked to the Gold Lady? Could the person who sent it not know my name?"

Farrow walked in with the box containing Farley's torn dog collar. He removed it with gloved fingers. I told myself it could be a cruel trick, and maybe Farley was unharmed, but I couldn't quash terrible images of the injured dog from charging through my mind.

I'd eaten very little, which explained why the walls caved in and the floor moved in sickening circles that didn't slow down until everything went black. When I recovered consciousness, I was sitting on the filthy steps, propped up by Jonah. Farrow fanned my face with his notebook.

Some investigator I turned out to be. I could almost hear Farrow thinking, *I told you so!*

I looked up at Jonah's partner and said, "Don't—you've got the wrong idea. I didn't faint. I, um, I forgot to eat. And, er, this dress, that was the problem. It's so tight, I can hardly breathe."

He stopped fanning me. "You passed out six months ago. If I remember correctly, it was at another one of these shindigs."

This was unfair. "I was knocked out, not passed out. That doesn't count." I rose to my feet and managed to stand without swaying. "I'm going to call Amber and find out if Farley is okay."

Jonah stopped me. "Farley is fine. The first thing we did was call the doggy hotel. The torn collar was a hoax. Amber is already back at the party."

"You talked to Amber? She checked up on him?" The relief was so intense, I had to grab the handrail to keep myself upright.

Jonah said, "Yes. Farley is resting comfortably. And you will be, too, once you get out of here. Time to go."

"Not a chance. I refuse to let myself be pushed around by this bully."

Farrow couldn't resist needling me. "You just fainted."

"You and Jonah and I know that. The person who sent the slashed dog collar doesn't. It'll be our secret."

Chapter Thirty-Four

Even today when I rehearse, I give it everything I've got. If I'm in a performance and the lights go out, I glow in the dark...That's the dancer within, reaching out.
—Mitzi Gaynor

I returned to my assigned place at the head table, where three plates filled with food were neatly lined up. Dr. Hurtado said, "I made sure they didn't remove your salad or appetizer. I hope you're feeling better, Ms. Siderova."

I thanked her, although ingesting more than a few bites would have strained my dress to the breaking point. I compromised by eating two crackers, four olives, and a couple of grape tomatoes to ward off another dizzy spell.

She peered at me through thick glasses. "I understand if you prefer not to tell me what happened, but I'm quite interested and would respect your confidence."

Dr. Hurtado's face was beautiful in its lack of artifice. Her gray hair fell in careless waves, and her black dress was without ornament. Her only jewelry was a gold wedding band and a steel wristwatch.

With genuine regret, I said, "I wish I could. But these are not my secrets to tell."

Bryan, who sat on the other side of me, stabbed at his broccoli as if he held a grudge against cruciferous vegetables. He hissed into my ear, "You don't have to tell her what's going on, but you should tell me. Amber was furious at how long it took for you to come back to the dinner table. She wanted you with her when she explained to the guests what happened. Were you with your boyfriend?"

The young choreographer had many talents, but perceptiveness wasn't one of them. "Amber isn't angry. You are. As for Detective Sobol, stop calling him my boyfriend. If you want people to think you and I are a couple, start acting like it."

The clink of a knife against glass stopped his angry rejoinder. The room quieted as Amber began her speech. Her tight grip on the lectern and a slight quaver in her voice betrayed her inner turmoil, but her fervent speech held the guests spellbound. She traced the history of her Design the Dream organization from its earliest days and thanked a dozen people for their contributions.

After extolling the generosity of her major donors, she beckoned to a server standing at attention at the end of the head table. With halting steps, the woman approached Amber, who said, "I also want to thank the people who never get enough credit."

She peered at the server's name tag. "Let's give a round of applause to Carol and all the Carols out there who have worked so hard to make this night so special." Keeping the reluctant, red-faced server close, she said to the rapt audience, "I'm going to let you in on a little secret. Like me, Carol is diabetic. Please open your hearts and your purses to help her live a happy, healthy, and productive life."

When the applause died down, she dismissed Carol and introduced Dr. Hurtado. Amber commended her contributions to diabetes research and presented her with a gold medal and a check. The room again erupted in applause.

With a wan smile, Amber made her final pitch. "I'm an actress, so you'll understand if there was a little extra drama added to the evening. For that, I apologize. This isn't the time or place for that. But if you want real, live theater, I'll see you next week at the opening for *Mad Music*."

One by one, the guests rose and gave her a standing ovation. She brought her hands to her lips and then extended her arms to the crowd.

Mac Rosen took her place and said, "Ladies and gentlemen, that was a tough act to follow, so I'm not going to try. After a break for dessert, we'll begin the auction."

Twenty minutes later, I got the call to report to the green room. The models, who'd been circling the tables to whet interest in the dresses, converged in a single line of silvery perfection.

We lacked only Mac's final approval before beginning our catwalk on an improvised runway that ran down the center of the ballroom. He was accompanied by a makeup artist toting a large case and Lynne Heller carrying a sewing basket. I was relieved to see the wardrobe mistress, having forgotten about her absence.

She gave me a sour look. "Some invitation this turned out to be. If I knew I'd have to work overtime for the privilege of showing up, I'd have ordered pizza and called it a night."

Mac snapped his fingers at her, which didn't improve her mood. The designer didn't notice Lynne's reluctance, because he was focused on the models. He circled each one with a pleased look and tossed them air kisses from two feet away.

His smooth procession ended when he saw me. "You look terrible! What in God's name have you done to your face? I've seen corpses with more color. And your hair? What's the point of a gold net if you're going to frizz out on me?"

I submitted to the ministrations of the makeup stylist, although I preferred to do my own stage makeup and didn't need help. After he plastered my face with foundation and blush, he dabbed gold glitter onto my cheeks, applied thick false eyelashes in the general direction of my eyelids, and painted my mouth in fire-engine red lipstick. Lynne removed the gold hairnet and smoothed my unruly hair with a quart of gel before using a dozen bobby pins to nail the hairpiece to my skull.

Mac kept up a running commentary, which he phrased in his idiosyncratic question-and-response mode. "Am I having a nervous breakdown? You bet I am. Is it my fault? *Puh-lease.*"

When the team of remodelers finished with me, Mac flashed a brilliant smile. "Voila! Perfection! Now go out there and be fabulous."

I followed the line of glamorous women into the darkened ballroom. Four black-clad servers wheeled black curtains in front of the head table, which provided a neutral background for the coming spectacle. Bryan, Dr. Hurtado, and the others joined friends in the audience to watch the show. Mac stood behind the lectern. Speaking over *Mad Music's* jazzy score, he recited an ode to each outfit. *This sweetheart neckline is anything but innocent...it says daring, it says desire, it says...*

I half-expected him to say *diabetes*, but the final adjective was *danger*, which was more apropos than he knew. When it was my turn, Mac intoned, *Gold, it is the eternal metal. Gold does not rust, it does not fade, it endures forever and forever. Like this dress, it is the ultimate luxury. Wear it, and be beautiful...*

I was more at ease in pointe shoes than high heels, but I made it to the end of the catwalk and back without stumbling. The slouching pose the other models used to flaunt themselves and the clothes was similarly uncomfortable. With Mac's reluctant approval, I walked as a dancer does and fixed my eyes beyond the crowd and the dizzying flash of lights. Amber, who'd been waiting offstage, joined us for the finale. She was still shaky after her earlier trauma and grasped my hand before standing, small and alone, under a single spotlight. She signaled Mac, who announced. "Let the bidding begin!"

When ABC held their auctions, they hired someone from one of New York's large art houses to preside, but in keeping with the bleeding edge vibe of Amber's gala, two men wheeled an electronic board in front of the black curtain, where it flashed and sparked with real-time images of Amber, me, and the models.

Mac instructed the guests to scan the QR code in the gift boxes, which would allow them to place their bids. Instead of the gowns being auctioned individually, people had the option of bidding on them simultaneously.

The room erupted in excited chatter as the dollar amount next to each dress climbed from four figures to five. Mac pulled me next to him and said, "I knew it! Your dress is going to break all kinds of records."

Bryan snaked his arm around me to share in the excitement. "You're so far ahead of the others. It's not even close." We watched the screen, riveted by the numbers.

As the bids for the dress I wore climbed higher and higher, the audience began chanting, *Le-ah! Le-ah!*

Although I was used to applause at the end of a performance, I found the cheering mildly embarrassing. Why were they calling my name? All I did was wear the dress. I didn't make it.

A cowbell rang, and a flood of confetti fell to mark the end of the auction. A spotlight circled the room and landed on me, nearly blinding me with its intensity. The guests clapped their hands, stamped their feet, and continued to chant my name.

I whispered to Mac, "I don't understand what's going on. You designed the dress, and it's Amber's fundraiser. Why are they applauding me?"

He kissed me on both cheeks. "Seriously? You, my precious, have enabled the world to see me as the genius I am. Is there another woman who could have made that dress an instant icon? No, there is not. And is there a single fashionista who isn't going to want a piece of this? No, my lovely, there is not. Plus, there's the whole diabetes research thing. But let's not think about that right now. Let's just soak this in together."

He put his arm around Amber's shoulders. "That's what I call a success. Take a bow!"

Amber evaded him and spoke in my ear. "Leah, can I borrow your phone? I can't find my evening bag." I handed her my phone, and she said, "I need Lynne. Do you have her as one of your contacts? She was backstage with me, and I think I left my bag there. It would be awkward for me to walk away now."

The timing of what happened next was unclear. I gave Amber my phone. The spotlight dimmed. The house lights came on. The music stopped. The screaming started.

Violence took center stage, like every other wannabe waiting in the wings for her shot at stardom.

Chapter Thirty-Five

He who cannot dance puts the blame on the floor.
—Hindu Proverb

The shrieks that interrupted the auction came from behind the dais. We ran down the steps, fighting against a mob of panicked guests. I swept open the curtain that closed off the green room. A group of police officers stopped us. They refused entry to Amber, Mac, and Bryan, but Francie let me and Dr. Hurtado through. At first, I thought Lynne was the victim. The wardrobe mistress's bright tunic bore irregular dark stains, and her hands were bloody. I rushed to her side, thinking she'd been hurt, but the blood wasn't hers.

It was Hugh Madden's. The server who dreamed of being an actor, and who'd played a pivotal supporting role earlier in the evening, was the tragic center of attention at its close. Dr. Hurtado crouched over him and tried to staunch the blood from a knife wound in his back. Her tense posture contradicted the soothing words she murmured to the injured man.

Lynne's sobbing drew my attention back to her. She breathed in heavy, ragged gasps.

Jonah stepped between us and addressed me in his detached, *we've-never-met* voice. "Ms. Siderova, please stand aside."

I answered him with my *don't-even-go-there* voice. "Detective Sobol, allow me to assist Ms. Heller. She's clearly not well."

Indeed, the wardrobe mistress looked quite ill. The confident woman, who'd formed so unlikely a connection with Aunt Rachel, was a trembling shadow of her former self. I brought her some napkins, which she used to wipe her face and hands. Her voice shook. "Detective, please let her stay. I-I can't. I'm not, that is, I don't know what happened."

Jonah let a hint of sympathy break through his impassive exterior. "It's best for all concerned if you concentrate on remembering. I understand how hard this is for you, Ms. Heller, but it can't wait. Take me through what happened, one step at a time. No detail is too small."

Lynne swayed as she spoke. "I got the text telling me to get Amber's handbag from the green room and to bring it to her on the dais. That's when I found, when I saw..." She turned to look at Hugh and shuddered.

Jonah prompted Lynne to continue. "We're almost done, Ms. Heller. How long was it before you called nine-one-one?"

Her words tumbled out. "Right away! I saw his legs sticking out from under the table. I-I was scared. He was half hidden under the tablecloth. I looked underneath, thinking maybe he'd passed out. When I saw, when I saw h-him, I called nine-one-one. Your officers arrived right away."

"Did you touch anything?"

Lynne's sobs increased. "I'm sorry, no, I didn't. I was afraid to touch the knife. Afraid to move him. I didn't even feel for his pulse."

Jonah pointed across the room. "What about the table? Did you move that?"

She said, through bloodless lips, "Yes. But that was so I could help him."

Jonah said, "You did the right thing. Officer Diaz will take your contact information and escort you out of the building. For your safety, as well as the safety of others, do not discuss what happened with anyone. That includes the people in this room. Remember that this is the second time you've been in close proximity to an attempted murder. We'll be in touch again tomorrow. That will be all for now."

I intervened. "Lynne, do you have someone who can stay with you?" She gave me a blank look. I persisted. "Can I call someone to pick you up? Take you home? You shouldn't be alone."

She swallowed hard and, in a weak imitation of her former self-sufficiency, said, "I don't need anyone."

"Yes, you do. I'm calling Rachel. She'd be happy to have company, and believe me, you could use a friend."

Lynne blinked back a fresh flood of tears. "That's absurd. Why would she want to go out in the middle of the night to help someone she hardly knows?"

I'd spent a good deal of my career hiding behind a mask of invulnerability, and I felt in my bones the emotions that tore at her. "You don't know her. I do."

Over Lynne's continued protests, I called Rachel and gave her a summary of what happened and what I wanted her to do. My loquacious aunt was, for once, brief. "Tell Lynne I'll pick her up and will text when I get there."

"Don't hail a cab. I'm going to give you the number of a driver who'll take care of you." I got Paulina's card out of my purse and read it off to my aunt. "Paulina is a friend of a friend, and she's someone you can trust. Give her my name and remind her that Rita referred me."

She said, "Got it," and rang off.

Lynne left to get her coat, and Francie Morelli took her place. Thinking aloud, I said, "Everywhere we look, we've got twins. It's as if everything is doubled. Two boxes. Two knives. Two threats."

Jonah spoke so quietly, I had to strain to hear him. "It's a mirage. Like a stage set. We're supposed to think everything is doubled, but half of what we think we see is pure fiction. A distraction from what's real."

Francie was equally philosophical in her judgment. "Yeah. Like Yogi Berra said, it's déjà vu all over again." She surveyed the room. "We've got statements from most of the staff working behind the scenes and in the immediate area in front. Do you want me to help out with getting contact info from the guests?"

Jonah said, "Kitchen first. See if you can find someone who knew Hugh. Maybe another aspiring actor."

She slapped shut her notebook. "Every waiter in New York City is an aspiring actor. But I'll do my best to find someone who was more than a work buddy to Mr. Madden."

His instructions for me were less specific. "The person who knows you're playing a double role is the only so-called twin we need to worry about. When we find out who it is, we'll have our assailant."

"That list is getting longer by the hour."

A muscle worked in his jaw. "Not for me. I'm down to one, possibly two."

I waited for him to keep talking. When he didn't, I said, "Don't hold out on me. Who made the cut?"

"Later. Still sorting things through, and it's better for me if I get your thoughts first. You know these people better than I do, and you have a way of stitching things together in ways I might never imagine. It's the ballerina in you, putting different steps together into a single dance."

I trailed behind him as he approached Dr. Hurtado, who spoke encouragingly to Hugh as she applied pressure to his wound. "Stay with me, Hugh. You're doing great. We're going to get you fixed up in no time."

A long table that held sewing supplies, makeup, an assortment of cups and glasses, and Amber's gold evening bag was pushed to one side.

Detective Farrow was on his knees. "Mr. Madden. Can you tell us who did this?"

The wounded man flinched and moaned.

Dr. Hurtado admonished him. "Not now, Detective." She resumed her gentle reassurances, but Hugh didn't appear to hear her.

Farrow straightened up. "Let's hope he recovers and can make a positive ID. I can't wait to nail this son of a—" He grunted. "This, er, this coward."

Jonah said, "Leah, you stay here and help the doctor. The ambulance will arrive any minute, and Farrow and I have to work quickly."

I ignored the painful pressure on my middle and stooped next to the wounded man. Dr. Hurtado handed me a pair of surgical gloves. "I hope you're not squeamish. You're not going to pass out or anything, are you?"

Once in a while, life hands out second chances, although not often within two hours. This time, I'd be strong. I held out a hand that didn't tremble. "Solid as a rock."

She instructed me to press against both sides of the knife. Hugh feebly resisted. Dr. Hurtado was sharp. "Don't move, my friend. You have to keep still." In a softer voice, she said, "You've got the most beautiful woman in the room taking care of you. Don't let us down."

Hugh's eyelids opened for a moment and then closed. We kept him still as blood dripped and pooled. She checked her watch. "When did Lynne call nine-one-one?"

"Can't be more than ten minutes ago, probably less. There was already a police presence when she made the call, which is why the cops were so quick to the scene."

Dr. Hurtado looked again at her watch. "Worst case basis, we've got another two minutes before the ambulance gets here and we get our guy to the hospital."

She continued to support Hugh in a slow, comforting cadence, although he stopped responding. "Hang on, my dear. Not long now." Her glasses slipped down her nose, and she pushed them back with her elbow. "You too, Leah. Hang on."

I needed better resources to keep myself calm than the ones the real me possessed. I exiled Leah Siderova to the furthest reaches of my mind and conjured up a vision of the magical forest in the ballet *Giselle*. Humming Adolphe Adam's music enabled me to block out the ugliness of the scene and keep it from crushing me. My hands remained steady, but a portion of my inner self floated far away.

I subdued my breath to the rhythm of a lilting waltz until the emergency technicians pushed me aside. Dr. Hurtado told them, "The knife punctured the lung."

The medic said, while lifting Hugh, "Got it. They're waiting for us in the ER."

They wheeled Hugh into the ballroom, down the runway, and past the gaping guests. Dr. Hurtado said, "Well done, Ms. Siderova. Perhaps we can meet again under less fraught circumstances."

"I'd love that. But I'm Leah, not Ms. Siderova."

She stripped off her glove. "And I'm Martina."

Detective Farrow approached and said, "Dr. Hurtado, we'll take your statement now." He looked at me and said, "You too, Ms. Siderova."

Martina said, "I'll be happy to assist in any way I can, Detective, but I would prefer to do so while sitting. These old knees aren't doing so well."

My knees, although much younger than Martina's, agreed.

Chapter Thirty-Six

Ballet is not technique but a way of expression that comes more closely to the inner language of man than any other.
—George Borodin

After the medics took Hugh to the hospital, the police tore down the curtain that divided the dressing area from the head table. I returned to the dais, where my suspects were gathered.

Mac, Bryan, and Amber huddled together in a tight circle. They shared the same dazed, shell-shocked expression. Amber rocked back and forth, her arms wrapped around her middle, as Mac and Bryan tried to soothe her. Sam wasn't with them.

When Mac saw me, his face turned a trendy shade of pale green. The designer leaped to his feet and wailed, "What have you done to my dress?"

The knees of that infernal gold gown were dark with rusty patches of blood. Mac's concern for the fabric, as opposed to the person wearing it, or the one whose blood stained it, momentarily stunned me. There were many possible responses to his complaint.

I chose one that matched his insensitivity. "Look on the bright side. It's probably more famous, and worth more, now. Attempted murder can do that."

Mac's words freed me from any lingering responsibility I might have felt for his prized creation. After getting permission to retrieve my wrap from the coat check, I returned to the table and unhooked the side fastenings of the dress, from the bodice to the waist, and wrapped myself in the soft velvet cloak.

Mac flapped his arms and fussed. "What are you doing? What are you thinking?" He appealed to his models, "Have you ever seen such an absolute travesty?"

One after another, the women unzipped, unhooked, and unbuttoned their gowns and sighed with relief at their restored access to oxygen. One of them, less addicted to fresh air, used her freedom from the corset to draw deeply at a vape pen.

Mac scolded. "You can't do that in here."

She blew a stream of smoke into the air. "Arrest me."

Defeated, he returned to his seat, muttering about the end of civilization.

A few quick stretches were sufficient to restore elasticity to my body and my brain. Time to get back to work.

After my brief expedition to retrieve the cloak, the police confined me to the head table. They separated the rest of the attendees into two groups. Officers moved quickly through the larger one, taking contact information and escorting guests and staff to the exit in clusters of ten or more. Gabi and Garret, who were seated with the *Mad Music* cast members, were not as fortunate. According to Gabi's text, Detective Farrow questioned each of them closely.

Texting was a poor substitute for the complex conversation we needed, but given my distrust of everyone at the head table, it was my only option. **Need info on Garret's movements previous to confetti fall.**

Gabi answered with a gif, a dark-eyed, dark-haired image that looked amazingly like her. The character had question marks over its head. Three dancing dots followed before she texted: **Call me asap.**

I slipped behind the dais and sat under the utility table in the dismantled green room, as far from the bloodstains as I could get. The hiding place wasn't ideal, but it was the best I could do under the circumstances.

Gabi said, "The room was dark, and there was a lot of movement. The sight lines were bad on this side of the room, and most people, including Garret, left the table to get a better view of the show."

I retreated further under the table. "Was Sam with you?"

"He spent some time with the *Mad Music* crowd. How long he was there, I couldn't say."

I spoke quickly. "Hugh Madden was stabbed during the fashion show. It could have happened up to fifteen minutes before it started and not more than five minutes after it ended. I'll explain more about it later, but the time frame is narrow. Ask Garret where he was and do your best to verify his claim."

Her voice was pitched so low I could barely hear her. "I'll take care of it. I'll also check up on a bunch of others who wandered in and out during the show."

"Good. When you're ready to leave, text me. I'll have a car waiting for you. Check the license plate before you get in. Don't leave with Garret, Sam, or anyone from the cast."

"I'll do better than that. I'll wait for you, and we can leave together and sort this out."

I was sweating under my black cloak. "No. I don't want you to be the next target."

Gabi blew a Bronx cheer into the phone. "Nice try, Sid, but that won't work. Your stalker has a picture of both of us on the loading dock."

So much for discretion. "I'm so sorry to have dragged you into this, Gabi."

"You didn't drag me into this. Garret did. If he hadn't invited me, I'd be snoozing on the sofa or reading Barbara's latest book."

"In that case, prepare for a long night."

Her voice changed and became cheerful as she rattled off a string of Spanish. I didn't speak Spanish, other than what I learned on *Sesame Street*. Gabi knew this. It was her way of telling me she could no longer speak openly.

I said goodbye, ending with an endearment I'd learned from her. "*Hasta luego, querida amiga.*"

It was too late to call most people, but Barbara and Rachel weren't most people. My mother picked up the phone before the end of the first ring. I said, "Get Rachel. If Lynne is still with her, then both of them should come to your place. Gabi and I will be there as soon as we can."

"I'll put on a pot of coffee and have some food ready. I just got off the phone with Rachel. She's at Lynne's apartment, but she'll be here shortly. We've been waiting to hear from you, and we'll be up."

I moved on to the next task. While Jonah questioned Amber, I zeroed in on Bryan. Like Mac, the choreographer's main concern was for himself.

He moaned, "This is a catastrophe. Poor Amber. Poor Sam. Poor me. This event was supposed to give a boost to *Mad Music,* and look what happened! You can bet the press will jump all over it, especially after Amber got swatted. We were already battling the impression the show was cursed."

I leaned closer to express completely insincere support, but Bryan shrank back when my cape opened to reveal the bloodstained gown.

I didn't let his revulsion deter me. "We can still turn this around." I pointed to the group of *Mad Music* cast members, still milling about in their confined space. "If you can help identify the person who attacked Hugh, you'll be a hero, as well as a brilliant choreographer."

He forgot his distaste in the excitement of the superhuman future I laid out for him. "You're a genius, Leah! But how can I do that?"

"The police are going to want to know if you saw anything or anyone who was backstage between the time the fashion show started and when the bidding ended and the confetti fell. Did you see anyone who didn't belong there?"

He looked as if he were about to break down in tears. "No. Like everyone else, I was watching you and looking at the screen. Those numbers were eye-popping. You really did look smashing. People couldn't stop talking about you. I hope I get half that much applause on opening night."

I said as if it were an afterthought. "Did you notice anyone who was missing?"

He shook his head. "No. Other than Sam, I don't think anyone left the head table."

My heart beat faster. "Where was Sam? Shouldn't he have been with Amber?"

"He decided at the last minute to spend a few more minutes with the *Mad*

Music cast as a way to bring people together. Makes him look like a good guy, someone who hasn't lost touch." Bryan rose from his chair and said, "Here's the big guy himself. You can ask him."

Sam embraced me, but his real concern was for Amber. "Glad to see you're okay, Leah. How is my girl doing?"

When Amber saw Sam, she ran from Jonah, threw herself into his arms, and sobbed. "Where were you? I needed you so bad."

He stroked her head and said, "I'm here now."

They made a striking couple, she with her flaming hair and he with his smoky gray eyes. The only thing missing from the tender scene was a Louis Armstrong soundtrack and a slow sweep of the city's skyline behind them to make it moving-picture perfect.

I wasn't alone in my cynicism. Jonah's blank expression didn't fool me. He regarded the magic couple as dispassionately as a fishmonger filleting a piece of salmon. I wondered if Sam and Amber were the two people headlining his list of suspects. If so, I wasn't yet in agreement with him.

Amber and Sam were guilty of many transgressions. Their relationships were transactional. They loved themselves more fervently than their most devoted fans. Artifice ruled their lives. And yet, that didn't make them bad people. In many ways, their concern with their public personae led them to pursue a more charitable and benevolent existence than those less concerned with fame.

Following the same advice I gave Gabi, I refused Bryan's offer to take me home. He pointed to the nearly empty hall. "You're not going to get a better bargain, unless it's from your boyfriend, and Detective Sobol looks as if he's not wrapping things up any time soon. The limo is paid for."

I was fed up with his niggling comments about Jonah. "You're boring me. What's worse is that you're putting me in danger. I don't care if you believe my relationship with Jonah, with Detective Sobol, is romantic. But keep it to yourself, unless you want me to be the next person to end up with a knife in my back."

He acted offended, as if I were the one in the wrong. "That's not funny, Leah."

CHAPTER THIRTY-SIX

"What makes you think I'm joking?"

He became, if not remorseful, less grating. "We've both had a tough couple of days. It's put a horrible amount of stress on all of us. Peace?"

With no desire to make an enemy where none, as far as I knew, existed, I gave the only answer possible. "Peace." If any unprintable words followed that concession, they remained unspoken.

Jonah waited until the last guest left to approach me. "I'll put you in a cab. There's nothing more you can do here. I'll call you in the morning."

I was anxious to learn what transpired during his interviews and who his two prime suspects were but was too tired to argue. I had plans of my own.

Chapter Thirty-Seven

A lot of people insisted on a wall between modern dance and ballet. I'm beginning to think walls are very unhealthy things.
—Twyla Tharp

As promised, Barbara had a pot of hot coffee waiting. She ushered us into the living room, where Lynne sat next to Rachel on the uncomfortable white sofa. The wardrobe mistress was still shaky but looked stronger than when she tottered out of the gala on my aunt's arm.

Barbara set out a plate of black and white cookies next to a pile of raw vegetables and a bowl of low-fat dip. I expected to see the vegetables, which were my mother's idea of an indulgent midnight snack. The cookies were a surprise. It wasn't often she allowed sweets to sully her home with their heavy load of calories and carbohydrates.

"Your aunt brought them," Barbara explained, as if we needed an explanation.

Rachel pushed the plate across the coffee table. "Eat up, girls. You need your strength. They're delicious. Got them from Zabar's this afternoon."

"Thanks, Aunt Rachel. I'll hug you as soon as I change my clothes." I took off my cape—Barbara's cape—and they gaped at the stained gown.

Lynne averted her face. "Leah, thank you for helping me out tonight. I needed it." She tried to smile. "And thank you, Rachel, for—" She nearly broke down again. Rachel handed her a cookie.

Gabi took off her shoes. "If you can spare some sweats, Barbara, I will be forever in your debt."

My mother didn't own sweatpants, but she had expensive, stretchy leggings and zippered jackets made of silky-soft cotton. She gave me a notebook and pen from her comprehensive stash of stationary, and after Gabi and I changed clothes, we settled down to work.

While Gabi gave Barbara and Rachel a complete account of the evening, I wrote it all down. Lynne was still too shell-shocked to contribute much. My mother handed the wardrobe mistress a snifter of brandy, which partially revived her.

Barbara selected one of her recently released books and flipped through it. "Although Amber may not see it this way, she is one lucky gal. Ketamine can kill someone in diabetic shock. I used that myself in *The Merry Knives of Windsor*."

Gabi helped herself to a cookie. "Amber has had more than one close call. So have you, Leah. And so has her dog."

My chest tightened when I thought of Farley. "The slashed dog collar was an attempt to intimidate Amber. Farley was never in danger. We have to establish the point of these threats. Who benefits from them? And why the attack on Hugh Madden? That's a radical escalation."

Rachel pushed a second cookie on Gabi, who didn't resist. "Someone who hates her and envies her might get pleasure out of tormenting her. If that's the inspiration behind it, there doesn't have to be a concrete personal benefit. Amber's fear and misery would provide the motive and would be an end in itself. Though that doesn't address Hugh's involvement."

Barbara returned to the bookshelf and chose one of her earlier novels for inspiration. "Professor Romanova makes a chart that details means, motive, and opportunity, and then uses literary analysis to unravel the mystery."

Rachel said, "Professor Romanova is a figment of your imagination. Real detectives don't work like that."

My mother, having heard this argument many times, remained undaunted. "Professor Romanova always wins in the end. And so will we."

I drank coffee and ate two bites of a wickedly delicious cookie. "We could use some creative thinking since forensic evidence for the poisoning wasn't helpful. The coffee cups that poisoned Amber and Marty had only their fingerprints on them, and the plastic stirrers the police recovered from the trash had multiple prints on them. The knife that was used to stab Hugh was the same one used to set the table for people eating meat. Hopefully, they'll get some good prints by tomorrow."

Gabi said, "Is there any point in getting a list of people who ordered steak?"

I rubbed my eyes, which felt as if they had sand in them. "I don't think that will help much, since the stabber could have used a knife from someone else's place setting."

Gabi looked over my shoulder at the growing list of suspects. "Have the police been able to do anything about the online stuff? I'm no techie, but would there be a marker? Like an IPO? Or some other trace?"

"I'll ask Audrey. The police are working on it, but nothing so far. The online threats have been made via anonymous accounts, and the stalker uses different burner phones. I wish I could persuade Amber to give us access to her social media accounts."

Rachel said, "Let's forget about stuff we don't know and concentrate on doing what we do best."

Barbara was still miffed at her sister's careless attitude toward *The Merry Knives of Windsor*. "What expertise, dear sister, do you bring to the table? More YouTube videos?"

Rachel didn't take offense. "Tomorrow is our first tech rehearsal in the theater. You're going to be in the front of the house with the directors, working on the script. Leah will be onstage with Abigail, Izzy, and Audrey, although the Weird Sisters will probably spend most of their time waiting in the wings. I'll be backstage with Lynne. Geographically, we've got the place covered. Together, we'll get to the bottom of this."

Gabi was plaintive. "What's my job? I'm feeling left out."

My friend's questions about getting evidence from the phones gave me an idea. "As Rachel said, we've got the place covered, including areas where there'll be no CC cameras. We can set our phones to record everything that happens behind the scenes. We'll stalk the stalker and beat them at their own game. Gabi, you'll be our command center, listening in via a shared meeting app."

I returned home in Paulina's cab. She said, "Whatever trouble you're in, it's not an abusive partner. What's going on?"

"I can't tell you yet, but I'm grateful. Rest assured, you're helping women in need." We drove the rest of the way in silence.

I gave her all the cash in my purse. When she protested, I told her to donate the excess money to the women's shelter. She pressed my hand warmly before we said goodbye.

I tiptoed up the stairs but didn't escape Mrs. Pargiter's ceaseless patrol of the hallway.

I was too tired to wrangle with her. "Mrs. Pargiter, it's four o'clock in the morning. Don't you ever sleep?"

She spoke through a crack in the door, using the three inches of space the chain lock allowed. "How can I rest when people stomp in and out at all hours? Tell me that."

"How about I tell you later? I'll call you in the morning."

Her voice was flinty. "It is the morning."

"Not to me. To me, it's still nighttime. If you can wait until eight o'clock, I'll make you coffee."

She unlocked the door and, with veined, gnarled hands, slowly opened it. She rarely afforded me this courtesy, which she freely extended to Jonah. I didn't count on her accepting my invitation since she loathed me.

It was a night of surprises. She said, "Coffee? I'll show you how to make a real pot of coffee. Eight o'clock. On the dot."

My body needed whatever sleep it could get, but my brain had other plans. I couldn't think or reason clearly without writing and had very little time left to organize my thoughts before reporting to the theater and beginning Operation Stalk the Stalker. Once upstairs, I opened my laptop and added to the list I'd started earlier with events that took place long before I joined the cast of *Mad Music*.

I began with our director. Sam hired Garret as the choreographer for *Mad Music* and then replaced him, possibly at Amber's request, with Bryan.

Attacking Amber would be an excellent way for Garret to hurt her, Sam, and Bryan. It gave Garret a double motive as a spurned spouse and rejected choreographer. If that were the case, going after me was a logical next step.

On my first day of rehearsal, I tripped over a dance bag, in a scenario similar to the one that injured Rose before I came on the scene. If Garret was guilty of either malicious booby trap, he couldn't have managed it alone. Carly had the most to gain by eliminating me, but this didn't explain what happened to Rose. The only way to connect what happened, both before and after my arrival, was to identify the person who benefited from each episode, not individually, but as a whole. That was the sticking point.

I called Barbara. "What sold Sam on hiring you? What changes does he want to make to the script?"

My mother answered as readily as if it were the middle of an idle day. "He wants an alternate script for the parts that connect you and Amber."

I drummed my fingers on the closed laptop. "I don't say anything. I just dance."

"You don't have any lines, but Amber does. The whole show revolves around the aptly named Leading Lady, and Sam is hedging his bets. As for you, you're leaving in three months, and he doesn't want to have to find a dancer who looks like Amber."

I looked at my list, trying to fit this new information into all that preceded it. "What you're telling me, then, is that the workaround in the script is a two-way street. If Amber drops out, Sam won't have to find an actress who looks like me."

Barbara said, "Correct. Best of all, it's not a big fix. According to Sam, it's closer to what he originally envisioned. Now turn off that brain of yours and get some sleep."

She ended the call, but I stayed awake. Jonah said he had two names, two people he suspected. From the start, much of the evidence pointed to Natalie and Carly. They were both ambitious, talented, and resentful at being passed over for a bigger star.

I hadn't wanted Natalie to be guilty, because she was kind, and funny, and a gifted actress and singer. A potent argument in favor of her innocence was her knowledge of Sam's insistence on hiring stars. She told me so herself. If I had any doubts, Bryan confirmed that fact during our dinner together when he told me the director's first choice was Lily Ferrante, who was a hotter commodity than Amber.

Carly's position was different. Although Sam was pleased with my decision to dance in *Mad Music*, he'd been equally content with leaving Carly in the role of Dreamcatcher. The dance captain had every reason to wish me ill, and with the support of the other dancers firmly on her side, she ran little risk of either discovery or punishment.

Unknown factors remained. Was each episode part of an escalating pattern? No one in the cast was likely to confide in me, but I now had multiple allies who could ferret out the truth. What I didn't have was an intimate knowledge of the theater, which was famous for its labyrinthine backstage area.

Garret was the prime suspect, but he wasn't working alone. Carly, Natalie, or Rose had to be working with him. At my first rehearsal, one of them tripped me up. It was my turn to entrap one of them.

Chapter Thirty-Eight

I may not be there yet, but I am closer than I was yesterday.
—Misty Copeland

A hot shower at seven thirty helped soothe a banging headache that woke me after less than three hours of sleep. I packed my bag for a full day at the theater and presented myself at Mrs. Pargiter's door at seven fifty-nine.

My neighbor's apartment was filled with photographs of her children and grandchildren. She didn't talk much about them, except to tell me they rarely visited. On a shelf next to the kitchen table was a picture of Mrs. Pargiter, holding a shaggy dog in a red knitted coat and an elf hat. Two gleaming, empty dog dishes were underneath.

I picked up the photo, which was inside a polished wooden frame. "Who's this, Mrs. Pargiter?"

She snatched the picture from me. "That's Sammy. He died." She cleared her throat. "I don't like going out without him. Too dangerous. You never know."

"Have you ever thought about getting another dog? There's a shelter around the corner, and they're always looking to find homes for the animals."

She traced the outline of the picture. "You don't understand. Sammy meant so much to me. You can't replace someone like him the way you change shoes or a hat." She coughed and blew her nose. "I suppose you think I also should have replaced my husband with a newer model."

Despite this unpromising beginning, we spent a pleasant quarter-hour together. She excitedly showed me the front page of the newspaper, which had a picture of Jonah carrying Amber after her collapse at the gala. She looked like a tragic fairy princess. His expression was more enigmatic.

"The article says Amber Castle has been attacked online, and someone is stalking her." Mrs. Pargiter nodded sagely. "I feel so sorry for her, but she's lucky to have Detective Sobol watching out for her." She rifled through the pages in search of a second article, this one in the Arts section. "Your show is sold out for months. They say it's going to set box office records."

I popped two aspirin tablets and washed them down with coffee. "Let's not talk about *Mad Music*. Why don't you tell me about yourself?"

Mrs. Pargiter regaled me with stories of her years as a community organizer. When I asked if she wanted to once again get involved in local politics, she didn't say yes, but she didn't say no, either. I didn't try to convince her to leave her apartment, but I put it on my list of things to do. Perhaps she would consent to go outdoors if I went with her. Another solution for her solitude and fear would be another dog. I put that task on my list as well, scheduling it for the day after I found the person or persons who'd attempted two murders.

The platform for the downtown train was packed with harried, impatient commuters. The presence of so many people was a good sign, because it meant I hadn't narrowly missed my ride. Nothing marked the morning or the passengers as atypical, but both felt different. I jumped when someone pushed past me and squelched a screech when a woman mindlessly ran her wheeled tote over my foot. I scolded myself: *The next thing you know, you'll be like Mrs. Pargiter, afraid to leave the house in broad daylight.*

Surrounded by dozens of people, I was surely safe, but the sense of swift-moving danger persisted. I surveyed the people closest to me. A young mother with two kids in tow. Three women dressed in tailored suits. A man with a scruffy beard, whose stale cologne, like a bowl of rotting limes, sickened me. All perfectly normal.

I couldn't recall the context, but a recent conversation about someone getting pushed in front of an oncoming train or into a busy street, teased my memory. This brand of violence happened rarely, but with enough frequency to have made me habitually cautious while riding the subway. No one in my immediate vicinity appeared to pose a risk, but this didn't guarantee safety, nor did it quell my fear. When the ground underneath vibrated with the rattle of an approaching train, I fled.

I was pressed against a building on Eighth Avenue, fighting for air, when Jonah called me back. His voice was hoarse. "How are you holding up?"

I didn't mention the panic attack that sent me running from a routine journey on the A train. "I'm fine. How is Hugh?"

Jonah delayed answering long enough for me to guess the tragic answer. "Hugh didn't make it. Never regained consciousness."

I was gutted and fearful of more bad news, but I forced myself to continue. "How is Marty feeling? Has he made any progress on recovering his memory?"

Again, Jonah paused. "You can ask Amber about him. She was on her way into the hospital as I was leaving."

Once again, I had to rethink my estimation of the woman at the center of our investigation. "That was very kind of her to visit him while she's going through so much herself. I didn't know the nurses were allowing non-family members to see him."

The background noise, on his side and mine, made communication difficult. After breaking for a passing siren, he said, "They didn't let her in at first. But according to his parents, she hasn't missed a day since he was admitted. He's improving, although he still doesn't remember anything about the day he was hurt."

Amber never mentioned visiting Marty, other than her first attempt to see him. She hadn't posted self-congratulatory updates on her social media or used Marty's plight to promote herself. This was unusual behavior for a woman who put no boundaries between her personal and professional life.

With this in mind, I reminded him, "You said last night you had one person, maybe two, on your list. Is it still Natalie and Carly?"

I heard the sound of a car door opening, and Jonah's tone became more guarded. "That's still an open question. We should be ready to move forward soon. Maybe by the end of the day."

"Is Farrow with you now?"

The older detective's raspy voice answered. "Yeah. I'm here. What's up?"

"I've got a plan."

The stage was set for the first act. Sam was seated in the audience, midway between the orchestra pit and the exit doors in the rear. The stage manager and set designer sat on either side of him, and the lighting and sound directors sat next to them. Barbara planted herself two rows behind the others.

The theater was a much smaller space than the soaring one at Lincoln Center. American Ballet Company performed at the Metropolitan Opera House, which could accommodate close to four thousand people. *Mad Music* would unfold before a more intimate audience of about eleven hundred.

The cast was familiar with the setup, having rehearsed onstage for a short while before Sam decided to delay the opening. I wasn't worried about the abbreviated schedule for tech rehearsals from a performance standpoint, but I wished I had a more thorough knowledge of the theater. For those details, I would have to rely on Rachel and Lynne. Backstage was their territory.

My aunt looked surprisingly well-rested, given our late night. The same could not be said of Lynne. The trials of the previous evening left their mark on the wardrobe mistress, whose bloodshot eyes were rimmed in dark shadows and whose shoulders slumped with weariness.

Rachel was true to her promise. She kept close to Lynne and avoided an open acknowledgment of our kinship. I was proud of my aunt, who limited herself to one stagey wink and two raised eyebrows.

The stagehands placed portable barres onstage, and Bryan gave us a ballet warm up. Like me, he'd trained with the famous Madame Maksimova, and he modeled his exercises on hers, which she'd learned from her teachers. It was a line that stretched back for many generations. After the shocks of the previous week, which culminated in Hugh's violent death, I needed the familiar rhythm and sequence to keep me centered and strong. *Plié, tendu, dégagé, rond de jambe.* Ballet terms are in French, regardless of where it's taught or performed, which enables dancers to take classes in any country and always feel at home.

When we finished the warm up, Sam came onstage to address us. "We all had a long and stressful night, but we're here now, doing what we do best. When I look around me, I see the most gifted performers on the planet. We're also among the most diverse. I don't know of another choreographer who could have meshed the range of talent, and levels of experience, as Bryan Leister. And congrats in advance to our three newest cast members."

No one clapped for Bryan, but a cheer went up for Abigail, Izzy, and Audrey.

Sam continued, "We've come through some tough times together. Let's make that our strength. Not our downfall. As for the, um, unpleasantness that happened after the fashion show, the police are conducting a full investigation. Don't be alarmed if you see them in the theater today. They have their work to do, and we have ours."

Unlike the controversy that erupted in the aftermath of Marty's injury, no one questioned Sam's decision to focus on the rehearsal. We knew the show must go on, despite the triteness of this most overworked theatrical cliché.

After the morning rehearsal, I went to the break room instead of my dressing room. Like Sam, I wanted to talk to the cast members when they were all together instead of individually. As usual, Carly dominated.

She clenched her hands as if spoiling for a fight. "Did anyone besides me think that Sam's speech was a little on the cold side?"

Rose sprang to Sam's defense. "What did you expect him to do? I would've thought you, of all people, would understand."

Carly sent Rose one of her marble-hard stares. "Listen, sweetie, I get it. I also get that we could be next. First Amber and Marty, and then that business with the busboy, or server, or whatever. Does anyone know how he's doing?"

I said, "Hugh. His name is—was—Hugh Madden. He died."

There was a collective gasp. Carly's hands trembled. "I'm so horribly sorry to hear this. Of course, we're shattered. Do you, er, do the police know who did it?"

I copied Jonah's mild tone and expressionless face. "I've got only one important piece of information to share. If anyone here has any questions or has seen something suspicious, don't tell Carly."

The dance captain erupted in an outraged yelp, and she squared off, ready to take a poke at me. I backed off, fearful of having to physically defend myself. I'm a coward, and Carly's resemblance to the elementary school kid who beat me up all those years ago made the situation worse. A war of words was more my style.

I spoke more quickly, hoping to head her off. "Don't trust me, either. Don't trust each other. The person who attacked Amber, Marty, and Hugh is probably in this theater right now. Maybe in this room. Be smart. You feel like sharing? Tell Detective Sobol or Detective Farrow, or any of the other police officers."

Carly didn't tackle me. She threw a tightly muscled arm around my shoulders and said, "For once, Ms. Twinkle Toes has it right."

I didn't know if Carly was faking friendliness or genuinely on my side. It didn't matter, because I accomplished my main goal, which was to make my fellow performers as suspicious of each other as I was of them.

Chapter Thirty-Nine

Life isn't about waiting for the storm to pass. It's about learning to dance in the rain.

—Vivian Greene

With very few minutes left before we resumed our rehearsal, I went to Amber's dressing room to ask about her early morning hospital visit.

She finished her vocal exercises before answering. "Marty was with the doctor, so I didn't get to see him. As of yesterday, he didn't remember anything that happened when he got hurt. A wasted trip all around. I suppose your Detective Sobol told you?"

I'd never admitted Jonah and I were romantically involved and had no plans to do so. "We didn't have time for a full briefing before rehearsal."

Something about her seemed off. Perhaps it was her way of dealing with stress, or maybe she was getting into her role. Her dressing room seemed empty, and I realized what was missing. "I'm disappointed Farley isn't here. You look like you could use a furry friend."

"Farley is still at the very expensive Pampered Pets doggy hotel. I have enough on my plate without having to worry about him. After all, I've been through, Sam and Bryan better not keep nitpicking every tiny detail. Carly is even worse."

Her abrupt manner precluded further questions. "I'll see you onstage. If you need anything, ask. I'm here."

She waffled a bit. "I think you had the right idea about Carly all along.

Watch out for her. I thought she was my friend, and I always trusted her. Now, I'm not so sure." Her voice lost its velvety cadence and turned ragged. "I'll be honest with you, Leah. I'm not sure I can finish out the day. I've had it. I've got nothing left."

Knowing what I was about to do was risky and that I might be wrong, I went ahead anyway. "Amber, I know who stabbed Hugh."

"Who? Was it Carly?" When I didn't reply, she rocked back and forth, as if in physical pain. "Sam. You think it's Sam."

"I don't have proof yet. As soon as I do, you'll be the first to know."

She pressed her hands against her eyes but couldn't stop the flow of tears. When I left, she locked the door with a loud *click.*

It was tempting to dismiss the panic that gripped me while I was waiting for the subway as irrational, the product of too much stress and not enough sleep. But I wasn't prone to flights of paranoid fancy. The premonition wasn't a random episode of unsubstantiated fear. It was my subconscious sending me a warning. Someone close to me was getting ready to strike again.

As I waited in the wings for the curtain to open, the three people I knew I could trust were by my side. We made whispered plans to meet in the costume room during our next break. I lost sight of them while I was onstage, but I knew they were watching over me.

Abigail, Izzy, and Audrey waited until the door to the costume room was closed and locked before speaking. My friends had spent the first half of the rehearsal watching the show, as they didn't have a role until the last act. True to form, they all had knitting needles, balls of yarn, and projects that were in varying stages of completion.

I read them the notes I'd written during my sleepless night. "We need a motive that ties together the spiked drinks, the threatening messages, the stalking, and Hugh's death. If we go after means and opportunity, the list would include almost every person involved in the show. Bryan, Natalie, and Carly all had the opportunity to spike Amber's coffee as well as attack

Hugh. As for means, anyone could have added sugar to Amber's drink or swiped a steak knife at the fundraiser. The ketamine that was in Marty's coffee isn't as available, of course, but it's not like you can't get black-market drugs. You could probably walk out this door and find someone who knows someone."

Abigail fingered a skein of thick pink yarn. "Have you eliminated Sam? He wasn't at rehearsal on the day the drinks were spiked, but he could have been working with someone. Rose would do anything for him, and he might have promised her Amber's role."

Izzy nodded in agreement. "His body language this morning was most interesting. He spoke to the group, but his eyes gave him away. I think he's obsessed with that chorus girl. She's no great shakes as a dancer, but she's lovely and not quite as dim as she pretends to be."

"I agree. Rose is sharper than she lets on. If you give her five minutes, she'll give you a Russian novel's worth of drama regarding her relationship with Sam, but I can't yet separate fact from rumor. Depending on whom you talk to, Sam is in love with her, and she's using him to get ahead. Or, Rose is in love with him, and he's using her for sex. We can come up with multiple motives, but we've got one piece of evidence that appears to rule out Sam. If he's guilty, why did he go to the police to file a report? The last thing a criminal wants is a police investigation."

Izzy observed, "It could be a double fake. He's powerful enough to think he can get away with anything, maybe even murder."

I closed my eyes and took myself back to the conversation we had at the gala. "Sam admitted he didn't think the police would do anything about his complaint, and he filed the report because he thought it would please Amber. If it wasn't for Jonah, who suggested I investigate, the police wouldn't have acted."

Abigail put down her knitting needles. "If Sam was guilty, he wouldn't have shared that information. I also can't see how stabbing Hugh fits in with the rest."

Audrey gave her head a shake, which freed several bobby pins unequal to the task of restraining her hair. "That part is easy. Hugh could have overhead something compromising. Since that motive won't eliminate anyone, I propose we put it aside and concentrate on the other actions and the consequences of those actions. We've got to look beyond immediate results and think long term, which I believe the killer has done."

She held up her phone, which had an image of a chessboard on it. "We need a strategy that will foil the Queen's Gambit."

I had a rudimentary knowledge of chess, but not enough for Audrey's reference to be meaningful. "Sorry, Audrey, that chessboard doesn't tell me what it's telling you, and we don't have much time."

She was patient. "The Queen's Gambit is a series of moves, usually by white, the dominant side. In brief, the player sacrifices a pawn early in the game to gain an advantage later. We have to ask ourselves how a temporary deficit ended up conveying a future benefit."

I'd come to the same conclusion. "What you're saying about the Queen's Gambit is in line with what I think happened, but I got there a different way. The music and the story in the ballet *Giselle* have been haunting me since last night, when I was helping Dr. Hurtado care for Hugh. Unlike the person who stabbed Hugh, Giselle's intentions are good, but her use of sacrifice as a source of power is the same. There are other parallels, like an innocent guy who gets in the way and dies, but what's most important is that the central character, who seems helpless, is manipulating the situation to her benefit."

Abigail wasn't yet convinced. "We shouldn't overlook the fact that we have two suspects who had the opportunity to gain everything they wanted without sacrifice."

Izzy finished her thought. "Carly and Natalie. With Amber and Leah out of the picture, they get their big chance."

I appealed again to Audrey. "Are there any chess moves that cover that possibility?"

She lost some of her certainty. "There are lots of other strategies, but most powerful moves involve sacrifice."

Audrey's theory validated what I'd hoped wasn't true. "There's one person who ruthlessly sacrificed herself and others to get what she wanted. It's the same person who had the most to gain by throwing suspicion on other people, making herself a trending topic on every platform, and creating an aura of danger and intrigue."

Audrey said, "The Queen."

I was bitter. "Not the Queen. The Castle. And I was the pawn."

A discreet knock was our signal that break time was nearly over. Izzy unlocked the door, and Lynne and Rachel entered, wheeling a long clothes rack filled with shiny costumes. Barbara brought up the rear, holding the pages of a marked-up script.

My aunt couldn't restrain herself. "Well, Leah? What have you come up with? We were dying to join you, but Sam's meeting lasted forever."

"Here's our new plan. We continue to use our phones to record conversations in places where people congregate, but we don't wait for our suspect to act first. Today, we turn the tables. Abigail, is Solly Greenfield here?"

At the sound of his name, she blushed. "He's with the stagehands."

Rachel was miffed. "How does a lowlife like Solly get access to a Broadway show?"

Abigail set her mouth in a prim line. "He knows people. But we're running out of time. Leah, hurry up!"

I was nervous. "Please don't think I'm getting all diva on you, but what stuck out to me about the sequence of events we talked about was how much I was involved in each episode. That seemed odd. The whole idea behind me joining the show was that I was an outsider and could investigate using my role as a cover. But two people knew from the start I was working a double role. And one of them always knew where I was and what I was doing. Today, instead of following her script, we make her follow ours."

I sketched out each role in our backstage drama and chose Audrey for the opening move. "You be the first sacrifice. I'll be the second."

Barbara said, "No! That's a bad idea. It's, uh, Professor Romanova would never, um she thinks—" Her voice trailed off.

I felt sorry for my mother. Her fictional character had never before let her down.

"It's not Professor Romanova's call. Or yours."

The gong sounded, calling us to the stage. I was in costume and had the hairpiece of red curls firmly in place on my head. *Showtime.*

Chapter Forty

Broadway...it's the World Series of showbusiness.
—Cyd Charisse

Onstage, Carly was in her element. Bryan had never been comfortable with allowing her to assume the full range of responsibilities Broadway dance captains were supposed to carry, but he was too busy blocking the scenes with the actors to interfere. Without Bryan looking over her shoulder, she dropped her combative attitude and bloomed with confidence.

Nothing escaped her, from the tiniest break in one dancer's line to a slight variation in the height of our leg extensions. She delivered her corrections impartially but gave Amber a wide berth. Perhaps she'd been warned to take it easy on her.

Actors' Equity union rules mandated that during tech rehearsals, we didn't have to work more than ten hours in a twelve-hour session. My friends and I began our version of a play-within-a-play twenty minutes before the clock ran out. Abigail, Izzy, and Audrey made their entrance for the finale. As they triple-stepped their way to stage left, Audrey appeared to stumble. She fell to the floor and cried out in pain.

The music stopped, and the dancers and actors rushed to help her. Bryan wrung his hands as the tiny woman writhed and moaned. "Is nothing going to go right with this show?" He shouted at Audrey, acting as if she'd lost her hearing and not her footing. "Should we get an ambulance? Can you walk?"

I took my place in the wings. When all eyes were on Audrey, Solly

Greenfield shoved a metal ladder off its mooring. It fell with a satisfying crash. I positioned my left leg in a gap underneath it and closed my eyes. I'd legitimately fainted at the Design the Dream fundraiser, and I talked my body into mimicking that same state of apparent unconsciousness. Solly and I didn't have long to wait before everyone came running.

Amber fell to her knees next to me. "Somebody help me move this!"

I half-opened my eyes as Solly pulled the ladder away. Sam reached his hand to my leg. I cringed and yelled, "No! Don't touch it! I'm fine!"

Sam took his phone from his back pocket. "I'm calling nine-one-one."

"Stop—no. Don't call anyone." I massaged my leg. "It's a sprain, which a doctor will make a big fuss over but can't do anything about. I've been injured before, and I know how to deal with my body."

Carly was gentler than I'd ever seen her. "Listen to me, Twinkle Toes. You may have sprained a muscle before, but not because a ladder fell on your leg. If you don't want an ambulance, Solly will carry you to a cab. I'll call my doc and tell him you're on the way."

Natalie was shaking, and her eyes brimmed with tears. "You have to see a doctor, Leah."

Amber pushed them away. She patted my shoulder and said, "I got you, my friend. Don't pay attention to them. How bad is it? Can you move your leg?"

Wiping real tears from my eyes, I said, "I don't want any fuss. Solly, if you could get me to my dressing room, that's all the help I need."

I'll always be proud that I was able to cry on cue, like a real actress. It wasn't as hard as I feared. I simply imagined myself as the White Swan, whose Prince betrays her by proposing marriage to her evil twin. As heartbreaking scenes go, that one is a doozy. Right up there with Rick's farewell to Ilsa in the movie *Casablanca*.

Bryan was white with shock. "Don't be so stubborn. If you can't dance, I'll have to rework the choreography."

I sniffled back a few more tears. I was getting good at this. "No. Please, everyone, give me some space. A few minutes of elevating my leg should do the trick. If it isn't better soon, I'll figure something out. Let's not panic."

Solly lifted me in his arms. Amber said to the assembled group, "Back off. Leah doesn't want a doctor." She rose to her feet. "I'm coming with you. And I'm not taking no for an answer."

With a grateful look, I agreed. Carly and Natalie followed us until Amber shooed them away.

Solly deposited me on a chair in my dressing room. "Anything else I can do for you?"

"No thanks, Solly. I've got an ice pack in my bag and can take care of this myself." He gave me two thumbs up and left.

Amber said, "I've got some pain meds that will help. Anti-inflammatory stuff that will have you feeling better in no time. I'll be right back." She opened the door, and Abigail, Izzy, and Audrey tumbled over each other's legs and into the room.

Amber failed to see the humor in the situation. She attacked Audrey first. "I thought you were injured."

Abigail spoke for her tongue-tied friend. "She's better. We're leaving now. Rehearsal is over. We wanted to check up on Leah."

Amber's voice was icy. "Go. All of you. Leah doesn't want you hanging around." She used the door to force them out of the room.

I called out, "Thanks a lot, ladies. Let everyone know I'm feeling better."

Izzy poked her head back in and retrieved two knitting needles from where she'd dropped them. "We'll see you tomorrow."

Amber stood at the threshold and waited until they exited the stage door before getting her red leather tote and dropping it on the table with a loud thunk. She withdrew a flask and shook two pills from a plastic, orange bottle. "Trust me. These go down a lot better with a good stiff drink. In fact, I'll join you." She poured two cups of whiskey. "Bottoms up."

I palmed the pills but couldn't fake her out where the drink was concerned. "I prefer coffee. The caffeine will help the pills work faster."

She handed me the coffee. My mouth was dry, but the remaining dregs were so bitter I managed only a few swallows. She put the glass of whiskey to her lips but didn't drink from it. From under downcast eyes, she watched as I used my arms to get to a standing position. When I got to my feet, I fell back into the chair, as if my leg couldn't hold me up.

I spoke calmly, although my heart was pounding, "The show's over, Amber. You screwed up."

She laughed. "What are you talking about? Maybe you do need to see a doctor."

After many days of close observation, I was finally able to see through her act. "I know you're the one who spiked the drinks. I know you're the one who sent those creepy texts. And I know you're the one who stabbed Hugh."

Amber appeared unmoved by my accusation. She said, as if it were a joke, "Hold that thought."

She selected a tube of lipstick from the collection on my dressing table and applied a thick coat of my color to her mouth. Using my brown eyeshadow, she darkened her brows. Looking at the mirror's reflection of our faces, she said, "You have no proof. And if you try and pin this on me, I'll make sure you never dance again, *ballerina girl*." Her tone turned dreamy. "I know all about you and your detective. If you'd listened to me, no one would have gotten hurt."

I had the two pills she gave me stowed under my chair cushion, but they wouldn't constitute sufficient evidence of her guilt. I needed a confession. "Tell me what happened. I want to understand."

Amber took a brown wig from her bag and fitted it over her red curls. With her darkened eyebrows and my lipstick, she looked like me instead of the other way around. Her cool demeanor betrayed no fear. She knew my plan to trap her was unequal to the one she'd plotted against me.

Satisfied with the result of her disguise, she reached back into the bag and withdrew a hammer, which she held with both hands. Her voice got deeper and throbbed with suppressed anger. "What you never understood is that I suffered more than you ever did. The whispers about me being too old, the rumors about Sam wanting a different star, the catty comments about my dancing—it was destroying me and my career. I was at my wit's end. And then, I realized I could turn it all around by beating the haters at their own game. I started planting threats against myself and against Farley. Once people thought my mangy dog and I were being trolled and stalked in real life, the whole narrative changed."

Amber's lips split into a bone-chilling smile. "The scarier the threats, the bigger the reaction. Let me tell you, Leah, the love and support was thrilling! It was brilliant, like a game with no losers. After a few weeks, the only negative comments about me were the ones I planted." She gritted her teeth. "And then you came along with your stupid questions."

In an excellent imitation of my voice and posture, she said, "Why don't you hire a detective? Why don't you get a bodyguard? Why don't you let me into your social media accounts?"

Switching back to her own voice, she said, "Marty wouldn't be in the hospital, and that pathetic busboy would still be alive if you hadn't gotten in the way. I did everything possible to scare you off. I stalked you and texted you, and locked you out of the gala. You should have seen your face after the ketchup attack. But you just wouldn't quit."

She used the hammer to slowly crush a tiny vase on my dressing table, turning the glass into powder. Her destruction of the fragile ornament was nearly silent and was scarier than if she'd smashed it.

"Your leg is next if you make a single move."

Amber had a weapon, but I had the tactical advantage. She didn't know I hadn't swallowed the pills or that my injury was faked. With one swipe of that hammer, however, she could shatter my leg and end my career. A shot to my head would end my life.

She was such a good actress. I couldn't hope to match her skill, but I had to try. I groaned and wiped away tears.

Amber gave the hammer a few practice swings and said, "Very soon, you won't be feeling any pain at all. It didn't have to end this way, but from the start, I was afraid you'd figure out I was behind the threats. Hah! You were afraid I'd blow your cover, but I was more afraid you'd blow mine. That was bad enough, but then people started believing you were the star. Sam, Bryan, the whole world acted like you were the secret of their success."

I needed no dramatic skill to get my voice to sound wobbly and scared. "I understand why you want to hurt me, but why stab Hugh? What did he do?"

Her beautiful features hardened into a mask of rage. "He walked in on me while I was putting the knife and the dog collar into the boxes. I told him it was a joke and promised him a role in the show if he kept his mouth shut. And then, he double-crossed me! And for what? It wasn't a crime! It was a prank. Like the ketchup. No one was supposed to get hurt. But after those dim detectives questioned him, he panicked. Said he was coming clean. He left me no choice. Traitors like him deserve what they get."

She patted the wig and stole a glance at her reflection. "It's good you brought that ugly puffer coat with you. The guy at the stage door is going to swear that he saw you leave the theater."

I spoke slowly and slurred the words. "Very clever."

Amber jerked her head toward the window. "Those pills are quick. You won't feel a thing. And when they find your dead body at the bottom of the air shaft, wearing my red wig, it will look like a case of mistaken identity. By the time anyone comes to check up on you, it'll be too late."

I ripped off the wig and threw it out the open window. "There goes your plan. No one is going to believe my death is a case of mistaken identity now."

She lifted the hammer over her head. I sprang out of the chair and tackled her knees. The resulting swing narrowly missed me, and the hammer fell harmlessly onto the chair cushion. If it had been a fair fight, she wouldn't have had a chance of overpowering me, but a wave of dizziness weakened my arms. My eyes were blurry, my tongue was thick in my mouth, and my brain felt foggy. She must have roofied my coffee the way she did Marty's. I hooked my foot around hers, and she lost her balance, which gave me time to grab the hammer before she could. I threw it, like the wig, into the air shaft.

Amber grabbed me from behind and, inch by inch, pushed me toward the window. We struggled for dominance. She muscled me over the ledge and tried to heave me over the side.

The body I'd trained for so many years didn't let me down. I elbowed her in the face and broke her nose.

That's the last thing I remembered before five ladies, one reformed mobster, and a certain homicide detective broke down the door and burst into the room.

Chapter Forty-One

Ballet is the body rising...Its disdain for the commonplace material world is the source of its authority and glamour.
—Camille Paglia

I recovered consciousness before I got to the hospital, but they put me in a bed and took pictures of my brain despite my protests. Jonah was by my side. Desperately thirsty and in the grip of an epic stomachache and headache, I opened my eyes and said, "Did you get her?"

He gave me a lopsided smile. "We did. And here's another bonus: we didn't lose you. What were you thinking? Downing a hit of ketamine wasn't part of the plan." He brushed a strand of hair from my forehead and said, "You should have yelled for help sooner. We could have spared you the fight."

Admittedly, that wasn't my finest moment. "I knew the stuff was in the whiskey but missed seeing her spike my coffee. It's possible she did it before we got to the dressing room as part of a plan she had in place before we started ours. The bigger surprise came when she tried to push me off the ledge. Most dressing rooms don't have windows and aren't so high up. I didn't yell for help before then because we needed a confession. Did you get the recording?"

Jonah pressed his lips to my hand. "We did. The techies are working to clean it up because, with the phone muffled under a cushion, the sound quality wasn't great. The worst part about that was we didn't know what was going on inside the room. I'm glad we didn't wait."

"How long were Amber and I together? It felt as if hours passed."

He kissed me, this time on the lips. "Five minutes. And we got it all."

I was pleased one part of my sketchy plot worked as planned. "I didn't know if Rachel was able to plant the phone in time and didn't want to tip Amber off by checking."

"If you're up for it, Rachel is waiting to see you, along with three Weird Sisters, one best friend, and a frantic mother. Oh, and Solly Greenfield is here as well. You really know how to throw a party."

"Will they be allowed in to see me? This hospital isn't known for hosting bedside picnics."

He opened the door. "This is your lucky day, in more ways than one. We got a one-time exemption, courtesy of your friendly, neighborhood NYPD."

Jonah stepped aside as Rachel and Barbara raced to get to me first. Gabi, Abigail, Izzy, and Audrey tiptoed in behind them. Solly stood in the doorway, looking ill at ease. I knew how he felt. Hospitals made me nervous, too.

Barbara kissed my forehead because she loves me and because she thinks she's more accurate than a digital thermometer at measuring my temperature. "You've been so brave, Leah. And so clever. I don't know how you deduced from the evidence we had that Amber was guilty."

I drank some ice water to clear my woozy brain and cotton mouth. "The first step was rethinking our original assumption, which was that the sugar and the ketamine were both meant for Amber. The combination was deadly for a diabetic, and Amber knew there was a good chance the police would treat what happened as an attempted murder, which was her goal. She wanted to authenticate her claim that her life was in danger.

"Jonah questioned that conclusion long before I did. He suspected it was no accident that the ketamine and the sugar went into two different cups, but until today, we couldn't come up with a motive. Marty, in either case, was never a target. I think Amber popped the ketamine into a random cup without caring who got it. She never intended Marty to suffer as he did, but after he collapsed, she found herself in a very scary place."

Barbara was incredulous. "Even I couldn't make up something that selfish and ill-conceived. What tipped you off?"

I looked at Jonah, and he picked up the thread of the story. "I questioned

Amber several times, as did Leah, but neither of us got much concrete information, which made me wonder what she was hiding. We now know she was afraid Leah would figure out the stalking and trolling was a hoax. Amber tried to sidetrack Leah's investigation, but your daughter is nothing if not persistent."

I said, "Amber knew Jonah and Farrow suspected—correctly, as it turned out—she was playing them as part of an elaborate publicity stunt. When I came onto the scene, she wanted to use me as a witness to prove the threats against her were legitimate. For a while, that's exactly what happened.

"I have to give some credit to Rose. She told me Amber's family had a horse farm, and I remembered reading something about ketamine being used for horses. Also, on the day Amber went to the hospital, she had an empty medicine bottle in her handbag, which she was frantic to have me get for her. She said she needed her phone, but it was the medicine bottle she wanted to get rid of. And what better place to do that but in a hospital?"

Barbara was thrilled. "That wasn't Rose who gave you the clue. It was me! I used ketamine as a murder weapon in *The Merry Knives of Windsor*." She informed the rest of us, "The Professor has to solve the murder of a dressage rider. I wanted to kill the horse, but people got upset."

Rachel squeezed in next to Barbara. "Keep talking, Leah. If you don't stop your mother, we'll have to listen to the entire plot."

Their sparring made me happy. It meant all was right in the world. "In addition to the medicine bottle, Amber also had a half-eaten candy bar in her bag, which she probably ate to make sure she had enough sugar in her blood. The last item she had with her was her dog's collar. Why was she carrying around an extra collar? The only possible answer was that she was waiting for the right time to enact the heartbreaking drama she ended up performing at the gala. Amber was always so mean about her dog. I wouldn't have put it past her to kill him and use his death to make herself look like a suffering victim."

Audrey looked up from what must have been a game of bullet chess, "Her sacrifices weren't real. She started by faking a threat and then became one herself."

I nodded, which made my head hurt worse. "She'd had a few flops and was humiliated when she learned she was Sam's second choice, behind Lily Ferrante. The dismal advance ticket sales were similarly embarrassing for her. That was bad enough, but then I joined the cast and gave *Mad Music* the boost she couldn't deliver. Aside from Amber's resentment over the attention I was getting, she had a young, gorgeous, talented woman in the chorus who was itching to take her place. She was jealous of Natalie's youth and talent. She was jealous of Rose's hold on Sam. She was even jealous of her dog. At our first meeting, she complained Farley was getting better press than she was.

"Things fell apart for her after I came onto the scene, because she lost control over what got reported. The police refused to investigate the online threats, and when she tried to convince me, nothing she claimed about her online stalker rang true. I've been there, and I know what that looks like. I couldn't understand why she wouldn't allow me access to her account or, on a more practical note, why she didn't hire a private detective and a bodyguard. Her only way to validate her claims was to manufacture a threat. She couldn't know how badly it would end for Marty."

I appealed to Jonah. "How is Marty doing?"

He relaxed into a smile. "Marty was discharged this morning. I told the hospital not to release the information, because I didn't want Amber to know."

Jonah's update reminded me of another clue. "Amber's professional and personal life were so intertwined, her failure to post about her visits to Marty's bedside was highly suspicious. Modesty wasn't her style."

Rachel said, "That's all well and good, but how did a publicity stunt end up the way it did? She might not have had evil intent regarding Marty or whoever drank the roofied coffee, but why kill Hugh Madden? Is there any evidence linking her to him?"

Jonah said, "We got hair samples from the room at the gala where Amber took pictures of Leah and threatened her. We also have a partial fingerprint on the trash can she threw out the window."

Rachel was disapproving. "You should have arrested her this morning."

All eyes turned from Rachel to Jonah. He remained his unflappable self. "That's not the way it works. Getting a strand of hair that looked like Amber's means nothing without a DNA test, and that takes time. Although her prints were on the trash can, they weren't on the knife. There were no eyewitnesses. It wasn't until we found another waiter who had talked to Hugh that we had something more to go on, but it still wasn't enough to charge her."

He left my side and walked to the window, which offered a view of a brick wall. "When Amber collapsed into my arms, I knew she was faking. It was the same feeling I had when we first met, but this time, there was no mistaking it. She didn't care about her dog. She cared about having people think she cared about the dog. And when I saw her at the hospital this morning, I realized she might have a very different motive to visit Marty than what she claimed. If he recovered his memory and could point to her involvement, that would've been the end for her."

Solly moved from the doorway to the bed. "I get the whole business with the PR stunts and the kid keeling over from the Special K. We still don't know why she iced the waiter."

Two small lines inside Jonah's eyebrows were the only indication of emotion. "To answer that, we have to go back to her original intent. What Amber wanted was a dramatic moment, something that would catapult her into the headlines the way the swatting did. And it worked. She opened the box with the damaged dog collar in full view of her audience, and she played it to the hilt. She was on the front page of the newspaper, and the department is fielding calls from every major news outlet about what happened last night."

Rachel interjected, "She'll have plenty of press now, but not the kind she wanted."

My mother shushed her, and when they finished arguing, Jonah said, "We're still building the case. We've got Amber on camera, giving Hugh the two boxes so we can establish a link between them, although that's almost worthless as evidence in the murder. Morelli found a witness, another busboy and aspiring actor, who said Hugh told him he was quitting the catering gig because Amber Castle was going to get him a part in *Mad Music*.

If Hugh ratted her out, she'd be box office poison. She killed him to cover her tracks. I knew he was lying. I shouldn't have let him go."

I felt in my heart all that he didn't say. "His death isn't your fault. I don't blame Hugh, but if he told you the truth when you questioned him, he'd still be alive. Amber murdered him. That's her crime, not yours. As for evidence, we've got it all on tape. When you recover the recording, you'll hear her say that Hugh double-crossed her, and she killed him. Without regret."

Gabi, like me, gets restless after staying still for too long. She stretched her arms and legs and said, "We thought Carly was guilty, because she had the best motive."

I was embarrassed at how thoroughly I'd misread the dance captain. "Carly made it clear to everyone that she hated and resented me, but that's not how a guilty person acts. A guilty person would hide how she feels. As for Natalie, I wasn't sure about her until the last minute. She, along with everyone except Amber, wanted me to wait for a doctor or ambulance. That proved her innocence. She was on my side all along."

Gabi went down the list of our other suspects, ending with Garret. "He was so bitter over the fact that Amber got him cut from the show. But if we use the same reasoning as you did for Carly, he wouldn't have told us he hated her and wished her ill if he was guilty."

Rachel had the last word. "Actors. You can't trust any of them."

A nurse entered and said, "The party's over, Ms. Siderova. The doctor is coming to check on you."

I held onto Jonah as the rest of my visitors left. "I need you to do something for me. It's important."

He caught his breath. "Don't tell me you're ready to commit. I might have to check myself into the hospital."

I wasn't sure if he was serious. "Think of it as a way station to commitment. I want to adopt Amber's dog. He needs a loving home."

"What makes you think she'll give him up, let alone give him up to you?"

"She won't give him to me, but she might give him to Garret, and if he doesn't want Farley, I do. One of the many clues I missed about Amber was her attitude toward the dog. The fact that I misjudged how she felt about me isn't something I want to think about. I prefer to think about Farley."

Jonah was gentle in his response. "I think it's a lovely gesture. I also think you're on the road a lot, and you work six days a week and think nothing of putting in a twelve-hour day."

"Do you trust me?"

He kissed me and said, "I do."

The following week, I brought Farley home. Mrs. Pargiter was so surprised to see the dog she opened her door without interrogating me through the chain lock. "What on earth are you thinking? You can't have a dog. They need love and attention, and you're constantly out and about."

I was regretful. "I know, Mrs. Pargiter. It's temporary. I'm taking care of him until I can find him a proper home. Although he's such a wonderful dog, I can't bear the thought of giving him away. Maybe I should bring him to the shelter."

"Don't be ridiculous. Bring him in, and we'll figure something out." She sniffed. "The very idea!"

I was back at work in time for *Mad Music's* opening night. Natalie was brilliant as the Leading Lady. My performance as the Dreamcatcher brought down the house.

In the end, a star was born. Maybe more than one.

Acknowledgements

For creative inspiration and unstinting support, I look no further than my kids and their partners. Gregory, Geoffrey, Jesse, Luke, Jacob, Becky, Emily, and Kris contributed their signature brand of humor, as well as their love of wordplay and intrigue, to make this story so much better than it would have been without them. I'm equally indebted to the newest generation: Sophie, Viola, Ava, and Alice. Like me, they love a good story.

If I had my choice of sisters, I couldn't do better than the one I grew up with and those I got through marriage: Karyn Boyar, and Barbara, Lisa, Jane, Gail, and Lolly Robbins. I also want to thank my talented Sisters in Crime.

Much gratitude is due to the many people who provided their expert advice. Chief among these is my editor, Shawn Reilly Simmons, who gave unstintingly of her time, talent, and patience. Many thanks as well to my longtime critique partner, Corey LaBranche, and dancer Elisa Heinsohn. Thank you, from the bottom of my heart.

To my brother Richard: I wish you were here to see the publication of this book.

This book is dedicated to Glenn, who still thinks—after all these years—that he's the one who got lucky.

About the Author

Lori Robbins is the author of the On Pointe and Master Class mystery series. She won the Indie Award for Best Mystery and two Silver Falchions for Best Cozy Mystery. Short stories include "Leading Ladies" in *Justice for All*, which was cited as one of the year's best in the 2022 Best American Mystery and Suspense anthology. She also is a contributor to *The Secret Ingredient: A Mystery Writers Cookbook*.

A former dancer, Lori performed with a number of modern and classical ballet companies, including Ballet Hispanico and the St. Louis Ballet. Her commercial work included featured spots for Pavlova Perfume and Macy's. After ten very lean years onstage she became an English teacher and now writes full-time. She is Co-President of the New York/Tri-State chapter of Sisters in Crime and an active member of Mystery Writers of America.

SOCIAL MEDIA HANDLES:
https://linktr.ee/lorirobbinsmysteries
https://www.instagram.com/lorirobbinsmysteries/

https://www.facebook.com/LoriRobbinsMysteries
https://twitter.com/lorirobbins99
https://www.pinterest.com/lorirobbinsmysteries/_created/
https://www.amazon.com/~/e/B077TTSCBH

AUTHOR WEBSITE:
https://www.lorirobbins.com/

Also by Lori Robbins

THE ON POINTE MYSTERIES
  Murder in First Position
  Murder in Second Position
  Murder in Third Position

THE MASTER CLASS MYSTERIES
  Lesson Plan for Murder

SHORT STORIES
  "Leading Ladies" *Justice for All: Murder New York Style*
  "Accidents Happen" *Murder Most Diabolical*
  "Killing it in the Catskills" *Murder Most Traditional*
  "Mirror Image" *Shotgun Honey*